DEADLY FARCE

DEADLY FARCE

•

Jennifer McAndrews

AVALON BOOKS
NEW YORK

Published by Avalon Books,
an imprint of Thomas Bouregy & Co., Inc.
New York, NY

Library of Congress Cataloging-in-Publication Data

McAndrews, Jennifer.
   Deadly farce / Jennifer McAndrews.
      p. cm.
   ISBN 978-0-8034-7464-2 (hardcover : acid-free
paper)   1. Women private investigators—Fiction.
2. Atlantic City (N.J.)—Fiction.   I. Title.
   PS3613.C2658D43 2012
   813'.6—dc23

                                    2011033153

      PRINTED IN THE UNITED STATES OF AMERICA
                ON ACID-FREE PAPER
      BY RR DONNELLEY, HARRISONBURG, VIRGINIA

For my daughters, with love everlasting

Acknowledgments

I am deeply grateful for the support and faith I experienced throughout this book's long and seemingly unending journey. Heartfelt thanks to my husband for insisting I keep writing, and to Ginger, Julie, and Linda for their unending confidence in this project. To my fellow writers for keeping me laughing; my wonderful agent, Michelle Humphrey, for keeping me sane; and my fabulous editor, Jennifer Graham, for making this process nothing less than joyous.

Chapter One

As I rushed along the boardwalk in Atlantic City, the early-morning breeze off the ocean filled my nose with the stench of summer seaweed and blew my hair into my eyes. My old pal Shepard had called at somebody-better-be-dead o'clock and begged me to meet him on set down in Jersey. I'd begged him to let me go back to sleep. When he'd said it was a matter of life and death, I'd dragged my body out of bed and headed for the shore. Despite building a career as an actor, he wasn't known for being dramatic.

On the boardwalk a crowd had gathered behind a line of saw-horses and stood gawking at the film crew beyond, no doubt hoping for a glimpse of someone famous. Heedless of any sort of first-come, first-see rules, I pushed my way to the front, ducked a sawhorse, and walked toward a guy wearing a lanyard heavy with pass-cards. He clenched a clipboard in his hands and juggled a stack of papers and a walkie-talkie.

His eyes popped when he saw me, as though he couldn't believe I'd dare violate the sawhorse barricade. Several papers slipped to the ground, and he stomped his foot on them to stop them from blowing away. "You can't come this way, ma'am," he said.

Ma'am? I hadn't even hit thirty. "Yes, I can." I pulled my shiny Diamond Security Services badge from the back pocket of my jeans and did my Joe Friday. "Tell me where I can find Shepard Brown."

His Adam's apple rose and fell at the glint of the shield. My good fortune this guy didn't know cop from square badge. "I don't think—"

"Look," I began. The wind kept blowing my hair into the corners of my mouth, and I worried that pushing it away would undercut my authority. Joe Friday wouldn't have cared about hair in his mouth, right? "Mr. Brown is expecting me," I said. "Would you like to be the one who makes me late?"

"Oh, I . . ."

"I suggest you make up your mind quickly." I slipped the tin back into my pocket and glared and tried to ignore my hair.

"The . . . uh . . . trailers are on the other side." He pointed his clipboard toward the gleaming white façade of a towering hotel. "Someone up that way will be able to find him for sure."

I thanked him and left him struggling with his paperwork. On an ordinary day I would have stayed to help. But this wasn't an ordinary day. No day with Shepard Brown in it had a chance of being ordinary.

I'd learned that lesson way back when. During an ordinary after-school outing to the skating rink, I had unintentionally freed him from the locker in which he had been trapped. Truth was, the boys' hockey team had folded him into my locker. All I wanted were my mittens. But from that moment on, nothing I said altered Shepard's belief in me as his heroic defender. And I repeated the role time and again on every nonordinary day, until the scrawny kid he had once been hit puberty—and the weight machines—with a vengeance. No doubt Shepard was part of the reason I was attempting to forge a career in executive protection.

Smoothing the tank top I was wearing under my shirt against my belly, I strode toward the hive of activity consuming a two-hundred-foot stretch of the boardwalk. All manner of persons scurried around the area, carrying all variety of equipment. In the heart of the chaos, a cluster of people stood in a tight circle. My razor-sharp, Maxwell Smart–like powers of observation told me the director was the guy in the center of it all, gesticulating madly while the wind and ocean made off with his words. A tiny bit of admiration rushed through me. If I could control a crowd with the skill of a Hollywood director, protecting a dignitary would be a million times simpler.

I drew level with a discount shop, where Holly Bellinger, modern Hollywood glam, lounged against an empty rolling chair and spooned a cup of yogurt into her mouth with remarkable speed. But no one else showed any sign of urgency or gave any indication that things were other than normal. Crewmen wandered in and out of the shot with light meters, measuring tape, and extension cords, but Holly ignored them and focused on her yogurt. Whatever had prompted Shepard's panicked phone call appeared unique to him alone.

One of the crewmen caught me gaping and placed himself in my path. "Help you?" he asked. He had faded blond hair, a scraggly beard that likely had sand caught in it, and a warm blue gaze. The gold-stitched name above the studio logo on the breast of his Windbreaker read DUTCH.

"Looking for Shepard. He around?"

Dutch took me by the shoulders and turned me forty-five degrees to face the entrance to the Steel Pier. "Skee-Ball," he said.

Huh. Fifteen million a picture and the guy was playing Skee-Ball.

I nodded my thanks and pounded farther along the boardwalk in search of Shepard.

Several yards shy of the Steel Pier, I spied a lanky figure casting a long shadow between two of the midway game stalls lining the entrance to the amusement park. The man of the hour, all in one piece. Relief allowed me the first full breath I'd drawn in hours.

Hands jammed into his pockets, Shepard loped more than walked. The wind pinned a lock of dark brown hair against his forehead and draped it in front of one eye. He pushed the hair away and smiled the smile magazine publishers had fallen in love with.

"Rainny!" he shouted.

I returned his smile and more than tolerated the bear hug he caught me in.

"Thanks for coming," he said.

"No problem." I stood back to look at him. Same floppy hair, same green eyes, same heartbreaking grin—different general shape. "You put on some weight?" I asked, fulfilling my duties as queen of tact.

"Yeah, it's for the part." He draped his arm around my shoulders and turned me away from the pier. We did the small-talk thing as we walked across the boardwalk and down the ramp to street level. A string of trailers hummed curbside along the closed road, making it look like a parking lot at an RV enthusiasts' convention.

"You wanna tell me why I'm here?" I asked, following him to his trailer.

"I got a problem," he said. "Come inside."

He opened the door and gestured me past, and I preceded him up the portable steel steps into the body of the trailer.

The entry dumped me into the road version of a dining room, and I blinked at the unexpected sight of a young man gathering bound scripts from the table and talking to himself.

"I inherited it from a man who was not the real Dread Pirate Roberts, either," the kid muttered. "No, that's not it. The man I was, not who—" He froze, arms full of screenwriters' children, eyes on the door. Evidently he'd caught sight of Shepard entering behind me. "Morning, Mr. Brown," he said.

"That's my assistant, Matthew," Shepard said. "Matthew, this is Lorraine."

Matthew lowered the stack of scripts to the table and squared their corners. "May I get you something, sir? Anything I can do for you?"

Shepard sighed as though greatly put upon. "Coffee. Large. Half-decaf. Toffee-flavored cream with some cinnamon sprinkled on top. And none of that white sugar. Get me the brown unrefined stuff."

His housekeeper, personal assistant, and paid slave nodded several times and scurried past us out the door.

I scowled at Shepard. "Are you an even bigger jerk than the tabloids give you credit for?"

Not that I read tabloids, mind you. But my best pal, Barb,

read them religiously and persisted in calling me at work to regale me with the latest gossip. It meant she forgave me for never introducing her to Shepard, so I listened and maintained the truce.

He peered out the narrow window beside the door, head turning as he tracked some movement—likely Matthew—outside the trailer. "I had to get rid of him. He might be in on it."

Safe behind Shepard's back, I rolled my eyes. "Anyone who misquotes *The Princess Bride* probably isn't in on much. And I know I'm going to regret this, but I came all the way down here to hear it, so, 'in on' what?"

He turned to me, and his brow creased with concern. "I think someone's trying to kill me."

As a bodyguard and private investigator I was trained to take that sort of thing seriously, but I still had trouble keeping back the giggles. I mean, come on. This was Shepard Brown. Who would go to the trouble of killing him? "Why?" I asked. "Have you contracted to do a Michael Moore–type exposé on greed and corruption in Hollywood studios?"

His lips pressed white, and his green eyes burned. "This is serious," he said. "Come look at this."

He took hold of my arm and dragged me into the kitchen.

"It's not a big place, Brown. I saw the kitchen from the dining room."

"In here," he said. He yanked open the refrigerator and pulled out a pizza box. He dropped it onto the counter, and I read the logo upside down. If you believe what you read, he'd bought the best pizza this side of Sicily.

"You're right," I said. "Pizza's serious business."

With a theatrical sigh, he turned to face me. "You know, I called you because I thought you'd be the one person in the world who would take me seriously."

Eesh. Guilt and the after-burn of strong coffee rolled through my stomach. "Oh. Thanks, I guess. And . . . sorry."

"Fuhgettaboutit," he said. And he nailed the accent. Really nailed it.

Guess the guy could act, after all.

"So what's up with the 'za?" I asked.

He flipped open the lid and pointed.

No slices were missing from the pie, but the bulk of the cheese had migrated to the southern hemisphere.

"Wow," I said, eyeing the cheese. "That *is* criminal."

His exhale could be measured in whole-number decibels. "Under the cheese, Sherlock."

I did a quick scan of the kitchen, grabbed a slotted spoon from its peg above the stove, and used it to lift some cheese. Firm red lumps appeared to be embedded in the dough beneath.

"Odd," I said. "What are the lumpy things?"

"Peanuts," Shepard said.

"Gross. Who puts peanuts on pizza?"

I swear I heard his eyes roll. "Someone who's trying to kill me. I'm allergic to peanuts. If I eat a peanut, I could go into anaphylactic shock and die."

Sixteen thousand wisecracks rolled through my brain. I refrained from voicing any of them. At the end of the day, Shepard was an old friend and a potential client. And peanuts might be a lame attempt at murder, but they hadn't gotten into the dough by accident. The queasy feeling curling the edges of my stomach had more to do with gut instinct than revulsion at the nuts in tomato sauce.

"Have you spoken to the police?" I asked. I brought it up because Diamond Security requires its agents to, not because anyone really wants the police nosing around too soon.

"Please. The police would be less tolerant than you are," he said, and guilt overwhelmed my belly again. "They'd laugh their badges off and call the *Star National,* and it would really suck to have to die to prove to everyone I was right."

I took a deep breath and flipped the lid on the box closed. "Okay," I said. "Give it to me from the beginning."

Chapter Two

Shepard leaned against the door of the fridge, his long legs crossed at the ankle, and told me the story of how he'd come to order a pizza at two o'clock in the morning. For an actor, he should have made the tale more dramatic.

"So your assistant went and got it instead of having it delivered, right?" I prompted. "Did you ask him about the peanuts?"

He scowled. "And what would he say if he's in on it? If I ask him, then I tip my hand that I know something's going on."

"Really? But not eating the pizza you sent him out for in the dead of night isn't suspicious?"

He waved a hand. "I do that all the time," he said. His nonchalant confession made me want to punch him.

To distract myself from thoughts of assault, I carefully closed up the pizza box and made sure all the flaps slid snugly inside the base. Though I'd feel like an idiot bringing a peanut-laden pizza into the lab, I needed to know if any other foreign matter lurked in the 'za. Plus, I could bill Shepard for the cost. Provided he'd called to hire me as a bodyguard and not as a food taster.

"Let me put this back," I said, lifting the carton.

Someone pounded on the trailer door as Shepard straightened and stepped into my path. "Aren't you going to take that with you? Have it tested or something?" he asked.

"Yes, I am, but I'm not leaving right away. I've got to talk to your assistant first."

More banging on the door, this time coupled with a deep, southern voice. "Shepard, you wuss, open the door."

"Are you sure you should talk to Matthew?" Shepard asked. "I'm telling you, he might be the one trying to kill me."

"Hell, you made him get you pizza at two o'clock in the morning, and then you didn't even eat it. *I* might try to kill you too." I smiled, just in case he had second thoughts about my dedication to his continued long life.

"Shepard!" the man outside called, and he pounded some more.

"Are you going to . . . ?" I said, pointing uselessly toward the door. Shepard Brown no more answered his own door than he did his own mail. With the loudest huff I could manage, I dropped the pizza back onto the counter, skirted around Shepard, and stomped to the door.

I banged it open with the side of my fist and hiccupped in surprise at the man waiting on the other side. Sandy hair, black T-shirt, and torn blue jeans. He smiled an easygoing, we're-all-friends smile. I couldn't stop myself from smiling in return.

"Hiya," he said. He squinted a bit, but the blue of his eyes shone through. "Shepard around?"

"Come on in, Eddie," Shepard called.

Holding on to my smile, I stood back to allow Eddie Gale to enter. The tingle I got as he brushed past me had nothing to do with the familiarity of his leading-man smile and everything to do with the clean, manly scent of him. And I was supposed to focus on a peanut pie?

He stopped inside the trailer and looked back at me, his brow narrowed with intrigue. "I don't know you," he said.

By some miracle, Shepard remembered his manners and introduced me while I tried to mentally collect myself.

"A pleasure," Eddie said. He took my hand in both of his, his grip strong and warm. A distinctly feminine flush dashed across my cheeks.

"Likewise," I said, happy for once that my flustered voice ran more to the husky, breathless end of the spectrum.

He held my hand and held my eyes as though the contact would solve some puzzle troubling his mind. Looking over my shoulder to where Shepard stood, he said, "I'm not . . . uh . . . ?" A slight hand motion added "interrupting something" to his question.

"Who, us?" Shepard asked. "No. No. Lorraine's an old friend. Can I get you something?"

Amazement shot through me as Shepard crossed into the kitchen, opened the fridge, and began reciting its contents as though he intended to serve. For crying out loud, he hadn't even offered me a place to sit down.

"Ooh," Eddie said, eyes bright. "Anything left in that pizza box?"

Shepard glared, bug-eyed. Evidently he needed some work on his improvisational skills.

"Oh, that . . . um . . . that's been sitting out all night," I said. "You don't want that."

"I don't?" Eddie said.

He looked at me with such focused attention, I thought he might bore a hole through me. My knees felt like ice in the sun, and a bead of sweat slithered down my spine. "No," I managed. "You don't."

He smiled. "All right," he said. "How about some coffee?"

The door banged open and slammed me out of my trance. A woman with wild blond hair stood in the doorway, eyes wide with fury. My instincts labeled her as *threat*.

"Shepard, you spawn of a mongrel!" she shouted.

Left-handed, I shoved hard against Eddie's chest. He staggered backward, and I sidestepped quickly to stand in front of Shepard. With my eyes on the door, my fingers curled around the waistband of my jeans, right where my gun should be. Cursed Jersey laws left me unarmed.

One foot on the doorstep, the blonde lifted herself into the trailer, and in the light I recognized Catherine Dawes. Gorgeous, British, and somewhat left of sane.

"How could you?" she shrieked.

Shepard stepped out from behind me and pressed his hand against the air in a "Down, girl" motion. "Hold it, hold it," he said. Uncertain whether he meant me or Catherine, I kept my hand under my shirt as though I clutched a weapon. Not that this would fool anyone with a brain, mind you. But Catherine Dawes had never been known for her intellect.

Shepard leaned on his hands against the narrow counter and regarded her with the same attention he paid to dust. "What do you want, Catherine?"

She clutched a sheaf of papers and waved them at Shepard. "How could you do this? To me?"

"Catherine—"

"Don't you 'Catherine' me, you ignorant, backwater peasant." She took a step in his direction, so naturally I did too. "You won't get away with this."

"Now, hold on," Eddie said, getting his feet back under him.

I'd shoved Eddie Gale. Oh, lovely. Heckuva first impression. Barb would laugh herself sick when I told her—you know, before she strangled me for not bringing her along.

"What's going on here?" Eddie asked.

"This . . . this . . . blackguard—" Catherine began.

" 'Blackguard'? 'Blackguard'?" Shepard said. "What script did you get that out of?"

"You're a fine one to talk." She brandished the papers once more. "Can't even think for yourself. You've hired people to think for you. To do your dirty work."

Figuring Catherine as angry but harmless, I eased my hand out from under my shirt, then sidled away from Shepard. Eddie's gaze rested on me rather than Catherine. I shrugged and tried a weak smile. Given the confusion creasing his brow, I doubted he understood my action as an apology.

"I don't hire . . . I do my own dirty work," Shepard said.

"Why doesn't someone just tell us what's going on?" Eddie said.

"I—"

"This . . . scum's solicitor has sent me notice." Eyes blazing, she attempted to straighten the papers against her thigh. "I am to cease and desist—*cease and desist*—or they will be forced to pursue a restraining order."

"For what?" Eddie asked. "What have you been doing?"

"I'll tell you what she's been doing," Shepard said. "She's been—"

"He's lying!"

"He hasn't said anything," Eddie said over a laugh.

"He's lied to me from the beginning," she said.

Now, this was drama. I hoped Shepard was taking notes.

He stood, scowled, and shoved the sleeves of his shirt up over his elbows. "I never lied to you."

"You always lied. You're lying still!"

"Now, there's no need to shout," Eddie said. "It's not as if there's a lot of space here."

"I never lied."

Catherine lifted her head and pushed the hair out of her eyes. A deep breath shuddered past her lips. "Everything you say is a lie," she said, holding up the papers. "And now you have Wilkinson, Hershowitz and Klein believing you."

"Oh, they're good," Eddie said, and Shepard nodded.

But Catherine fixed her searing gaze on me and narrowed her eyes millimeter by millimeter. "And just who are you? His latest bit on the side?"

I opened my mouth, but she didn't stop long enough for me to get a word out.

"You think I'm raving mad, don't you? Admit it. You think I'm a nutter."

The thought had crossed my mind. But I had a job to do. Maybe. It might be in my best interest to keep relations between myself and the Psycho Brit cordial. "No, Miss Dawes, I don't think you're crazy."

Her nostrils flared, and she jerked her chin up as though something distasteful had wafted her way. "Why should I believe you? You're obviously taken with this wanker," she said.

Behind her, the trailer door opened, and Matthew stepped into view. Laden with a cardboard takeout tray holding three coffee cups, he eased his way up the stairs. The divine aroma of gourmet brew filled the area.

"Well, I have news for you, all of you," Catherine said,

wielding the papers. "I've got my own solicitors. And you'll have them to answer to, I can assure you."

Glaring at Shepard, she executed a neat about-face and ran up hard against Matthew. Coffee streamed from the upturned carrier. Matthew gasped. Catherine shrieked. And behind me, Eddie Gale failed to suppress a chuckle.

"You stupid, stupid fool," Catherine hissed at Matthew. "You did that on purpose. Look at my shoes. Just look at them. Out of my way, you insignificant little man."

She shoved Matthew out of her path and stomped out of the trailer while he wheezed and struggled to get his shirt off. Steam rose from its folds and curled in the breeze from the door.

"What's her problem?" Matthew gasped, carefully rolling his sodden shirt into a ball.

I eyed Shepard, and he crossed his arms, then shrugged. "She's . . . got issues."

"That's putting it mildly," Eddie said.

Matthew bent to retrieve the empty coffee cups from the floor and, with assistance from Eddie and me, managed to clear away the physical mess Catherine Dawes had made.

Shepard huffed. "I really wanted that coffee."

Matthew looked at Shepard with a poorly concealed mixture of disgust and disbelief and went off to his hotel room to change into a clean shirt and dry pants.

With Eddie occupied wiping splattered coffee from the window, I cornered Shepard in the kitchen. "Look," I whispered, "I need to know what's going on with you and Catherine Dawes."

"Jealous?"

"Painfully." I took a breath. "Shepard, what am I doing here?"

"I need you here."

"In what capacity?"

"We'll go over it." He shot a quick glance over his shoulder. "Not now, though, okay? I gotta get to makeup. I'm due. Stick around. We'll talk when I'm done on the set."

"No, Shepard—"

"Eddie," he said, moving away from me. "I gotta go to work."

And what did he expect me to do in the meantime? Collect autographs? Fetch him more coffee? Hit the slots at the Taj? Maybe I could find some gossip columnists beyond the barricades who knew what lay at the root of the Shepard-Catherine conflict. Or maybe I should just put in a call to Barb.

"You sure? No time for a replacement cup of coffee?" Eddie said, shaking the hand Shepard offered. "I wanted to run something by you."

"Can't, man. Besides"—he tipped his head in my direction—"I got company."

"That's fine. Happy to have her along." Eddie shrugged. "I don't have any national secrets to divulge."

"Well, walk over with us, then," Shepard said.

I followed Eddie out of the trailer and stopped outside and waited for Shepard to lock the door. But he came down the steps and stood silently beside me as though waiting for me to lead the way.

I opened my mouth, hoping words would follow in a timely fashion.

"What?" he said. "What are we waiting for?"

"Aren't you going to lock that?" I asked.

He glanced at the trailer and shrugged. "What for? There's nothing in there. Why would I lock it?"

I lifted my hands in surrender. "Hey, no reason. I suppose it's easier this way. You can come and go as you please—"

"Yes, I can."

"Yeah, good. Matthew too. And me, come to think of it. You know, and if Catherine wanted to leave you any love notes—"

Shepard scrunched his eyes shut and pinched his lips together. "Okay. I get it. I'll get a key."

"What do you mean, a key?" Eddie said over a chuckle. "What do you need a key for?"

Shepard squared his shoulders. "Rainny says I need one."

A soft *O* rounded Eddie's lips. He narrowed his gaze, squinting at Shepard and me in turn. "Maybe I should catch up with you later. Seems you got a few things to work out. But you best listen to this lady," he said, without a hint of humor. "Get a key."

With a soft grin and a twitch that might have been a wink, he turned and strolled back toward the boardwalk.

We both watched him go, the rumble of the RV air-conditioning motors filling our silence. Eddie Gale had a really great swagger. And I only got to appreciate it live because Shepard had sent him on his way.

It suddenly became very important to me to find the guy who wanted to kill Shepard. Because I wanted to help.

While Shepard relaxed in the makeup trailer getting pretty, I surveyed the environment, mentally cataloging building heights, site access, and the constant, chaotic foot traffic on the film set. Ceaseless movement and enough unknown faces to fill the stands at a Knicks game set my nerves on edge. How could I possibly do a threat assessment in a place like that?

I could have started by calling Barb and getting the dish on Shepard's relationship with Catherine Dawes, but I lacked a cell phone. I'd had one—right up until an involuntary swim during a Fourth of July beach party. Someday I'd get around to replacing the phone. Till then, I relied on pay phones and face-to-face discourse. How primitive.

At the sound of a hammer on nails, I shifted my attention from the rooftops to the vacant parking lot beside me that the film crew had cordoned off. Holly Bellinger clacked toward me in shoes with heels so narrow, they might have been made of straight pins. My toes twinged in sympathy.

She approached with her head turned slightly to one side, announcing her suspicion by watching me from the corner of her eyes. Finally close enough to address me, she lifted her chin in a mute rendition of "Hey, you." Aloud she said, "Who are you?"

She had to be talking to me—after all, she hadn't taken her eyes off me—but still I glanced around, trying to spy someone more likely to be the object of her attention. "Who, me?"

"I saw you before, hanging on Shepard Brown." She stopped

less than two feet before me, near enough to encroach on my personal space and make my backing off a sign of weakness. I stayed put.

Even in five-inch stilettos she stood only a couple of inches taller than my sneaker-clad five-foot-six, making her work hard to achieve the challenging glare she angled down at me.

"You were also standing around staring while they were lighting my shot. And you don't belong here," she said.

Interesting. "How do you know I haven't been here on the set all along?" I asked.

"I pay attention. Now, are you going to tell me who you are, or am I going to have to call security?"

The fact that they had security surprised me; I had seen no indication of protection. Either Holly B. was more observant than I—a deeply frightening thought—or there were too few members of the security team to make an impact.

I answered her question as truthfully as I dared without tipping my hand. "I'm a friend of Shepard's," I said.

"You're lying. Shepard doesn't have female friends," she said. "He has ex-girlfriends who hate him and one-night stands who want him back."

"Really? Which category do you fall into?"

"We're not talking about me. We're talking about you."

"I told you, I'm a friend."

"Which is a lie."

"So nice to see we're making progress. Go into the makeup trailer and ask him," I said. "He's right inside. Maybe you'll get lucky and he'll be showing off his biceps."

An irritated pinching around the eyes made me think she wouldn't find that prospect appealing, which actually I found rather endearing.

"Fine." She struggled to pull a haughty demeanor into place but circled wide around me on her way to the trailer entrance. "I'll just ask him, then."

I turned to wave at her retreating figure. In so doing I spotted Dutch, the crewman I had spoken with earlier, whistling as he rounded the corner. A coil of electrical cord hung from his shoulder. His gaze met mine, and his whistle faded away.

I smiled, but his nervous glancing—at everything but me—indicated his displeasure at my presence. He scuttled toward me, shoulders hunched. "You shouldn't be here," he said.

Oh, here we go again.

"I never should have let you pass before." He hiked the electrical cord higher on his shoulder.

"You don't look like a security guard," I said. I realize this was a bit of Mrs. Kettle and Mr. Pot, but . . .

"I'm not, but we all help out where we can. So I'm afraid I have to ask you to leave."

"I'm not leaving."

"Now, don't make this difficult, all right? You're going to have to leave."

"I can't leave. I'm waiting for Shepard. If I'm not here when he comes out of this trailer, they're not going to get a decent day's work out of him." I didn't know if my absence would affect Shepard in any such way, but the implication sounded good.

He shook his head slowly, the ends of his pale blond beard grazing his shirt. "Sorry, but I don't know that you're not lying. There are a lot of women who would like to get their hands on Mr. Brown."

As repulsive as that sounded, it was true. Millions of women across the nation thought Shepard was the greatest thing since call waiting. Thank God I wasn't one of them.

Sighing, I reached into my pocket.

"You can't bribe me," he warned.

I gave Dutch a tight smile and presented him with my badge and ID. "I'm here to make your job easier," I said. "You worry about . . . whatever it is you worry about . . . and I'll make sure no one gets their hands on Shepard without his permission, okay?"

He ignored the badge but took my ID in hand. "Diamond Security Services, Executive Protection and On-Site Guard Force. Sounds important," he said, reading from the ID. He squinted at the little photo in the corner, then squinted at me for comparison. "You're blond in this picture," he said. "I like the brown better."

"Gosh, thanks."

"You're welcome, Ms. Keys."

"It's just Lorraine, okay?"

"Okay." He handed me back the ID case and smiled. "Stay for today," he said. "But if you're coming back tomorrow, make sure Mr. Brown arranges a pass-card for you."

"I don't think Mr. Brown is capable of arranging anything on his own," I mumbled.

Dutch laughed, knocked me sideways when he patted me on the shoulder, and continued on his way.

As he resumed his whistling, Holly emerged from the trailer exit and started down the steel steps. She pitched slightly forward, balancing her weight on her toes to keep the heels of her shoes from catching in the grating. She tried to toss her hair, but it was lacquered motionless, so she huffed, rolled her eyes, and came to stand beside me, this time keeping a respectable distance.

"Shepard says you're just friends," she said.

I wanted to say "I told you so" so badly, I bit my lip.

"He also says you've known each other since grade school and I should be nice to you."

"Well, tha—"

"So, what size dress do you wear?"

"Sorry?"

"Dresses. What size? I asked my assistant to send me the cocktail dresses I keep in the blue garment bag, but she sent the navy blue garment bag instead of the royal blue garment bag, and the navy blue garment bag has a dress and a couple of blouses and jackets that don't fit me after my last enhancement procedure. I planned to give them to a thrift shop, but they might fit you, in which case my assistant will have done a good thing instead of something I should fire her for. So, what size?"

Huh. There was a difference between royal blue and navy blue?

"My dress, uh . . ." I said.

Holly shrugged. "Well, you'll let me know. Shepard said you'd be staying around for the next few days, so we'll work something out. I have to get back inside now." She pressed her fingers to her nose, where a spray of freckles shone through her foundation. "I'm flaking."

This time she smiled and waved as she went by, and I wondered what Shepard had said to make her turnaround so complete. Looked like I'd have time to find out. Shepard had told her I'd be staying around.

Guess that meant I was on the job—for better or worse.

Chapter Three

Shepard emerged from the makeup trailer looking just like himself, only intensified. "This way," he said.

I hustled after him, trying to keep pace. "Why are we hurrying?" I asked.

"I'm late."

"You were late before. Why are we rushing now?"

"I gotta beat Holly up there. I bet her twenty bucks." He took the ramp up to the boardwalk at double-time, long legs making the movement effortless.

"Hey, what did you say to her anyway?" The metal railing burned beneath my hand, and I peered at the sky in some surprise. The haze that had muted the sky earlier had burned off and left behind an endless, washy blue and the promise of a scorching day ahead.

"Told her we're old friends," Shepard said, flashing a grin.

"No, about me staying."

He waited for me at the top of the ramp. "You are staying, right?"

I pushed my hair back off my forehead, wishing for a taste of the wind that had irritated me earlier. "Let's get this on the table right now, okay? So there's no confusion. What is it that you want me to do?"

He glanced briefly over his shoulder. "I want you to stay and make sure"—he checked over his other shoulder—"make sure nothing happens to me."

"You want to hire bodyguards?"

"No, just you."

"No, not just me. I can't do this alone. I'll need help."

Shepard folded his arms against his chest, broke eye contact, and shook his head. "No. I don't want anyone else."

"Shepard. Though it pains me to admit it, especially to you, I'm only human. You want me to stay sharp, I'm going to need someone to relieve me."

He had his lips pressed firm, but they twitched as he considered.

"One more person," I said. "One more or I'm not doing it."

He snorted in displeasure. I'm not sure whether the guy was being cheap or whether he really did believe I could do it all—making him either a jerk or my biggest fan. "Okay," he said. "One."

"One."

"At night. When I'm sleeping."

"Yeah. Whatever. I'll make that part of the deal."

"Okay. Only at night."

"Only at night," I said. "I'll take a ride back now and square it with my boss." And score instant points for bringing in a high-profile client. Go, me.

"What do you mean 'now'?" he said, waving to the crowd gathered behind the barricades. Several dozen screeching women called his name and waved back. "You're not leaving right away, are you? Why don't you stick around for a little while? You'll have fun. Trust me."

I hung around the set till late morning before I decided Shepard had no understanding of "fun." The scene-shooting process amused me for the first thirty-five minutes. After that, it excited me as much as watching a cat sleep. In front of the cameras, Shepard had looked earnestly at Holly and said, "How long has it been?" sixteen times before I surrendered. If I had to watch the scene one more time, I was going to shoot myself—which would make Shepard a wide-open target for the pizza killer.

I flagged down Shepard to let him know I was leaving and

assure him the bright lights and rolling cameras guaranteed his safety. Anyone who would choose poison as a means to murder wouldn't be likely to get too close to their target, especially in a place as public as a film set.

I almost made a clean getaway too. But smack in the middle of my "Don't worry, you'll be fine" speech, Eddie Gale ambled by on his way to try to catch a ride to the Gardner's Basin location. Without consultation, Shepard volunteered my services as driver. He also volunteered the use of his car. If I'd been in my right mind, I would have declined the car, but trying to recover from the idea of driving around with Eddie Gale made it tough to argue.

Shepard dispatched his assistant, Matthew, to retrieve the car from the valet at Resorts while I dashed over to the trailer to wrap a sample of the suspect pizza. Along the way I told myself a dozen times that Eddie Gale was just a man like any other. It didn't matter how good he smelled or how sweetly he smiled. He was just a guy. I didn't quite believe myself, but I got close enough to be functional.

I tried not to look directly at Eddie when I met up with him and Matthew beside a glossy black SUV with hubcaps polished to a mirror finish and dark-smoked windows.

"This is Shepard's?" I asked.

Matthew nodded, and a tiny burst of dread centered itself between my shoulder blades. My personal vehicle hovered in that awkward stage between classic and heap of junk. If I drove my car into a sandbank, it would be no great loss. If I drove the SUV into anything other than a mountain of cotton . . . different story.

Handing me the keys, Matthew solemnly wished me safe travels.

As he jogged off in the direction of the boardwalk, I took a deep breath and turned to face Eddie.

Sunshine nestled in his hair and brightened the blue of his eyes. He looked tan and healthy and fit. And I was expected to speak?

He studied me for a long moment, as if trying to figure something out. "You want me to drive?" he asked, before I could get body and mind in sync.

"Get in the car," I managed to say. Juggling the pizza slice, I shrugged out of the shirt I wore over a black tank top to save the silk from major wrinkling as I drove.

He smiled a lopsided smile. "Should I undress too?"

I thought I might swoon and completely ruin my tough-girl 'tude. I looked him in the eye, hoped my body wasn't telegraphing "take me now" messages, and said, "Get in the car please."

Grinning, he circled around to his side of the vehicle, and I did a very slow count to three and tried to collect myself. Only months had elapsed since I split with my last boyfriend, and it wasn't as if Eddie Gale's fame made him undeniable. Rather, I blamed the shortness of breath and tiny trembling on that unnamable something, that appeal, that chemistry sizzle. It was a basic boy-girl thing. Happened all the time. I just wished it wouldn't happen while I was working.

With pizza slice and silk shirt stowed behind the driver's seat, I climbed into the comfort of soft leather and the lingering fragrance of new car. Shepard had told me he kept the car at his folks' summerhouse so he would have his own vehicle whenever he visited. From the shiny-clean look of things, he kept his visits infrequent and brief.

Pulling the seat belt across my body so that it looked as if a bandolier bisected my breasts, I blew out a breath and tried to overlook the hum in my bloodstream.

Eddie buckled into the passenger seat as I threaded the key into the ignition. "This is a great car," he said. "Three hundred forty-five horse, V-8 engine, rear-wheel drive, and ABS with hydro-boost."

"Thank you, *Motor Trend*," I said, grateful for this proof of his ordinary-guy status. I could handle that. As soon as my heart stopped beating so hard. Lord, did I smell his cologne or just his natural, sexy scent?

The engine caught, and a hellacious noise roared within the cab. Club music vibrated the windows, the bass beat lodging in my throat and making me doubt my ability to swallow. I reached to shut off the noise, but Eddie reached the volume control first.

"Sorry," he said, glancing in my direction. "Did you want to hear that?"

"Good grief, no. See if you can find something with a lot of metal, will you?" Maybe a little classic rock would help soothe my nerves.

Eddie smiled softly, further turned down the volume on the radio, and started searching for a station.

Focusing on the car, I eased away from the curb, anxious not to do any damage to the vehicle. I spent a couple of seconds familiarizing myself with its handling. It leaped ahead at the slightest tap of the gas pedal, and each time I tested the brakes, we came to an abrupt stop.

"You sure you know how to drive?" Eddie asked.

"Nope. This is my first time." I adjusted the rearview mirror and urged the vehicle to cruising speed.

His hand stilled above the radio tuner. "You're joking, right?"

I sighed. "Yes. Sorry."

"Just give me a little while to get used to the humor, okay?" he asked over a chuckle. "It's not what I'm used to."

"How sad."

He lowered his hand. "ZZ Top okay?"

"Turn it up loud. Which way at the light?"

With classic ZZ filling the car, we headed north on Atlantic and began to weave our way through the less-glittery portions of Atlantic City. While most of me focused on not crashing a car that cost more than I made in a year, the other part of me relaxed at the idea of having Eddie in the passenger seat. After all, it wasn't as if I'd never had a man in my car. Then again, I wasn't in my car.

"Tell me something," I said over the music. "Don't you guys have car service to get you back and forth? A limo or something?"

Scowling, Eddie shook his head. "There's a limo. I'm not into it. Any of it. Turn right."

I bit back a complaint and made the turn. I much preferred a navigator who gave heads-up directions rather than springing turns on me like a surprise party. But this navigator I was willing to forgive.

"Now you tell me something," Eddie said. And before I had time to panic over what he might ask, he continued. "Shepard said you guys go way back. That so?"

"Yeah, forever."

"How long?"

"Grade school. So that's—what?—almost twenty years." Wow. I rarely thought of it in terms of actual years. Somehow "forever" sounded like less time.

"And you and Shepard are just friends, or . . . ?"

My laughter echoed in the cavernous confines of the car. "No, there's no 'or.' Just friends. Seriously, do I look like Shepard's type?"

"Well, aside from that great laugh you have, I'd say no. He's got a thing for fragile, anorexic chicks, and you . . ." He trailed off, and I glanced over to find his gaze slowly tracking every curve of my body, the corners of his lips rising in appreciation. "You are definitely not anorexic."

His eyes met mine and popped in shock. He shook his head quickly and fixed his gaze out the window. "Sorry," he said, as his neck and the back of his ear flushed red.

This line of conversation warranted pursuit. "What—?"

"Here," Eddie said suddenly. "Left. Take this left."

Squelching a profane outburst, I slammed on the brakes and hauled the wheel hard to the left. An alarmingly loud pop sounded from the engine of the SUV. The tiny seed of fear I carried about wrecking the car began to grow. I sucked in a quick breath and held it, waiting to find out what horrors lay ahead. The vehicle shimmied into the straightaway and stayed on course.

"Did you hear that?" Eddie asked.

I shot him a glance and met intense blue eyes gone dark with concern. "Turn the radio off."

Silence cocooned us, a silence so complete, I marveled at the car's engineering.

As I eased off the accelerator, I tried my best to forget Eddie's presence and tune in to the vehicle. The car slowed as expected, then, when I got up the nerve to resume pressure on the gas pedal, increased speed. A check of the instrument panel showed no illuminated warning lights, and the needle on the tachometer held steady. I softened my grip on the steering wheel, telling myself my nerves had made me jump to conclusions, that the noise had been nothing. A squirrel pitching acorns. A couple of months early. At the undercarriage of the car.

"You want to take this left," Eddie said softly.

I gaped at him. "*Now* you're going to start giving me advance warning?"

"Seemed the best plan. How's the car feel?"

I shook my head. No sense telling him about the squirrel.

At the corner I spied a break in traffic that would allow me to make the turn. I flicked the blinker with one hand and pulled on the steering wheel with the other. The SUV turned fifteen degrees to the left, then moved straight ahead, headed directly for the corner pawnshop. Beneath my hands, the response of the wheel went from instantaneous to nonexistent. "Crap," I spat.

I put extra muscle into turning the car, but still the vehicle altered course no more than five degrees. I slammed on the brakes. Eddie lurched forward in his seat.

"What's wrong?" he asked.

"No power steering!" I shouted, eyes on the oncoming traffic.

He shifted and took hold of the wheel as I gave the car a little gas. The blue sedan headed for us honked its horn as though we were unaware of our predicament. Shoulder-to-shoulder, four hands on the wheel, we cussed and muscled the SUV around the corner with less grace than a Patton tank.

In my rearview mirror, traffic streaked past my rear bumper. "Thank God," I breathed, foot on the brake to slow the speed of our turn.

"Must have been what that noise was," Eddie said.

I choked back a "duh," chiefly because the brake pedal was rising against my foot. "Losing power brakes," I said, trying to keep the panic from my voice. I didn't know the line between not having power brakes and not having any brakes at all. I had no desire to learn the hard way.

"Maybe it's time to pull over."

But on one of Atlantic City's many one-way roads, each curb was lined with parked cars.

"Where do you suggest?" My voice cut with unchecked sarcasm, while my chest constricted with anxiety.

"Maybe . . ." He reached to the button for the onboard GPS, and we both watched the display screen remain dark.

While I pumped the brake, I resumed looking for somewhere to pull over. "Leave it to Shepard not to keep his account current."

"And I can't think of anyone I know who needs vehicle-navigation help more," Eddie said, leaning forward a bit in his seat. "Let's take this left."

"No. Let's please avoid any turning or stopping until we have no choice."

"Well, I don't want to alarm you . . ."

I tore my attention away from the endless string of parked cars to glance at Eddie. His gaze rested on the hood, where puffs of smoke crept out of the seams.

A renewed stream of sweat trickled between my shoulder blades.

"Got any ideas?" I asked.

"I have some ideas about what could go wrong next."

"You're right. We need to get off this road. Help me make this turn."

Half off his seat, he cursed the burled-wood console that divided us. Eddie once again took hold of the wheel and added muscle to get us around the corner.

We rolled in a straight line into the left lane of the one-way. Even at idle speed the speedometer crept over twenty mph. "Do we have fire or just smoke?"

Eddie leaned close against the dash and peered at the hood. "I don't see any flames—"

"Don't say 'yet.'"

"All right. But I'm thinking it."

Sweat made my hands slick on the wheel. "We need to find a way to stop this car."

"Controlled crash."

But we'd rolled into a residential area. The distance between the street and the front porches was mighty narrow. Should the smoke indicate fire and the fire spread, I didn't want the fire consuming anything more than the car.

A single flame licked out from under the hood, and I clenched the steering wheel tighter.

"Ahead on the left," he said.

At the upcoming corner, orange plastic fencing blocked undeveloped property from trespassers. I figured the fencing was no match for the SUV. I also figured there was no need to make a pretty turn into the driveway.

"Give me a hand," I said.

Eddie shifted toward me, his hands beside mine on the wheel. We forced the car left, then grunted when the vehicle jumped the curb. The SUV threatened to tip. Cursing, I pressed both feet against the brake and aimed for a mini-mountain of dirt. The side of the vehicle scraped against the dirt, and still we rolled. The property line lay ten feet ahead. Fifteen feet would put us into the neighbor's yard, into the side of their aboveground pool. One more pile of dirt to our right. The SUV caught it at the headlight. Dirt and pebbles flew up over the hood of the SUV, clattered against the windshield, and the vehicle ground to a stop. Clouds of dust surrounded us, and flames crept onto the windshield.

"Out, out, out," I said, as if there were any other option. I cut the engine, pulled the key from the ignition, and rolled out of the car.

Dirt and smoke swirled into my eyes and filled my throat. Squinting against the assault, I hustled to the sidewalk, coughing and sputtering.

Eddie met me there, breath shallow, brow coated in sweat and dirt and creased with concern. "You okay?" he asked, resting a hand on my shoulder.

I nodded and swiped at my eyes, tearing from the force of the coughing.

"You sure?"

"Fine."

We stood for a moment side by side, watching smoke rise from the vehicle. Safe. We were safe. I let out a shaky breath, then sent a silent thanks heavenward. Nothing like a brush with disaster to make a person grateful to be alive.

"Holy smoke," Eddie said. "What do you think caused that?"

I shook my head. I wasn't thinking about *what*. I was thinking about *who*.

Eddie made all the appropriate phone calls while a helpful AC resident rushed to our aid with a pair of kitchen fire extinguishers. The police radioed for a tow, but with no injuries and no damage to anything but the SUV and a plastic fence, they departed in short order to attend to more pressing matters—like getting Eddie Gale to Gardner's Basin.

I sat beside Matthew in his economy rental car, heading back to the boardwalk. I needed to get back and explain to Shepard about his car, even though I had no idea what to say and no confidence the right words would occur to me. The adrenaline rush I'd felt earlier had long since faded, and the experience of wrecking the SUV had taken on the quality of a surreal memory, an event I had imagined rather than lived.

Shepard turned out to be more concerned about me and Eddie than about the car but continued to give me a wide-eyed gaze that conveyed his conviction that this adventure proved someone was trying to kill him. I hated that he might be right.

The episode gave me reservations about leaving Shepard on his own, but he planned to go straight from work to the safety of his hotel, to catch up on the sleep he'd missed the night before. And I had to see my boss, present the job proposal, and swing by my house to pick up an Atlantic City wardrobe. Well, okay, a few changes of clothes.

I took another sample of peanut pizza from the trailer and left with Shepard promising to get some pass-cards for me and my yet-to-be-assigned partner. I wondered if we'd need some kind of cover story for being on the set and hoped that, if we did, my boss would come up with one. After all, aren't former spies supposed to be creative thinkers?

Okay, so maybe Dave du Comte hadn't actually been a spy. But nothing else explained his slight limp and classically non-descript appearance. In the two years I had been working for him, I had only ever seen him wear brown suits, for Pete's sake. When was the last time a guy in a brown suit drew your attention?

By the time I got back to the offices of Diamond Security to drop off the pizza sample, the night shift was on dinner break. One of the on-call guards, playing solitaire on his break, informed me that Dave had headed out to the local diner.

I found him sitting at the far end of a string of booths, slicing into a plate of gravy-smothered . . . something. A tiny jukebox hunkered in silence at the end of his table, but I could just make out Elvis singing "A Little Less Conversation" from a nearby machine.

I dropped onto the vinyl-covered bench seat opposite my boss. Brown hair, brown eyes—you wouldn't give him a second glance. But let your gaze hold his for a moment too long and you couldn't tear yourself away, not until the certainty of someone peering into your secrets made the connection unbearable.

I set my elbows on the table and leaned in. A hole in the vinyl wheezed air as my weight shifted. "You're not eating meat loaf, are you?"

He brushed his lips with a corner of his napkin and looked up at me. "I need you at the Guggenheim warehouse tonight."

Few security posts were as tragically boring as the Guggenheim warehouse. I was almost grateful to Shepard for getting me out of the assignment. Not that I planned on thanking him or anything.

"Can't," I said, hoping to keep both the relief and pride out of my voice. "I've gotta get back to Atlantic City."

Dave didn't speak. He simply raised his eyebrows in a way that implied "Explain yourself."

I ordered coffee and pie from a passing waitress and told Dave the story, from Shepard's middle-of-the-night phone call to his agreement to contract two bodyguards. Through it, Dave did a lot of nodding and eating. He had nothing to say until I put the first forkful of apple pie into my mouth.

"I'll send Joe and Frank down," he said.

My mouth went dry around my food. "No. Not Joe and Frank," I said through a mouthful of sweet apple filling. "Me and Frank. Or me and Joe. I'm on this."

"No, you're not."

"Yes. I am."

"This is an actor, right? The job goes to A-division. You go to the Guggenheim."

A-division consisted of eight men who handled high-profile clients. They got the important assignments, the international travel, and the big money. In short, they got what I wanted. But Diamond Security required each guard to complete five hundred hours of bodyguard work before being eligible to apply for A-division. With all the time I spent square-badging and standing watch over inanimate objects and sign-in books, I was about 442 hours short in actual bodyguarding. Spending a week or more as Shepard Brown's shadow would seriously whittle down that number.

I spit the gooey filling into my napkin and glared at Dave. "This is my contract. I brought the client in. I work it."

Calm as you please, Dave laid down his knife and fork and sat back. "You've done—what? Four, maybe five airport transfers?"

"I've done more than that." To date, I'd been in on nine assignments involving safely moving a high-profile client from an airport to his or her hotel. I'd done two alone for Shepard, along with a handful of black-tie fund-raisers. In a world where celebrities and politicians alike take desperate chances to avoid paparazzi or worse, protection is never as easy as it appears.

"Rainny, you're not qualified."

At the sting of his words, my cheeks flushed with heat. "I've completed all the training, Dave. All of it. Even the stuff that's not required."

"Training isn't experience."

"I won't get the experience if you spend another year assigning me to museums and banks and smelly labs." I forked more apple-pie chunks into my mouth, trusting the food to keep frustration at bay.

"I'll assign you wherever I please."

"Then assign me to my client."

"He's not your client. He's the company's client."

"Not if I advise him to use another company." Granted, this would have sounded more menacing if I hadn't been talking with my mouth full, but I hoped the puffy cheeks added a certain Brando-in-*The Godfather* quality to my speech.

Dave picked up his knife again and dragged its tip through the gravy puddle on his plate. A hint of the dark capability of the man lurking within Mr. Nondescript flashed in his eyes. "Listen to me. You screw up in training, they lower your marks. You screw up on a security patrol, we fire you. You screw up guarding a principal, and the principal can die."

His dire observations hung in the air while I chewed. Make no mistake, I knew the consequences of failure. Were this any other assignment, Dave's words might have done more than sour my stomach. They might have made me forget how badly I wanted to be the first woman on the A-division.

The difference was, no faceless foreign dignitary needed protection. Shepard Brown needed protection. My Shepard. My childhood pal. How could I not be the one to keep him safe? How could Dave suggest sending Joe and Frank instead of me?

Forcing that last bite of pie down my throat, I looked away from Dave, unhappy with where my thoughts were straying. "Tell me something," I said, " 'cause I want to know. Is this about my experience, or is this about something else?"

"I suggest you refrain from insinuating."

I hated it when he talked like that. "I'm not insinuating. I'm asking. Is this about—"

"It's nothing to do with your gender. This is about a man's life. Focus on that."

A man's life was precisely what I was focused on.

I reached for my coffee cup, white-knuckling the porcelain handle. I lifted my gaze to Dave's and practically fell into the endless dark pools of his eyes. He didn't move. I didn't move. Activity continued around us. Cutlery tapped on earthenware. Busboys chattered in Spanish. The register bell dinged with a sale.

"You and Joe," he said at last.

Tension whooshed out of me so fast, it should have been audible.

"Work it out who's on days and who's on nights."

I squelched the urge to thank him effusively. Frankly, I squelched the urge to thank him at all. Instead I nodded and did my best to appear professional while my toes did a happy dance inside my Keds.

"I hope you're right and there's nothing to this," Dave said. "But if you're wrong . . . first sign of trouble . . ." He jerked his thumb like an umpire signaling a runner out. "Guggenheim warehouse."

I stood before my kitchen stove and carefully turned sizzling strips of bacon. My heavy-duty duffel bag slouched beside the living room door, ready to be thrown into the trunk of my car and whisked away to Atlantic City. I'd stuffed the bag with my usual summer wardrobe of cutoffs and funky shirts for off-hours and khakis and polos for working. All I needed to do was down a hearty breakfast and I'd be off.

"You look so calm."

I spun at the sound of the voice. Barb stood at the door, nose pressed against the screen, scowl visible.

"You look so annoyed," I said. I set down the spatula and went to let her in.

"I take it you haven't seen this morning's paper," she said when I reached the door.

"Would reading the paper spoil my calm?" I punched the latch with the side of my fist and pushed the door open. "Want some bacon-and-cheese muffin?"

She shouldered into the kitchen, overstuffed purse dangling from her elbow and a newspaper clutched between her palms. "Shouldn't there be something else in there, like egg or hamburger or . . . ?"

Back at the stove, I shook my head and tugged at the pull cord that switched on the exhaust fan. I loved the smell of bacon, but the smoke was starting to collect. "No eggs today," I said as I tugged in vain on the chain. "Today is for consuming perishables like bacon, bread, and chocolate pudding."

"I don't know how you don't weigh four hundred pounds."

"Is that what this attitude is about? My metabolism?"

"No, I'll tell you what's . . . I'll tell you why." She struggled with the newspaper, trying to fold it open without its pages touching her nails.

I eyed her polish, liquid crimson and shiny new. And did her hair look a little blonder and a little straighter? She looked lovely; why was she stomping around like I'd stolen her boyfriend? "Tough morning at the salon?" I asked.

With a huff she crossed the room and dropped the paper onto the table. "Why didn't you tell me you saw Shepard Brown?"

Uh-oh. I almost wished I had stolen her boyfriend. I needed to stall while I thought up a plausible alibi. "Seriously, I need to get rid of the chocolate pudding. Are you sure you don't want some?"

Barb separated one newsprint sheet and held it in front of me. Page six. In a photo below a headline that read ON LOCATION, Shepard smiled as he embraced a woman with her back to the camera. Clarification: *my* back, Shepard's bear hug nearly eclipsing my favorite shirt, the silk one I'd worn yesterday.

"Nuts," I muttered. I grabbed the page from her and squinted at the grainy photo. Nose against the print, I still couldn't accurately identify the woman in Shepard's arms, and I would go so far as to say I knew her pretty well. How had Barb figured it out?

"Aha! So it *is* you!" Her brown eyes flashed in triumph.

"Wait. You didn't know it was me?"

Barb's face said *sarcasm* better than words could. "How could I possibly tell from that picture?"

"So you *tricked* me? I can't believe you did that." This was the sort of thing my mother would pull. But Barb had been my best friend since I'd decked Regis Colper during our freshman field trip. From her I expected direct questions, not subterfuge.

"Jeez, Rainny, I wouldn't have had to if you'd just told me. How come you didn't?"

I made a rapid scan of page six. If Barb was out-of-joint over the Shepard Brown meeting, I didn't need her stumbling over any photos of me with Eddie Gale. "I got in late," I said, searching the caption for a mention of Eddie or the episode with the burning car. But all it said was *Shepard Brown greets unknown woman on the Atlantic City set of* Boardwalk.

"Hey," I said. "Does this 'unknown' mean they couldn't identify me, or does it mean I'm a nobody?"

She sighed. "Both. It means they don't know you and don't need to. Be thankful. If it said 'mystery woman,' then you'd be in trouble. 'Mystery woman' says you and Shepard are involved. You're not involved, are you?"

If being "unknown" meant I didn't have Shepard's skivvies between my sheets or his paparazzi at my door, I'd take it as a good thing.

"No," I said. "Not involved. Don't be ridiculous."

"I'm not being ridiculous. Number one, this is Shepard Brown we're talking about. I mean, c'mon, Rainny, most normal American women would crawl through broken glass to sleep with him. He's gorgeous. And he's got abs you could bounce a quarter off."

Now, I wanted to correct her regarding the physique of Mr. "I'm putting on weight for the film," but I thought it kinder to allow her her illusions. She had so few. She taught public school, after all. Summers off provided only so much consolation.

"Second of all, you lied to me about seeing him in the first place. Why shouldn't I think you're lying about the nature of your relationship?"

"Oh, for the love of . . . Barb, I didn't lie to you about seeing him."

"Well, you didn't tell me about it. Same thing."

"Different thing. I would have told you, but like I said, I got in late."

"Because you were out with Shepard."

"I was not out with Shepard!"

"What else aren't you telling me?"

"I was—" The whistle of the smoke alarm split my eardrums, and I realized that, worse than my breakfast being reduced to cinders, I'd nearly blurted out the story of crashing a burning SUV with Eddie Gale. "You'd better sit down," I said, shouting over the shriek of the alarm.

I shoved the frying pan onto a cool burner and dragged a chair into the hallway. Climbing atop the chair, I twisted the cover off the smoke alarm, removed the mechanism from the ceiling, and ripped out the battery. Ah, blessed silence.

Assuring myself that I would remember to replace the device, I left smoke-alarm innards on the seat of the chair and left the chair in the hallway.

"Look," I said, as I returned to the kitchen. "My relationship with Shepard is purely professional."

Barb sat in the remaining chair, ankles crossed, hands folded in front of her, and raised one eyebrow.

I sighed. "Okay, it's friendly. But certainly not physical. He's also a client, and you know the rules, Barb. I can't give you any information about him." I threw open a window and tried to wave the smoke along its path to freedom.

"I don't see why not," she said. "You know I wouldn't tell anyone. I'm good at keeping secrets."

"This isn't about your ability to keep secrets. It's about my job, and it's about policy and rules. And call me crazy, but I'm a real fan of rules."

"Are you?"

"Yes." I took a spatula to the ruined bacon, chiseled it out of the frying pan, and dropped the over-fried pork into the trash.

"Then why did you disconnect your smoke alarm?"

My first instinct was to slap her with the spatula. I'd known her a long time; I could get away with a little. Instead, I smiled as sweetly as I could manage and laid the pan and spatula on the stovetop. "Thank you. You're right. Excuse me for one minute, would you?"

Back in the hallway I snapped the battery into place and clambered up on top of the chair. I pressed the cover to its track in the ceiling and turned it clockwise, but the device weighed heavily in my hands. Huh. I had removed it counterclockwise; it should go back on clockwise. I tried again. And the battle began. "Nuts," I muttered.

"Everything okay?" Barb called.

"Fine. Everything's fine, drat it."

Once more, with feeling. I lifted, twisted, and hoped. No dice.

The phone rang, and I looked down at the chair, wondering if I should get off the thing and answer the phone or let the call go to voice mail.

"You want me to get that?" Barb called.

"Yeah, would you? It's probably my boss. Tell him I'm not here." If Dave was calling to tell me he'd had second thoughts and had decided to send me to the Guggenheim warehouse, I could pretend I'd already left for the land of sand and casinos. Good thing Barb had stopped by. And, damn, I had to remember to ask her about Shepard and Catherine Dawes. When it came to celebrity gossip, Barb held more facts at her fingertips than a database operator at the *Star National*.

I heard Barb use her ultracalm schoolteacher voice to tell

the caller "one moment please." The phone clattered onto the countertop, and Barb appeared at the end of the hallway, hands braced against her hips, lips pinched in bitterness. "It's for you," she said. "Eddie Gale."

Chapter Four

As though Eddie could see along the phone lines, I tried for poise as I clambered down from the kitchen chair.

Smoke alarm in one hand, I grabbed the telephone receiver with the other. Since that left me nothing to cover Barb's mouth with, I tried to glare her into silence.

She smiled a wicked little smile and plastered her shoulder against mine so she could hear the conversation. Great. Lucy and Ethel talk to a movie star.

"Eddie," I said, trying to keep Barb from tipping the receiver in her direction.

"Lorraine," he drawled. Most people slur my name. He actually got the *o* in there. Impressive. "How are you doing today?" Every word out of his mouth came slow and steady, in no particular rush.

"Fine—just—I—what can I do for you?" So much for poise and composure.

"I was wondering . . ."

I waited, wondering a bit myself. What had compelled Eddie Gale to call me? How had he gotten my number? And where had he grown up that he had that voice? Mercy. Parts of my body that hadn't melted in eons softened just at the sound.

"Wondering what?" I said, as I tried—and failed—to edge away from Barb in the confines of the hallway. I could feel the bubble of enthusiasm building in Barb seeping out of her pores. Any second now she'd be squealing.

"Is Shepard with you?" Eddie asked.

I shot Barb a stern look that assured her Shepard Brown was nowhere on my property. "No, he's not. Have you tried his trailer?"

"I'm in his trailer. In fact, I'm using his cell phone," he said slowly. "He has your number on voice-command dialing—did you know that?"

It figured. I couldn't even maintain possession of a cell phone, but Shepard got his to function like a *Star Trek* communicator.

"See, he was due on the set at eight this morning," Eddie went on. "But no one's seen him. Are you sure he's not with you?"

That fast, the warm, relaxing-in-the-sun feeling that Eddie's voice gave me evaporated, and anxiety filled the void. "What do you mean, no one's seen him?" I asked.

"Just what I said. He missed his call."

Missing. Shepard was missing. Oh, sweet mother of all that's holy. Visions of Shepard bruised and gagged flashed through my imagination like a slide show at a torture training camp.

I clutched the phone tighter. "Eddie, please tell me someone's spoken to him, someone knows where he is."

"No, no one. So I thought maybe he headed up by you."

Sweat sprang out on my forehead as the Shepard in my visions began to bleed. Barb edged away from me, confusion wrinkling her brow. I had to do something. But what? I was in Staten Island, and Shepard was . . . somewhere.

The police! I'd call the police. I just needed a phone not currently in use.

Free of Barb, I dropped the smoke alarm onto the kitchen table and grabbed her purse. "Eddie," I said, in a voice favored by demon-possessed virgins, "when was the last time someone saw Shepard?" One-handed, I attempted to upend the purse in hopes its contents would spill helpfully onto the table.

"What are you doing?" Barb screeched. Heedless of her manicure, she ripped the purse from my hands and hugged it to her chest. Nuts!

I extended thumb and pinky, holding my hand to my free

ear in the universal sign for *telephone*. She huffed and pointed to the phone I held to my other ear.

"Your cell phone," I mouthed. Argh! What was the area code for Atlantic City? 608? 609? Could I just dial 609-911? How did that work?

"Oh, no," she said in an intense whisper. "You keep Shepard and Eddie from me and expect me to trust you with my things?"

"Barb," I snarled.

"No." Eyes closed, she held her hand up, palm out, and shook her head. "I can't talk to you right now."

"I haven't seen him since last night," Eddie was saying. "I left him in the casino playing some poker."

"What time? Any idea?" Time mattered. The police were funny about missing persons.

"Maybe one thirty. Two o'clock."

Not quite eight hours, then. Mercy.

I closed my eyes, pressed my hand against the top of my head, and crouched a little. What in heaven's name had I been thinking? Why had I gone home? I should have stayed with Shepard, should have made sure he went back to his hotel and slept like he said he would. Guilt flooded my chest, making it hard to draw breath.

"Lorraine?" Eddie prompted. "You still there?"

"Sorry," I said. "Sorry, I, uh . . . Matthew. Have you seen Matthew? Shepard's assistant?"

Barb shot me the sort of haughty look only blondes and Brits can pull off and headed to the door.

"I thought I saw him down by—" Eddie said.

"Good. Find him. Find out from him the last time he heard from Shepard, and call me—" Drat. I didn't have a cell phone. I gambled on talking Barb into letting me borrow hers and gave Eddie the number even as I watched Barb heft my duffel bag over her shoulder and bang out of the house.

"Everything all right, Lorraine? You sound tense."

"Yeah. Fine. Sure." I tried to pursue Barb out the door, but the phone cord didn't reach much farther than the threshold.

"All right, then. I imagine I'll be seeing you shortly?" Eddie's tone shifted to all-business.

And Barb sat cross-legged on the hood of my car, clutching my duffel bag like a body pillow.

"Wait—can—I'm very sorry, Eddie. Would you give me one moment please?" I didn't wait for his answer. I pressed the receiver against my thigh and shouted out the door. "What are you doing?"

Barb raised her chin. "I'm going to Atlantic City with you," she said.

"No, you're not."

"Oh, yes, I am. If I have to sit here all the way there, so be it."

"Barb!"

She sent me a frighteningly serene smile. "I'm going to Atlantic City. And I'm going to meet Shepard Brown once and for all."

Bottom line, I was too worried to argue with her. Making her see reason would take too much time away from my search for Shepard. Plus, I needed her phone.

I hung up with Eddie, tossed the frying pan into the trash, and locked up the house. I told Barb in no uncertain terms we wouldn't be stopping for any of her things and made her swear that as soon as she'd met Shepard Brown, she'd go straight home. When she agreed, we climbed into the car and lit out for Atlantic City.

"I don't get it. I mean, you might want to explain to me why we're suddenly in such a rush to get down there," Barb said. From the corner of my eye I could see her studying her manicure, trying to act cool and not at all like a devotee of the *Star National*. "Is Shepard in some kind of trouble?"

"No, no. He's fine." What else could I tell her? Certainly not the truth. I needed to distract her. "Tell me about Shepard and Catherine Dawes," I said. "What's the story there? What's the history?"

"Oh, you know." She waved a hand, dismissing my query.

I read the road signs long enough to get into the correct lane for the outbound bridge, and still she didn't continue. What was it with people needing to be prodded?

"No, I don't know. You know these things. That's why I asked you," I said.

Wisps of hair detached themselves from her sleek style and floated around her face. She reached for the vents in the dashboard and carefully angled them away, then smoothed the wayward hair back into place. "Well, they had been dating for about two months, Shepard and Catherine, and she was doing the talk-show circuit for her latest movie. So she goes on that morning talk show, you know, the one with the weird hostess? And she starts yammering about how Shepard is her one true love and they're planning on slipping off and getting married quietly. After which, of course, neither one of them can make a move without the paparazzi on their tails."

"Naturally."

"Naturally. And then Shepard went to Mexico to shoot that movie from Elmore Leonard's book. The one with the guy with the money and the girl and the plane?"

"Uh-huh." I knew neither the book nor the movie, but I knew Shepard had been in Mexico. He'd sent me a postcard of some ancient pile of rocks. He's thoughtful that way.

"So of course they get a picture of him with that Mexican actress, that Malena, and plaster it all over the newsstands."

Finally something I knew about. I might not read the tabloids, but you can't miss the headlines when you're standing in line at the supermarket to pay for your hamburger meat and tampons.

The story went that Shepard and Malena had been "caught" exiting her hotel room together. Sources reported they both looked "rumpled." There's a slim chance they might have gotten rumpled moving furniture or having a pillow fight. But Shepard did have a reputation, and even I had to concede that Malena was drop-dead gorgeous. She made Catherine Dawes about as appealing as yesterday's bubble gum.

"I gather Catherine didn't take it well," I said as I steered the car toward the prepaid lane. "What'd she do?"

Barb's lips curled in sarcastic speculation. "Depends who you believe. According to her supporters, the breakup devastated her. She tried to woo Shepard back by being everything he could possibly want in a woman. She sent him flowers, boudoir photographs, expensive gifts—"

"What about Catherine's detractors? What do they say about her behavior after the Mexico thing?"

Barb huffed so loudly, it might have been a snort. "They accused her of everything from calling at all hours to setting fire to his sports car. Wait a minute. Wait." She struck a stop-in-the-name-of-love pose. "Is Catherine Dawes a problem for Shepard? Is that why you're involved with him now?"

I signaled a lane change and considered. From what Catherine had said, I had to imagine Shepard had found some portion of her behavior disturbing enough to warrant his taking legal action. Maybe she really had set fire to his sports car. Was she capable of doing more?

"I don't know," I said, and I shook my head. "If Catherine really has done those things, why are they working together on this movie?"

Barb shifted in her seat, doing her best to face me despite the restriction of her seat belt. "Seriously? Are you telling me Catherine Dawes is there too? Jeez, Rainny, maybe we could take a few minutes and you can tell me everything you didn't bother to tell me last night."

No way could I tell her the nature of my business with Shepard Brown, but giving her a rundown of the cast-in-residence provided enough distraction that she stopped asking why we were going and started pestering me about the length of time till our arrival.

As far as I was concerned, we couldn't get there soon enough. But once we did . . . Where was I supposed to go looking for Shepard that Eddie hadn't thought of? How was I supposed to find a man whose notoriety had turned him into a pro at not being found?

Cursing silently, I stepped on the gas. I had a few hundred miles to come up with a plan.

By the time we rolled down Brigantine Boulevard, the sun hung high overhead, and the glare off the Borgata blinded unsuspecting tourists and passersby.

I left my luggage, my car, and my best friend in the capable hands of the valet at a massive casino/hotel. If it were up to me, I'd have chosen someplace that couldn't accommodate a small country. But Atlantic City on short notice in the summer made for a tough ticket, and I'd been forced to flex the Diamond Security account at one of the larger establishments.

"Lorraine." Barb grabbed my elbow before I could dodge away. Her eyes shone bright with an anticipation usually reserved for a 70-percent-off sale. "You're going to introduce me tonight, right?" She cut a glance toward the valet, pitching her voice soft so he wouldn't hear. "To Shepard."

Oh, mercy. If I found him. If he was alive. "I'll talk to him about it," I said. "I don't know his schedule."

She sighed and dropped my arm. "Okay, I guess that works, since I have to shop for something to wear. What should I wear?"

I wanted to tell her I didn't care. To me, fashion meant clean clothes. But it meant more to Barb, who set a lot of stock in appearances. "Think about the women he's dated, figure out whether he goes for classy or—"

"Slutty?"

"Sporty. I have to go."

She nodded and followed the bellhop who'd come to collect my bags, and I pushed my sunglasses higher on my nose and turned toward the boardwalk.

I skirted the edge of Brighton Park—a postage stamp of benches and greenery, with a soothing water fountain that did little to soothe me—then hung a left and headed toward the film set and the cluster of trailers at the far end.

A pair of police officers, with shiny badges clipped to the breast pocket of their short-sleeved shirts and with tanned legs peeking out from beneath their uniform blue Bermuda shorts, stood watch at a string of wooden sawhorses. Each barricade had ACPD stenciled along its length to keep the general public—or, in this case, a group of giggling teenagers—off the set.

Since they were real cops, my cute little security-guard ID failed to impress them. Neither were they inclined to consult with any of the dozen or more film assistants scurrying around on the privileged side of the barricades who could let me onto the set.

"I understand," I told them when they flatly refused me access. Were our roles reversed, I would have refused me access too. "Would you happen to know, though, if Shepard Brown is on set right now?"

Movie Cop One shook his head and crossed his arms against his chest, massive muscles flexing with the action. "I don't know anything about that, ma'am."

What was with the whole *ma'am* thing?

"No, he's not there." This from a girl who couldn't have been more than fourteen, dressed like a woman who couldn't be less than twenty. I waited for her to pop her gum bubble before she continued speaking. "We've been, like, waiting for him to show up, but so far only Eddie Gale's come by, and some other, like, really old guy."

I forced a smile past the knot of anxiety threatening to choke me and thanked her for her help.

Sweat gathered against my scalp and pooled at the small of my back. I checked the time on Barb's cell phone. Cast and crew would be breaking for lunch shortly if they hadn't already. My own stomach rumbled, but it wasn't hunger causing the noise. Worry would continue to roil through my belly until I found Shepard. Then I might pass out with relief.

Putting some distance between me and the police barricades, I backtracked to the nearest ramp leading to the beach and headed down to the sand. With the boardwalk on my right and the ocean on my left, I jogged along the beach toward the piers, passing under the massive concrete beams that supported the piers over the crashing waves.

Past the Steel Pier I took the first ramp that returned me to the boardwalk. I continued my jog, hanging a left turn and

passing between two games-of-chance booths. There should
have been obnoxious carnival music playing, attendants hawk-
ing their games. But midday, midweek, the amusements stood
empty and practically silent. Only the sound of my panting
troubled me as I slowed to a stop. That, and the complete absence of any sign of Shepard.

The pounding of my heart as I started back toward the
boardwalk may have been caused by the exertion or the worry.
Or both.

What else? If not Skee-Ball, then what?

Minutes later I swung open the doors at his hotel. Up the
escalator and down a quiet corridor, I took a right into the
private gaming room and came to a sneaker-screeching halt.
Save for a bored-looking waitress and a dealer doing card
tricks, the room held no other life.

Snake eyes.

Bent at the waist, hands on my knees as I gasped for air, I
tried to focus on where to find Shepard, tried to figure out
where else he might be if he were someplace of his own
choosing. While I fought to catch my breath, my mind reeled
of its own accord, rapidly retracing the years I'd known him,
the stupid things he used to get into.

After grade school he'd gone off to a private high school,
the kind of exclusive *école* attended by Arabian princes and
sons of pharmaceutical owners. He'd gone out for football, baseball, and archery. We'd continued to cross each other's paths,
not because I was a cheerleader and he was a running back, but
because he was a darn good shot with a compound bow, same
as me. In fact, I'd gone on to be a darn good shot with a .9 mm.

A new thought brought me upright. If my hobbies had progressed to semiautomatic handguns, and Shepard and I had an
eerie tendency to share interests . . .

I dashed down the escalator, made a beeline for the concierge's desk, and asked the location of the nearest firing range.
It was a long shot, but it was all I had.

Barb's cell phone chirped to life in my pocket as I half ran
two blocks of Illinois Avenue toward Frederickson's Rifle

Range. I wiped the sweat from my temple and helloed politely, if a bit breathlessly.

"May I speak with Lorraine, please?"

It was the *o* in Lorraine that tipped me off. "Hi, Eddie," I said. "Have you found him?"

"I was hoping you had."

"Working on it."

"You still on the road?"

"No, I'm here. I'm on—" I looked up at the street sign. "Atlantic. Not too far."

"All right. We're breaking for lunch here. I'm gonna check out a couple of . . . um . . . eateries . . ."

I had a swift vision of the "eateries" in question, known more for the scantily clad ambiance than for the food. "Thanks. Keep me posted," I said, and I snapped the phone shut. Just my luck. I had Eddie Gale calling me, repeatedly, and the only reason he kept punching my number was because he was looking for Shepard.

Midway up the block I located the establishment the concierge had recommended. I barged right in, setting the electronic door chime into bleeping spasms that echoed my blood pressure.

Frederickson's was Dirty Harry's candy store. Rifles lined the walls, and handguns filled display cases along the perimeter. I passed by shelving in the center that offered a variety of paper targets, cleaning products, and hunting gear, and I spotted surveillance cameras mounted in each corner, their monitors lining the back wall behind the register. I felt oddly at home.

"What can I help you with today?" the proprietor asked. He had dark hair and sallow skin and a surprisingly warm smile.

"I'm looking for—" I said. And stopped. Why couldn't I be looking for Joe Smith? Nobody would bat an eye if I leaned casually on the counter and said, "You seen Joe Smith today?" But I was looking for Shepard Brown. Even a friendly shop clerk might protect Shepard's anonymity for one morning. Nuts. I never should have left him the day before in the first place.

"You have a range on the premises, right?" I asked.

The proprietor nodded and proudly informed me that he kept the range up to code. Of course, I wasn't up on the code, so I nodded in return, acting as if that was good news.

"Would you mind if I take a look?" I fished my gun license out from behind my ID and handed it over. "I'm moving down here in a couple of weeks and need to get some things lined up."

I didn't like to lie. But I believed in doing whatever it took to get a job done. Sometimes that meant getting creative.

He studied the license, then tipped his chin in the direction of my ID. "Who you with?" he asked.

Holding out my Diamond Security ID for his inspection, I bounced my toes inside my sneakers, caffeine-fueled impatience mounting. What if Shepard wasn't here? How much time was I wasting? What if he was slowly bleeding to death somewhere and time was critical?

The shopkeeper handed my license and ID back a split second before I grabbed them. "You folks have to qualify regularly?"

"Absolutely." If the guy thought I'd be shooting once a month just to keep my job, I might improve my odds of a tour.

Fingers rubbing his chin, he considered the facts and finally nodded briefly. "Okay. Through that door." He pointed to a blue-painted door at the rear of the shop, labeled, no surprise, RESTRICTED ACCESS. "Down the steps will put you in the range master's office."

I thanked him and forced myself to walk to the door as if I had nothing but time. Beyond, the concrete stairs were painted glossy gray, dimly lit but not dark. Making up for lost time, I jogged down the steps and pounded open the door at the bottom.

As promised, I landed in the range master's office, where a gentleman considerably rounder than his friend upstairs perched on a stool, roast beef sandwich on the counter in front of him. While he chewed, he interrupted his perusal of his domain to turn to me. "Help you?" he said through a mouthful of food.

I smiled and gave him the routine about checking out the range, one eye on the thick bulletproof glass closing us in. "How many stations you have here?" I asked, casually strolling away, hands clasped behind my back. Beyond the glass I could make out a half dozen or more stations, but to see which ones were occupied, I'd have to walk the length of the office. Someone inside the range was firing, slowly, deliberately. Large caliber, judging by the popping noise that penetrated the glass and soundproofing.

He repeated what his partner upstairs had told me about being up to code and gave me the specifics for the eight stations. Each stretched a standard twenty-five yards long. The walls and ceiling were soundproofed, the glass before me bulletproof.

At sight of the broad-shouldered gunslinger on position five, relief washed through me, followed by a surge of something not unlike fatigue. Worry exhausted me. Feet braced and elbows perfectly angled, Shepard squeezed off two more rounds, and the slide on his semiauto locked back. Habit made me want to knock on the glass to get his attention. But with those orange headphones in place, he'd never hear me.

I did a quick scan of the range master's workstation and spotted the button I wanted. While the range master went on about the best times to shoot, I reached for the button and gave it a good long push.

The cease-fire tone sounded within the booth and along the range. Pavlov couldn't have done better. Shepard laid down his firearm and stepped back from his station. He turned to face the booth, and a seriously goofy smile stretched across my face.

The range master sputtered a protest, pushing himself to his feet. He blustered on about how I shouldn't touch anything and how I'd have to leave if I didn't behave myself, and he might not ever let me back in, and I didn't give a rat's teeth if I never saw the range master again. I had Shepard in sight, upright, whole, and looking just as pleased to see me as I was to lay eyes on him.

Throwing down the headphones, he loped toward the range master's booth. He waited with his hand on the door until the range master buzzed him through, then charged into the space with the exuberance of a puppy. He grabbed me in yet another crushing hug, and a tiny bit of relief morphed into irritation. I couldn't do him much good if he cracked my spine, could I?

"Hey, not here, all right?" the range master said. "Take it outside, huh?"

I wriggled out of Shepard's grasp, gave him a great big smile, and punched him hard on the shoulder.

He covered the offended spot with his hand. "What was that for?"

"Where the hell have you been all morning?"

He shifted his gaze from my eyes and seemed to focus on the tip of my ear. "I've been here for a couple hours, I guess. I'm not really—"

"You were supposed to be . . . at work," I said, catching myself before I said "on the set." I wasn't sure if the range master recognized Shepard. Judging by the pinching across his forehead and at the corners of his mouth, he didn't have a clue. And I didn't want to be the person who gave him one.

Shepard rubbed his arm a second longer. "I know. I overslept. So?"

"If you didn't stay out so late, you wouldn't oversleep."

"I was out because I couldn't sleep in the first place. I finally had to take some sleeping pills. So I had trouble waking up this morning. What's the big deal?"

"What's the big deal? People are looking for you, dummy. All kinds of people." I added extra stress to "kinds," hoping he'd pick up on the clue.

He nodded and looked around. "Yeah, but I'm safe here. I can defend myself here."

Leaving aside the fact that I wanted to beat the crap out of him for scaring me the way he had, he had a point.

"Who else knows you're here?" I asked.

"No one." His grin was enormous. "I'm pretty clever, right?" He caught my elbow. "Come shoot with me. It'll be great."

"There are other people waiting for you," I said.

He waved his hand, unconcerned. "I'll call my agent—he'll straighten everything out. As soon as I find my phone."

"Eddie has your phone."

"That's good news. I thought I left it in—" He cut himself off, and his eyes flared wide for a moment before he recovered his cool. "In the casino."

I crossed my arms and tried to give him a know-it-all glare. "You know, you're a rotten liar. Where were you when you took those sleeping pills anyway? I'm certain Matthew checked your room when you didn't show for work."

"I was . . . I . . ." Shepard pushed his fingers through his hair, which seemed only to encourage more of it to cover his forehead. "I can't tell you right now."

I took a deep breath and continued to work on that glare.

"Seriously, if I could, I would. But right now . . . I promised."

Sounded to me like his evening involved a girl. Or some secret movie deal that I wouldn't understand or care about anyway. I got a vengeful kick out of making him squirm, though, so I kept the glare going, adding a raised eyebrow for impact.

"No, don't. Don't look at me like that."

A few more moments of me being patient ticked by.

"Rainny," he whined.

I huffed. "You know, you have to be honest with me, or this whole relationship we've got going is never going to work."

Reflected in the glass, the range master smirked. All right, I guess I knew what the conversation sounded like, but it really wasn't important enough to try to set him straight on his assumptions.

"I know." Shepard hung his head, looking suitably contrite and not at all unlike an altar boy caught with more than his share of sacramental wine. "I'll try. As soon as I can, I'll tell you. I promise."

"Well, I guess that's all I can hope for. Come on, then," I said. "We really need to get you back."

I expected compliance, maybe a slight delay while he finished up his ammo on the range. Instead, he visibly balked.

Shoulders squared and chin high, Shepard shook his head

in brief, determined motions. "I don't want to do that right now. I need to be alone for a while. No crowds, no press, none of that. I can't take any more people wanting a piece of me right now. You understand, right?"

Of course I didn't understand, not really. The only time I had to put up with crowds wanting my attention was at family reunions. I couldn't imagine what it would be like to live with that sort of pressure day after day, but maybe I might hide out at a pistol range too—take out a little frustration.

"How long are we going to be here?" I asked over a sigh, because no matter how much this new incarnation of Greta Garbo wanted to be alone, I wasn't letting him out of my sight.

"Another hour, maybe? I haven't had lunch. I'm starting to get hungry."

I braced myself, waiting for him to ask me to fetch him some food, but he tipped his head in the direction of the range and repeated his request that I shoot with him for a while.

"C'mon," he said. "You have to be here anyway, right?"

I nodded. "Let me just . . . I've got to call Matthew and let him know you're safe. He can spread the word."

Rather than taking this as par, Shepard did his panicked bit again. "You can't. Not Matthew. I'm telling you, he's in on it. He's the one who brought me that pizza. He can—"

I held a hand up. "I won't tell him where we are, okay? I'll just tell him you're with me. How's that?"

"No. Don't. Just don't."

"You know, as hard as this is to believe, there really are some people worried about you." All right, so no names came to mind. But somebody other than me had to be worried, right? Behind the anger of the bosses, crew, and fellow actors toward Shepard for not showing up for work, there had to be some concern.

"Fine. Call Eddie. He can spread the word."

Shepard read out the number, and I punched it into the cell phone and then headed up to street level and hit SEND.

As I listened to the ring on the other end, it occurred to me that I'd just put Eddie Gale's private cell number into Barb the Tabloid Subscriber's phone. I needed to figure out how to delete that. Right after I figured out how to introduce Barb to Shepard, the man someone wanted dead.

Chapter Five

We spent another hour and a half at the range, falling hopelessly back into childish "I can top that" patterns that made me remember how we'd become friends in the first place. For that little while Shepard relaxed into a regular guy, not a Hollywood legend-in-the-making whom someone was trying to kill.

A cab took us to the production offices, where Shepard expended a great deal of effort smoothing things over with the irate and vocally profane producer, Karl Moyne. Seems Shepard's not showing up for work was not only rude, it cost money—something Moyne and the production in general were short on.

Shepard took his lumps and apologized masterfully, and before we left the offices, he tracked down the abused assistant whose job entailed issuing pass-cards. I sneered for the camera, signed my name a couple of times, and, bingo, I had a set of all-access passes for which the *Star National* would pay thousands of dollars.

Okay, so it was kinda cool.

We headed back to Resorts and spent the remainder of the afternoon in Shepard's hotel suite. Shepard passed the time watching televised poker and talking on the phone. Now and then he interrupted his conversations to share with me some unsavory fact about the celebrity guests on the poker show, and I'd nod and try to figure out if it were the sort of thing I could share with Barb without fear of slander. And then I'd go back to flipping through the many scripts strewn about the area.

"What's with this one?" I asked, holding out a script in Shepard's direction. "You've written all over it."

"Which one?"

I checked the cover. "It says *The Whispering Gallery*."

He nodded. "*Gallery*. I like that one. Director's a first-timer, though. I kinda want someone else, you know?"

He shrugged and turned up the sound on the poker game, effectively ending the conversation, and I put my feet up beside his on the coffee table and flipped through the script. The potential director was listed as Ko van Weer. Not as appealing as, say, George Lucas, I guess.

I waited for a commercial break before I hit him with the question. "What do you have planned for tonight?"

Shepard explained his intent to attend a private gambling party at de la Vega's Hotel and Casino. Several members of the cast and crew would be there, and he figured he'd be safe. "You're not going to tell me I can't go, are you?"

I shook my head. "No, not at all," I said, and then I took a lengthy pause. "It's just that I wanted you to meet my friend Barb."

"Cool." He changed stations on the television and slouched lower into the couch. "Meet me in the lobby at around nine."

Wow. That was too easy.

At six forty-five on the nose, Joe Collins, my night relief, arrived at Shepard's suite, backpack in hand. I introduced the boys, and they launched immediately into a power handshake. Shepard might be bigger, but I'd put my money on Joe in a brawl. The guy spent every nonworking moment in the gym or the dojo. He was on the diminutive side, just over five-five, but his shoulders were as wide as my legs were long.

Joe fished a white plastic bag out of the backpack and handed it to me. "Yours," he said in his typically abbreviated fashion. "From Dave."

My stomach clenched at mention of the boss. I'd been on the job no more than ten hours; what possible issue could he have with me that early in the game?

Holding my breath and cringing, I reached into the bag. I came up with a brand-new cell phone, still in its box. A sheet of computer-fed business cards, company logo discreetly set in one corner, showed my name and new number. One card was already missing.

"Took one," Joe said, pointing to the page. "This too." He pulled a folded sheet of paper from the front pocket of the backpack and handed it to me.

The computer printout from the lab listed the results of the chemical tests on the peanut pizza. An unpronounceable string of words ran along the left side of the page, percentages to the right. I didn't understand much beyond the summation at the bottom: *No foreign or controlled substances found.*

Good news. I still lacked an explanation for how the peanuts got into the pie in the first place, but one thing at a time.

With Joe the bruiser standing guard over Shepard, I shoved the printout into my pocket, said my good-byes, and escaped the luxurious confines of Shepard's suite. Free at last, I headed for the boardwalk and tested my new cell phone with a good-news call to Barb.

After the glitz and glam of Shepard's hotel, the soft lighting and faux balconies of de la Vega's Hotel and Casino seemed almost refined. Even the greeter, dressed in traditional Spanish garb and touching the brim of his hat as we passed, managed to look classier than the feathered and sequined hostesses at some of the other casinos.

"This is amazing!" Barb bounced down the soft, carpeted steps beside me, hands clasped before her as though she could barely resist applauding. "Atlantic City and Shepard Brown all in one day. I don't know which I'm more excited about."

I tugged at the hem of my white blouse, settling it neatly over the waistband of the black trousers Barb had been good enough to pick up for me. I always felt put-together in clothes she chose for me. "Maybe you should get out more. This Shepard obsession you have can't be healthy."

"I'm obsessed with Shepard, and that's unhealthy? Oh, please. You're practically phobic about the man. No way can *that* be normal."

We turned to our right and circled the cream half wall that lined the entrance corridor. Shrill bells assaulted us, coupled with electronic whistling and the rattle of slot machine cylinders coming to rest. The sounds ricocheted across the casino floor until the noise surrounded us on all sides and seemed to sneak up my spine via my shoes. Overhead, dim lights allowed the bright-colored glow of the slot machines to illuminate the room.

While Barb fed a fifty-dollar bill into the slot on a change machine and selected the denominations she'd like in return, I eyeballed the security guards wandering the casino floor. The older, square-badge types wore bright white shirts and navy trousers and smiled at everyone. The younger, armed-and-dangerous types wore dark shirts and dark blazers and made eye contact only with the surveillance camera domes overhead.

Ready to gamble, I followed Barb on a quest for a pair of free slot machines—no small feat. By the time we found a vacancy, I was snarling at old ladies and rotund men and trying my best to give them the evil eye. I dropped into the chair and held a twenty-dollar bill taut for the machine to gobble.

"How much time do we have?" Barb asked as she centered herself on her chair.

I checked my watch and did some math. "A little over two hours."

She pulled in a deep breath and fanned her face with her fingertips.

I chuckled. "Relax. He's just a guy."

She shook her head slowly, lips pressed tight. "Look, Rainny, I know this is no big deal for you. You see the guy all the time. Just try to understand how exciting this is for me, will you?"

Okay, so probably my lack of enthusiasm carried in my voice. But really, I'd known the guy since grade school. How jazzed was I supposed to be? "I'll try," I said.

"Think about it like the time we had to go into the city so you could get Jackie Chan to sign his book for you. Remember?"

"A little different, Barb. I didn't have any plans on schtupping Jackie Chan. I don't even want to know what you have planned for Shepard."

She flashed a smile. "I'm not stupid," she said. "I'm not looking for a lifetime with the guy. Not even a weekend."

"Just an autograph and then you're gone?"

"One night." She tipped her head so her blond hair glistened in the violet glow of the slot machine. "All I'm hoping for is one night."

My mind rolled back to Holly Bellinger's lesson on the women in Shepard's life. She'd said the one-night stands wanted him back, and the girlfriends wanted revenge. The way she'd said it, I couldn't tell which category she fell into—or hoped to join.

"Tell me something," I said as I watched the slot machine debit twenty-five cents from my hard-earned cash. "Shepard ever have anything going with Holly Bellinger?"

Barb tapped the button to start the cylinders turning, the rhinestones set into her nail polish winking in the low light. "Not that's been in any of the papers. Why?"

I shook my head. "Just curious."

"I could check it out for you," Barb said. "I'm sure the hotel's got a computer I could use, or maybe there's an Internet café nearby. I'll ask on a couple of the forums for you."

"Thanks," I said, smiling. "Not yet. But I'll keep it in mind."

A little while and a lot of quarter debits later, I checked my watch again, waking the butterflies in my stomach. Shepard and company were due to arrive in less than half an hour.

"We should think about cashing out," I said.

We changed the paper vouchers the slot machines had given us into the sort of paper that other businesses accepted as currency. Barb tucked half the cash in one pocket and half in the other. Well, at least she had a system.

"Do you think I have time to hit the ladies' room?" she asked.

"I'll wait for you out here."

I stood at the edge of the gaming floor, hands clasped behind my back, waiting and wondering when the nerve-jangling noise of the casino had reduced itself to background noise. Too late it occurred to me that I should have taken Barb's cash from her. I had a dim recollection of slot machines just outside the restrooms.

The casino's greeter rushed past me on his way to the entrance and bowed so low his serape brushed the floor. "Welcome to de la Vega's, sir," he said to a new arrival. "We're happy to have you."

Shepard Brown, the object of this obeisance, smiled his warm, magazine-cover smile. At his elbow, Joe Collins swept a gaze over the entryway and the gaming pits two steps below. "Nice to be here," Shepard said.

"Is there someplace I can escort you to?" the greeter offered.

Matthew, stumbling in behind Shepard and Joe, caught sight of me and waved, a broad smile on his face.

All eyes turned to where I stood, and I heartily wished for a potted palm or a sumo wrestler to hide behind. As I smiled in return, a very feminine shriek sounded above the regular ring and buzz of the slot machines.

"Oh, my God! He's here!"

My heart stopped, and I turned slowly. By some miracle, the uproar was not coming from Barb.

Bleached blond and deep in her cups—judging by the manner in which she stumbled off her bar stool—a woman well past forty pitched herself in the direction of the lobby. "Shepard Brown!" she screeched.

Oh, nuts. She was heading his way.

I sidled over to where Shepard stood, aggravation and resignation warring with the line of his lips. Joe looked quickly at me before snapping at the greeter, "Let's move."

Flustered, the greeter looked from Shepard to the bleached blonde and back again, as though trying to estimate how long it would take them to collide.

"Where are we headed?" I asked.

"The Toledo room," Matthew said.

"Right this way, sir." The greeter nodded and turned to lead the way.

Two steps and the bleached blonde reached us, joined by a short, frizzy-haired woman who wore a MOUNT ST. CLAIR CHOIR AND BIBLE STUDY T-shirt that matched the blonde's.

"It really is you," Frizzy said.

"I told you." Bleached Blonde grinned, baring her teeth from between ultraslim coral-colored lips. "I just wanted to tell you, my daughter loves you."

"Only your daughter?" Shepard said, a gracious smile frozen across his face. "What about you?"

Bleached Blonde laughed too loud and tottered forward on her spike-heeled sandals. Joe stepped up with a strong arm to keep her from falling and to get her to step back if possible.

"Oh, she's crazy about you too," Frizzy said.

"Shepard Brown!" A male voice now. I looked around to where a bull-shaped man in his early thirties clomped toward us, beer in hand. "You owe me!"

"Let's keep it moving," Joe snarled.

"Owe you what?" Shepard called.

"Do we know him?" Matthew asked.

"Back it up, ladies," I said, shooing them away with my hands. "There you go."

"I took my girlfriend to see your last movie," Bull-man said. "You owe me forty bucks."

Over my shoulder, Shepard laughed. "Hey, I'll take the blame for the movie, but someone else owes you for the popcorn."

"Let's go, let's go," Joe muttered. But even his verbal urgency couldn't stop the crowd from forming a circle around us. Shepard had walked into an establishment where people at leisure could easily spend hours upon hours. No one there was in any rush to be someplace else. If they didn't have a slot machine or a seat at a blackjack table, they had the time to spare to shake Shepard's hand and ask for an autograph.

Joe and I fought the crowd back as best we could, while

Shepard continued to smile patiently and trade banter with fans and detractors alike. Our forward progress felt more like a pitched battle, and sweat trickled down the center of my spine as I looked out at the growing crowd and remembered a poisoned pizza and snapped power-steering line. The muscles of my stomach clenched as a burning sensation spread across my chest. Every nerve in my body sprang to attention, adrenaline surging. "Back it up," I growled at a chippie who looked too young to be in a casino to begin with.

"Hey!" she snapped. "Who are you to tell me what to do?"

"Just take a step back, ma'am," I advised. Young. Pretty, despite a gap-tooth. Did she look like a killer?

"I don't have to listen to you. Who do you think you are, giving me orders?"

Firm male voices reached us from the back of the crowd. "Okay, let's go. Move along. Break it up. That's it."

I looked away from the charm-school graduate to the string of blue-blazered hulks wading through the crowd, forcing it to disperse. Casino security. *Mi compadres.* I had to smile.

"Hey, I'm talking to you," the chippie said.

A weight landed on my shoulder. I held a hand up to keep the chippie at a distance and spun around to see Shepard at my back, smiling down at her. "This is my guardian angel," he said, shaking my shoulder a bit. "Show her some respect."

I went all soft and gooey inside at his sentiment. I didn't even have the anger left to feel righteous when security took hold of the chippie and demanded to see her ID.

Flanked by uniformed security, with the greeter proudly leading the way, we trooped along the perimeter of the casino, up a half flight of stairs, and to the doors of the Toledo room. Security formed a column at either side of the doorway, and we passed through them like a bridal party walking through a double-columned honor guard.

Joe and I slowed at the door. Inside the room the crowd was on its feet, shouting at the wide-screen monitor mounted on the far wall. On-screen, a trio of harness horses, drivers going to the whip, thundered up the home stretch. The air inside the room crackled with the thrill and anticipation of the moment. I felt as if I'd jumped onto a roller coaster midride.

"Why are we waiting?" Shepard asked from behind us.

"Making sure," Joe said.

The horse on the inside pulled into the lead and trotted under the wire half a length ahead of the second- and third-place finishers. Shouts of triumph and curses of loss replaced the unified cheering of seconds before, and the crowd swiftly restored itself to milling, partylike behavior.

Joe looked to me and nodded, and we pushed forward into the room. A wave of invitees surged in behind us with mumbles of "about time" and "finally." Matthew trailed in last, tossing me a smile as he pursued a petite blonde with a pixie haircut.

"Thanks for the help," Joe said to me, with a "You can go now" tone to his voice.

I smiled and tried to force myself to say "No problem," but the words wouldn't come. Relief silenced me.

"This is why I count on you," Shepard said, hand on my shoulder once more. He gave it a good squeeze and grinned happily at me. "Where's your friend? What's her name . . . ?"

"Barb," I said, with an "Oh, crap" tone to my voice. I envisioned Barb pacing the lobby, cursing me as soon as she heard that Shepard Brown had arrived on the scene. "She's downstairs," I said.

"So go get her, and bring her up," Shepard said. "I'll go get you a drink in the meantime. What'll you have?"

Shepard himself would get me a drink? Wow, this was one for the record books. "I'll have, um—" I tried to come up with a drink suitable to the occasion, but the sight of Joe scowling and reaching for Shepard proved too much of a distraction.

"I'll figure it out," Shepard said, and he stepped away, leaving Joe to close his fist around a piece of paper he pulled from Shepard's back.

As Shepard moved off in the direction of the rolling bar stationed in a corner, I moved closer to stand shoulder to shoulder with Joe. He opened his hand and smoothed the paper with his fingers.

Someone had taken a magazine picture of Shepard and drawn the crosshairs of a rifle scope over his head and chest.

"Nice," Joe said.

My eyes popped, and my heart constricted. Despite Joe, me, and casino security, someone had gotten close enough to Shepard to stick a life-threatening *kick me* sign on his back. Once again I scanned the room, no longer seeing a simple group of people enjoying themselves. This time I needed to see the particulars: Holly Bellinger waylaying Shepard on his way to the bar; the producer, Moyne, studying the field for the next horse race; Matthew's shoulders sagging and his smile melting as the petite blonde pointed to her engagement ring. Couples and groups and singles, laughing or scowling or brooding. Nothing to distinguish this gathering from a hundred innocent others. Unless, of course, you counted Eddie Gale peeling away from the betting window as remarkable.

Unfortunately, the woman in me really did find him remarkable. The bodyguard, however, had to look right past him.

"Coulda been outside," Joe said, crumpling the picture in his fist once again.

"Someone would have seen it. Someone behind him." Had Matthew been behind him when they entered the lobby?

The lobby. Barb. Oh, nuts. I had to go get Barb. But Shepard . . .

I reminded myself I was off duty. Joe had the room covered. It would help for me to relax and be a regular person for an evening and go drag my best friend to a party. My best friend who was probably cursing me as she paced the lobby. I turned for the door and said, "Keep an eye on things, huh? I have to go find Barb." I took a step, but someone slung an arm across my shoulders.

"Not so fast," my captor said, in a slow, easy drawl that could only belong to Eddie Gale. "You only just got here."

Oh, for the love of all that's holy. Eddie Gale had his arm around my shoulders, applying subtle pressure to move me closer to him. His warmth bled through my blouse, and he smelled deliciously of spice, whiskey, and fine cigars. And I had to go find Barb.

"I'm pleased you decided to join Shepard this evening," Eddie said.

"Well, I . . . it wasn't . . ."

Drink in hand, Eddie waved away my failed protests. "You need to relax. You've had a rough couple of days." He lifted his arm from my shoulders and ran his fingers along my back until his palm rested at my waist. "Start with a drink. This way."

I really needed to find Barb. I needed someone to screech with amazement at the sight of me with Eddie Gale. "I really should—"

"Don't worry. Shepard will find us," Eddie said, steering me into the crowd.

"No, it's not Shepard," I said. "It's Barb. My friend Barb, she's—"

"She'll understand."

"Eddie." Much as it pained me, I dug in my heels, no longer allowing his warm touch at my waist to rule my forward motion.

"Hey," he said, turning to face me. He put his arm around me again, kept me from the crush of the milling crowd, and moved in close, the space between us feeling solid and alive. Beyond the cocoon he created, someone laughed too loudly, someone cursed like a teamster, and a champagne cork popped. "I just thought you might like to have a drink, take it easy for a little while, and I could explain about Shepard's car."

Silent alarms went off in my head. "The car?"

"A drink first."

"The car."

He pulled in a deep breath and took a tiny step back. "I did some reading today," he said. "Seems the '06 model of that vehicle was recalled for a problem with the power-steering cable snapping."

Shepard's SUV was barely a glimmer in a car designer's eye in '06. "But the manufacturer—they can't still be having the same problem, can they?"

"Either they do, or you triggered the problem."

"Me?"

"If you had been a better driver and had better control of the vehicle, none if it would have happened." He took a sip of whiskey while I blinked at this unexpected insult. But then I spotted the light in his eyes and realized he was holding the whiskey glass in place to hide a smile.

"Oh, I see. Is this you joking?"

"Yeah, how am I doing?" He took a mouthful of whiskey, and the blond-haired pixie creature Matthew had been bickering with earlier came to a halt beside us.

"Let go of the waitress, and put the whiskey down, Eddie," she said.

Eddie swallowed before giving in to laughter and took his hand off me. "This isn't a waitress," he said.

"She's dressed like one." The blonde's gaze raked me head to toe as a waiter slid through my peripheral vision. Black trousers, white blouse. All I lacked was a bow tie.

"I'm Lorraine Keys," I said, keeping my chin up. "And you are . . . ?"

"This is Kim Lloyd," Eddie said. "Kim's our assistant director."

"Pleasure to meet you," I said, reaching to accept the hand she offered.

"So if you're not with the hotel . . . ?" Kim asked, brow creased as though my face tested her memory.

"Lorraine is with Shepard," Eddie said.

The fold in her brow softened as her eyes popped wide. "You're with Shepard? Are you the reason he missed his call this morning?"

Again her gaze swept over me, assessing, and the subtext of her question became clear. "Oh, good grief, no," I said. "Shepard and I are just—"

"Well, good. Friendly advice? Keep it that way. Trust me on this one. The guy is total player slime. I could tell you stories that would turn you into a ranting feminist."

"Now, wait a minute. I've known Shepard a long time," I said.

"But all's well that ends well, right?" Eddie asked, his joviality slightly forced. "You're engaged now to a great guy, right, Kim?"

She flinched and reached for the phone clipped to her belt. "I'll see you in the morning, Eddie. Seven." She scowled at me as she raised the phone to her ear and helloed into the receiver. Looking back to Eddie, she said, "And don't show up hungover." Then she put her back to us and wandered off, intent on the incoming phone call.

Eddie turned to me and shook his head. "I would never show up for work hungover."

"Good to know," I said.

A series of bells chimed, as though intermission had ended at the Metropolitan Opera House.

"Two-minute warning," Eddie said, and he knocked back the remains of his drink. "I gotta put some money on a horse."

He ducked into the swirl of people heading for a makeshift betting window and left me gaping in his absence.

I needed to find Barb. Barb was like Kansas. Everything would be okay if I could just get to Barb.

I turned and tried to orient myself. With the raceway monitor to the north, the exit would be to the south. But Shepard was heading toward me, smiling a goofy smile, holding a pair of longneck bottles in one hand and dragging Holly Bellinger along with the other.

"Beer," Shepard said, arriving at my side. "I figured I couldn't go wrong. You remember Holly, right?"

Dressed in a tank top and a pair of camouflage capri pants, with her hair falling softly around her freckled face, Holly smiled and tapped her glass against my beer. "We've met," she said, before turning to chat with someone behind her clamoring for her attention.

"Was that Kim you were talking to?" Shepard asked.

"I was talking. She was threatening."

"What did she tell you? What did she say?"

One eye on where Joe hovered, watching our exchange, I explained Kim's belief in my responsibility for Shepard's missing his morning call.

"Is that all? She didn't say anything else about me? Are you sure?" His eyes narrowed, and his brow creased.

"Is it important?"

A deep breath cleared the concern from his face and left room for a distasteful grimace. "Sorry. It's just . . . She's been bad-mouthing me since the Mexico shoot."

"Any particular reason?" I asked.

"We kinda had a . . . you know, a thing."

I huffed out a sigh and shook my head. "Shepard . . ."

"How was I supposed to know she didn't understand the basic principles of hooking up? She can't let go, and it's starting to tick me off."

"Do you have no luck with women or just bad taste?"

"I'm working on it. Right now, you don't have to worry about Kim," Shepard said. "She can't do a thing to you."

I wanted to give him a "well, duh," but Holly laid a hand on my arm before the sarcasm could escape.

"Hey, you know, I still have those clothes for you if you want," she said, an easy smile lighting her eyes.

"Clothes?"

"I told you. My stupid assistant who sent the wrong garment bag. Wait." She released my arm and pulled a teeny pink cell phone from the pocket of her capris. "Where are you staying?"

"I'm down at Bally's with a friend of mine. But listen, you really don't—"

"Hey, yeah, where is she?" Shepard said. "I thought you were going to go get her."

"I was, but—"

"Concierge?" Holly shouted into her cell phone. "This is Mary May, suite six. I want you to get someone to pick up a garment bag that's on the back of my bathroom door and bring it down to Bally's, room—?" She raised her eyebrows at me, and I gave her my room number. "Room ten-oh-four. Got that? Thank you."

She snapped the phone shut. "All set. Anything you don't want just, you know, sell it on consignment or something."

Shepard smiled down at her. "You're giving Rainny some clothes?"

Holly blushed an attractive shade of pink. "Just . . . trying to be friendly."

"That's really sweet."

"It's nothing."

"Yes, it is."

"Okay, you guys," I said. "You're making me ill, and I have a friend to find, so . . ."

Shepard laughed and caught me in a half hug. "Sorry, sorry. It won't happen again."

At that point I caught sight of Eddie, sipping his drink and studying his betting ticket.

"I gotta bail," I said. I lifted Shepard's arm from my shoulder and turned him so that he could drape it around Holly.

Holly said good-bye, and Shepard protested my departure, but I stepped away all the same. I needed to follow up on something.

I worked my way steadily through the room, gripping the longneck beer as though it gave me confidence and dodging the odd drunken gambler. By the time I reached Eddie, the horses were lining up behind the truck that led them to the starting line.

"Did you bet?" he asked.

"I was coping with Shepard."

His gaze found Shepard as though he'd known all along right where he was. "He's lookin' kinda cozy with Holly."

"And may they live happily ever after. Listen, before, when you were joking, which part was the joke? The recall or my driving?"

He tipped his head and sighed. "I really didn't mean any offense to you or your driving. It was a joke, that's all. You have my word."

"So the recall you were serious about?"

He squinted a bit, as though that would help him follow my train of thought. "What's this all about?"

"It's nothing," I said. "I needed to be sure, that's all. The race . . ." I lifted my chin in the direction of the screen as the truck keeping the horses in place drew away. The race was on; the crowd turned its unified attention to the monitor.

"Speaking of being sure . . ." Eddie began. Eyes on the screen, he stood close beside me, unwittingly wrapping me in the welcome scent of him. "Did you tell me the truth about you and Shepard?"

"About what?"

"That there's nothing . . ." He waved a hand to gloss over the words he wouldn't say, but *intimate* hung in the air all the same.

I huffed. "It is possible for a man and a woman to be friends without any romantic or sexual elements, you know."

He shook his head. "No, it's not."

"How can you say that?"

"Because it's true."

The horses rounded the final turn and pounded down the stretch. I watched them, numbly, waiting for words that weren't coming. "It's not," I managed to mutter.

"I'll prove it to you," Eddie said, as he moved in real close, his voice soft below the excited shouting of the crowd. "Tonight, you and I, we're friends. We'll do friends stuff. And tomorrow, you can tell me if you still think it's possible for us to remain just friends. How does that sound?"

"Sounds suspiciously like a bet."

"You up for it?"

"You going to play fair?"

He grinned, broad and dazzling, and the short space between us crackled. "I doubt it."

Oh, Lordy. The air between us sizzled. Add in the soft sound of his voice, the heat rising off his skin . . .

"You in?" he asked.

Oh, yeah. I was *all* in.

* * *

"You're making it up," Barb said. She slid the key card into the door. When the lights went green, she turned the knob and led the way into our hotel room. "I can't believe you're making up this elaborate story. No, no, not a story, an excuse. A great big bulging excuse. I can't believe you ditched me. What the heck is that?" She stopped at the foot of the first bed, gaze on a blue garment bag laid neatly across the spread.

"Is that navy?" I asked.

"Why?"

"If it's navy, it's for me. If it's some other shade of blue, I don't know whose it is." I did my best impersonation of a debutante swanning into a room and perching on the edge of the bed.

I pulled the garment bag to me and drew down the zipper.

"What's in it?" Barb asked. Curiosity outweighing her anger, she edged closer to me and tried to peer inside the bag.

I did my best to smile devilishly at her. "Holly Bellinger's cast-off clothing, if you don't mind."

"No!"

"Yes!" Okay, I admit it. I went all girl. My hands trembled as I pulled the first item free of the bag—a bright blue spring jacket with a starched collar and stunning appliqué work.

Barb wrapped her arms around the jacket and sank to the floor with it, Miss Scarlett in a swoon. "Heaven," she crooned.

The garment bag yielded two more blouses and another jacket—denim with impossibly tiny beads worked up the sleeve, forming rows of creeping ivy. And finally there was a black dress, all lace and flounce, with capped sleeves and a narrow bodice.

"It's not!" Barb gasped. She snatched the dress from me and turned it inside out, searching for a label. "It is. Oh, my God." She turned the garment so I could read the designer label. "It is! Can you believe it?"

Frankly, I couldn't even pronounce the name. Whatever. It looked pretty. "I'm going to try it on," I said. I grabbed it from her and ran for the bathroom.

"Don't think this bounty excuses you for earlier. I'm not going to forget you ditched me, you know," Barb said.

Through the open doorway I could see her standing in front of the mirror, holding the little blue jacket against her body and admiring her reflection.

"I didn't ditch you. I got—"

"Yeah, yeah, 'caught up.' And so you invented this elaborate lie about some snotty assistant director called Kim and about watching horse racing with Eddie Gale all night. For future reference, Rainny, you need to come up with excuses that don't sound like fantasies, okay?"

Shirt off, I shucked off the black trousers and caught sight of myself in the over-the-sink mirror as I reached for the dress. Next time I indulged in fantasy, I would choose more alluring underwear.

"You know, Barb," I said, pulling the dress over my head, "if you want to continue to believe I could make up something like that, go right ahead. I won't stop you."

The dress slid over my shoulders, and I tugged it gently down over my hips. It fell low on my bust, hugged my waistline, and draped over my hips to fall midthigh. I loved it instantly. And more, I loved me in it.

Hauling the door open, I padded out of the bathroom and back into the hotel room entryway. "Okay," I said. "What do you think?"

Barb looked away from her own reflection, and her jaw softened in astonishment. "Holy moly, Rainny. You look amazing."

I laid a hand against my stomach, trying to hold in all the confident, classy feelings the dress evoked in me. "You think?"

"Oh, yeah." Her smile faded, leaving an unusual solemnity behind. "You're not exaggerating about this threat against Shepard, are you?"

Pretty dress forgotten, I folded my arms against my chest and shifted my weight onto one leg. "I'm not going to let anything happen to him."

"I heard about what happened at the casino, about the crowd."

She picked at a loose thread on the bedspread, and then her eyes locked on mine. "Rainny, you really think you can keep him safe?"

I took a breath, reconsidering my typical boasting. The moment a man's life was in your hands was the worst time to learn your best wasn't good enough. I needed to step up my game.

Chapter Six

My alarm went off five minutes after I'd fallen asleep.

Okay, so it just felt that way. But there was something deeply wrong about crawling into bed at eleven and being woken by the electronic shriek of a travel alarm at one. I know it was wrong, because every nerve and muscle in my body protested. Drat that Shepard Brown. Why couldn't he have ordered a poisoned pizza in the middle of the afternoon?

I crawled out of bed as quietly as I could and grabbed some clothes from my duffel bag. Barb continued to snore in a soft and ladylike manner that I could only hope I emulated while I slept. I dressed and dragged a brush through my hair, grabbed ID, cash, and my room card, and slipped out.

Of course, one A.M. by no means meant the dead of night in Atlantic City. The hotel lobby was bustling, and the casino was jammed. Up and down the boardwalk, bright, colorful lights reached for the sky and reflected off the water. The atmosphere said seaside party chic, brilliantly tempting.

With a sigh, I turned the other way, away from the lure of the boardwalk and toward the slightly dicey exterior environs.

That deep into the night, the air had cooled considerably and a strong wind helped push me along the sidewalk, past the scant pedestrians who made me wish I'd brought my gun. I wrestled the hood of my sweatshirt onto my head and shoved my hands into its front pockets, but I could do nothing to ward off the wind on my bare legs. Denim cutoffs had seemed like a good idea, but halfway around the block they made my legs feel like I was skiing in a bikini.

At Benvolio's Gourmet Pizza Palace, I hauled open the door, and a blast of warm air assaulted me with the gorgeous fragrance of fresh-baked pizza, just a hint of parmesan with an undertone of garlic. My stomach yawned and stretched itself awake, suspecting that this trip might prove worthwhile.

I walked past a series of scarred tables, vacant save for one where a disheveled older gent sat slowly turning the pages of a newspaper. At the back of the store, a glass-and-chrome display counter that had lost its luster stretched along the left wall. Above the case hung an illuminated menu that gleamed as though fresh out of the factory. The wall behind it could do with a fresh coat of paint, and I became instantly convinced Benvolio's was fighting to keep up in a changing fast-food world.

The gooseflesh on my thighs settled down in the warmth of the shop, and I pushed the hood of my sweatshirt back and nodded to a bored-looking guy behind the counter.

"Help you?" he asked.

I looked up at the menu, and my stomach did an entirely different kind of roll. Benvolio's menu featured every conceivable way to order a pizza, from every corner of the globe.

Jaw hanging low, I met the guy's gaze. "Do you have any normal pizza?"

"Normal?"

"You know. Red. Round. Nothing more daring than olive oil?"

He nodded. "You mean 'traditional.' "

"I prefer 'classic.' "

"Yeah. We still got that."

I ordered a slice. "You work the night before last?" I asked.

The guy slid my slice into the oven and jerked a thumb at his fellow staff member. "He was here."

The "he" in question lifted an orb of pizza dough and slammed it back down onto the wood worktable. "What can I do for you?"

He was somewhere between forty and sixty years old, with dark hair that barely grayed and Mediterranean skin that concealed wrinkles. I couldn't peg his age. He wore white pants and a white T-shirt, and his arms were dusted with enough flour to bake several cupcakes.

"I was hoping you might remember a call that came in a couple of nights ago, probably around this time," I said.

He paused long enough in the pounding of the dough to scan the empty expanse of the pizzeria. "You figure?"

I smiled. "This would have been for a medium pie—"

"I make two medium pies last night," he offered. "One onion and garlic, one with broccoli."

More smiling. "Not *last* night. The night before. A friend of mine called you, ordered a medium pie—"

"Yeah, yeah, sure." He slugged the dough a couple of times. "Your friend, medium pie, night before last . . . lemme see."

He conferred briefly in Italian with his coworker. I don't speak a word of the language, but I managed to pick up the gist. The cadence of questions made me think the older guy wanted help remembering. The defensive noises and offended posture of the younger guy convinced me he didn't know a thing and wouldn't be inclined to help even if he did.

"Okay, okay. I remember now," the older guy said, slamming the dough around a bit more. "I make a medium pie almost like a Thai pizza. Special order for your friend, yes? You want I should make you one?"

Traditional girl that I am, I didn't know what was in a Thai pizza. I looked up to the sparkly new menu.

The younger guy folded his arms and leaned back against the cash register. "It's got onions and chicken, and it's supposed to have peanut oil," he said with a brief glare in his boss' direction. "But here we add chopped peanuts."

"Night before last I make Thai pizza, extra peanuts, hold the chicken."

"You made a pie with peanuts in it?" I asked, hoping to keep the disgust from my voice.

"We make to order," he said, his tone somewhere between pride and resignation.

"Yes, but don't you think peanuts is kind of a strange order?"

He leaned one hand against the dough and gave me his full

attention. "Lady, with all the crazy diets these people are on, I'm just happy they order crust and sauce, okay? Okay."

All I could do was nod my agreement.

"She like the pie?" he asked, as his buddy slid my oven-warm slice of classic pizza onto the counter.

"Who?" I asked.

"Your friend with the peanuts. Kelly," he said, eyes bright with the joy of recollection. "Her name was Kelly. She like the pie, or no, she didn't like it?"

Kelly. Who was Kelly? No one Shepard had ever mentioned. "What did she look like?"

"Who?"

"Kelly. What did she look like?" I asked, and then I remembered I had identified myself as her friend. "I mean, uh, how did she look? Is the diet working out for her, or is she still a double-wide?"

"How would I know? She send her boyfriend to pick up the pie."

I did my best TV-cop-describing-a-suspect routine, filling in the particulars with facts about Matthew, and before long the pizza maker was nodding and confirming that the guy I described had picked up Kelly's pie.

Not that that told me much. Who was Kelly, and why did Matthew pick up her pie and give it to Shepard?

I paid for my slice, thanked the older man for his help, and headed back to the hotel.

The wind, though still as cold, was slapping me in the face now. Which worked out great, since I had a fresh-from-the-oven slice to eat and didn't need my hair blowing into my mouth.

I chewed and tried to apply my sleep-deprived brain to the puzzle. I had Shepard, Matthew, Kelly, and a peanut pie that nobody but Shepard and me seemed to think strange. The made-to-order cleared Benvolio's Gourmet Pizza Palace of any wrong-doing or foul play, which in turn left out any possibility of me getting the police in on the act, even if I had Shepard's consent. That meant there would be no one to work the other end to find out where the threat against Shepard was coming from. I was relatively certain I could keep him safe, but it sure would be nice to remove the threat. I wondered if Dave could assign me any help in the poking-around business . . .

I also wondered if I could use the "Who is Kelly?" angle to wake Shepard up at three A.M. You know, payback and all.

But no, I didn't have the heart. Sheesh. First I'd let Barb come to Atlantic City with me, and then I decided to let Shepard sleep through the night.

I'd picked a bad time to go soft.

At 6:20 I headed to the set to relieve Joe. I desperately wanted a cup of coffee and deeply regretted that pizza slice from the night before. Its consumption had resulted in some truly bizarre dreams of which I clearly recalled monkeys loading bananas into professional movie cameras.

The usual organized chaos of a film set was under way by the Steel Pier, with a palpable current of anxiety. Cast and crew alike kept shooting nervous glances skyward, where black clouds had massed on the horizon like an invading army. Several industrious grips had begun wrapping equipment in heavy plastic.

I pulled up the hood of my sweatshirt and scanned the area for a sight of Shepard. I located him standing in a small huddle of actors, each looking more miserable than the last as they shivered against the cold.

With Shepard sighted, it was easy to spot Joe. He stood like a sentinel at the edge of the action, eyes in constant motion. For just a moment he held his gaze on mine, enough to acknowledge my arrival, and then he went back to scanning.

I checked my watch. If I found the craft services table in the next four minutes, I could grab a cup of coffee before changing places with Joe. Trouble was, I didn't see the table anywhere.

"Dutch," I called, as my favorite on-set electrician ambled into view.

The wind sent his blond beard off to the left, giving his face a Dali-like quality when he smiled. "Hope you brought an umbrella," he said, closing the distance between us.

"Nah, I figure if it rains, I'll just take shelter under some of the egos out here."

He barked a laugh, then looked around to see if anyone had heard us. "Your property's over there," he said with a nod in Shepard's direction.

"Yeah, I see him. What I don't see is coffee. Where is it?"

His face composed itself into caffeine-dependent understanding. "The crafties are all behind the makeup trailer. It's got an awning. Nobody wanted the donuts to get wet."

I couldn't fault them on that one. But neither did I have time to get to the makeup trailer and back again before I had to relieve Joe, and I had no intention of screwing up the assignment by doing something as trivial as failing to show up on time.

I thanked Dutch for the information and headed off in Joe's direction, consoling myself with the thought that surely Shepard, of all people, would be looking for a donut before long.

"How'd it go?" I asked Joe.

He looked me up and down, face registering displeasure. I wasn't sure if he had a problem with me simply being on the job or with the fact that my narrow slacks and fitted sweatshirt failed to underplay my figure. Maybe if I had a hunting knife strapped to my thigh . . .

"No further excitement," he said. "This guy doesn't sleep much, though."

I squinted in Shepard's direction. Sure enough, little puffy bags hung below his eyes, complementing the little puffy love handles hugging his waist. "He's got a lot on his mind," I said, almost automatically. Of course, I'd been losing sleep myself, wandering off to struggling pizzerias in the dead of night, so my sympathy didn't stretch as far as one would expect.

"Gonna crash," Joe said. He gave me one more once-over and sighed heavily. "Keep your eyes open," he said, and he walked away, the muscle-bound mass of his upper arms making his gait look almost like a waddle.

I waited until Joe disappeared down the boardwalk before I crooked my finger in Shepard's direction.

He made a face that showed his displeasure at being summoned, but he ambled my way all the same.

"What is it?" he said when near.

"Oh, and good morning to you too."

His eyes narrowed, accentuating their puffiness. "I was up half the night reading scripts," he said.

"No sympathy here, dude. I was up too. Got a couple of questions for you."

A crew member hustled by, hauling rolls of plastic sheeting and shouting "Heads up!" Something went splat against the top of my head, and I hoped like mad it was a drop of rain and not a drop of seagull.

Shepard looked up and down the boardwalk, scanning the area as though worried who might overhear. "Shoot."

As I had been half expecting him to put me off or tell me to mind my own business, his invitation—if you could call it that—threw me a bit off balance. "I need to, uh . . . tell me, who's Kelly?"

His eyebrows shot up. "Kelly?"

"Guy I talked to at the pizzeria said the peanut pie was a special order for Kelly. So who's Kelly?"

It was too much to hope that she would turn out to be the same woman whose room he had slept in the night before he failed to show for work and whose identity he was protecting. It was also pretty frightening to think he'd fallen asleep in the same room as a woman who might be trying to kill him.

"Oh, so you went to the pizza place? That's great," he said, clearly pleased at my initiative. "What'd you find out? Who messed with my dinner?"

I shook my head. "No one messed with your dinner. Your pie was a special order—that's what I'm trying to tell you. Ask you. Whatever. Who's Kelly?"

Shepard smiled a little, just enough to expose the lower half of his teeth. He leaned close, and I caught the scent of aftershave and makeup. "I'm Kelly," he said.

"I— What?"

"I'm Kelly."

"You're Shepard," I said. "You were tortured for that name straight through to junior high."

He huffed, annoyed at being reminded of his less-than-illustrious beginnings. "Yes, but I can't check into a hotel as Shepard Brown, can I?"

I gave myself a mental kick in the pants for that one. I mean, duh, of course he couldn't. If he did, then any Liz, Ted, or Barb could simply call the front desk and ask to be connected to his room. And it explained a heckuva lot about Holly calling herself Mary May. "Okay, but 'Kelly'?"

The grin returned. "You know, like *Kelly's Heroes*."

I had a vague memory of a war movie . . . or maybe I was thinking of *Hogan's Heroes* reruns.

Perhaps sensing he was losing me, Shepard continued. "World War Two? Clint Eastwood moving gold bullion out of Paris?"

"Let me guess—Clint played Kelly?"

"It's a great movie."

"So, then, you checked in as Kelly, right? For privacy. Do I understand that?"

He shrugged and nodded. "Yeah, that's about right."

"But you yourself didn't order the pie."

His curled lip and narrowed brow reminded me how dumb I could be. "No," he said. "Matthew ordered the pie."

Of course. As any good assistant would. Except, according to the pizza maker, Matthew hadn't. Matthew had only picked it up.

"Yeah, I don't think he did. Where's Matthew now?" I asked. I did a quick scan of the area and tried to ignore the trip of my pulse when I caught sight of Eddie. Even in the police-detective wardrobe calculated to make him appear unkempt and underpaid, his natural self-confidence made him appealing. My heartbeat went a little erratic, and I dragged in a deep breath. I needed to focus, not fantasize. Not that his friendly wave helped matters. And not that the sparkle in his eye and his broad grin didn't threaten to push me over the edge.

I smiled briefly and kept scanning, reminded myself to check not only for Matthew's presence but for the presence of anyone who looked like they didn't belong.

"I don't see him," I said, as a big honking raindrop broke across my nose.

"He was supposed to get me coffee," Shepard said, and a whole new set of longings coursed through my veins. Could I justify going off to search for Matthew as a work-related activity? Grab a cup of coffee for myself while I was at it?

Another raindrop on my face brought me back to reality. I couldn't leave Shepard. For the next twelve hours no more than six feet would separate us, ideally. "It'll have to wait," I said.

But Shepard pulled his cell from his pocket. "He should be back by now," he said. "I'll see what's keeping him."

He shouted, "Where's my coffee?" into the phone a split second before the heavens opened. Great sheets of moisture rolled along the boardwalk. Little shrieks and loud cussing could be heard as people scrambled for cover. Dutch threw a sheet of plastic over a camera as though he were trying to tackle the equipment to the ground, and Catherine Dawes let out a wail as her high-piled Jersey hair flattened instantly against her skull and mascara streamed down her cheeks.

Shepard grabbed my arm and hauled me toward the video-playback tent, and I cursed louder than anyone not a union worker. Chaos made for the worst security nightmares.

I wrenched my arm free of Shepard's grip and instead took firm hold of him and spun him away from the tent. "That way!" I shouted above the rain, and I pushed him toward the entrance to the ninety-nine-cent store. I couldn't have him doing anything predictable and couldn't have him pressed in with any huddled masses.

We caught our breath in the doorway. I did my best to block Shepard's bulk with my body as I peered out at the boardwalk. Director Riley Jacks and a cluster of his minions huddled beneath the open-sided tent, actors and actresses farther inside. Kim, the assistant director, clutched a clipboard to her chest and pointed to each actor in turn, lips moving and head bobbing, clearly counting heads like a second-grade recess monitor. She consulted her clipboard, and a crease of annoyance bisected her brow as she scanned the group again.

"What is this place?" Shepard said over my shoulder.

It's a shame, really, that he couldn't see the face I made. "It's a dollar store, Sherlock."

"It's filled with junk."

I indulged in an eye roll for my own personal benefit before going back to the activity on the set. Rain drenched the crew as they rolled equipment into a cluster and threw an additional tarp over the collection.

Of the faces I was accustomed to seeing, I'd lost sight of Catherine Dawes. Eddie, too, seemed to have vanished. "Now what?" I muttered, as the walkie-talkie feature on Shepard's phone chirped.

"Go," he said, and I peered over my shoulder to see whom he was speaking to.

Matthew's voice crackled from the speaker on the phone. "Did you just try to call me, sir?"

"Yeah, where are you? Where's my coffee?"

"I've been trying to a find a coffee shop with unrefined sugar," Matthew said.

"Why?"

We waited a moment before Matthew responded, and I had a quick mental impression of him trying to squeeze the life out of the cell phone in lieu of Shepard's neck. "Because that's what you prefer," Matthew said, his voice measured.

Across the boardwalk, Kim's gaze locked with mine for a split second before her eyes flicked over my shoulder to where Shepard stood. Something flashed in her eyes, a look I thought I knew, the same look Barb had whenever she saw a Hummer pull up to a gas pump—envious and indignant all at once.

Kim looked down at her clipboard, then bent her head to the director's. Shepard had had a thing with her in Mexico? Before or after the Spanish actress?

I leaned back and got my head close to Shepard's without looking at him. "Ask him to get me some coffee too."

"Lorraine needs coffee too," Shepard said.

"How does she take it?" Matthew asked.

Shepard tapped my shoulder. "How do you take it?"

I answered carefully, lest he miss my message. "I can hear him," I said.

"Oh. Right."

"Give me the phone." Seized with a thought, I grabbed the phone from him and switched off the point-to-point feature, rendering my conversation with Matthew private. I needed to ask him a string of questions. I started with, "Have you heard from the mechanic?"

His sigh came through a split second before the low-battery warning beep. "Yeah, he said he hasn't gotten to the SUV yet. I'll call him again after lunch. I'm really sorry. It's my fault you and Mr. Gale . . ."

"We're fine. No harm done." The phone beeped its warning again. The rest of the questions would have to wait. I told him how I preferred my coffee and said good-bye.

I closed the phone and passed it back to Shepard. I was no closer to determining if the episode with the SUV was intentional or accidental. I hoped Matthew would have enough information about the pizza that I could start putting things together.

Taking a deep breath, I returned to my observation of the crowd now dispersing from beneath the tent. Holly emerged and turned her face to the sky, smiling as her makeup streaked off her face. Behind her, Catherine Dawes appeared, sheets of newspaper held above her head. She dashed across the boardwalk in the direction of the hotel, snarling at a harried-looking woman I took to be her assistant.

"No wonder you cheated on her," I said over the drumming of the rain.

"Who?" Shepard asked.

"Catherine."

"Oh, right. Catherine. Yeah."

I turned to gape at him over my shoulder. "Who else have you cheated on?"

He had the grace to look sheepish.

I shook my head. Unbelievable.

"I think we're taking a break," Shepard said, studying the

goings-on across the way. Beneath the tent, Dutch stood, hands on his head, eyes squinched shut, while Riley Jacks threw a tantrum. The normally charming and reserved director ripped the clipboard from Kim's arms and threw it to the ground. His shouts carried clearly across the space between us, leaving no doubt of his familiarity with vulgarity, nor of the fact that he was bleeping losing three bleeping hours to the bleeping rain.

"Let's go," I said to Shepard.

"Back to the hotel?" Shepard shuffled out beside me. "Thank God. I need to get my publicist on the phone, and this battery is just about dead."

"No. We'll go to your trailer first." I flinched a bit as the easing rain pelted me in the face.

"Why? Everyone else is going to the hotel. Why can't we?"

"One more time, let's review. You are not supposed to do what people expect you to."

Thunder rumbled. "You're right. You're right."

He trudged along beside me down the boardwalk and over to his trailer. Along the way, we met up with Matthew. The sight of three extra-large coffee cups nestled in the cardboard carrier did wonders for my drowned spirits.

With a twitch and a shrug serving as an apology to me, Matthew handed Shepard the first cup of coffee.

"I hope this has the right cream in it," Shepard said.

"Toffee-flavored, I promise." Matthew handed me my coffee, then pulled his own from the carrier. "You want to give me the keys to the trailer? I'll go ahead and open it up."

Shepard handed over the keys and went to work prying open the cutout on his coffee cup lid.

"Matthew, let me ask you something," I said, falling into step beside him as we headed for the trailer.

"Shoot," he said.

"The other night Shepard asked you to order a pizza." I tried to watch his face for any change of expression, but with his head bowed against the rain, I couldn't quite see. "Who made the call?" I asked.

"I did. Who else?" But a flush crept up his neck and along his jaw.

"You were with someone."

"I was alone."

"Don't lie."

"I'm not."

"You were with someone, and you told her about Shepard's being registered as Kelly."

Matthew's wide-eyed gaze met mine. "I did not. She knew. Mr. Brown must have told her when they—" He cut himself off, stopped in his tracks, and looked around.

Rats. Shepard was still twenty paces behind us, sipping his coffee, his face creased with puzzlement. "Hold that thought," I said, then double-timed it back to where Shepard stood smacking his lips, the crease in his brow distracting me from my purpose. "What are you doing?"

He faced me, the corners of his mouth turned down. "I don't think this is toffee-flavored."

"Oh, for the love of—"

"It's not vanilla. I don't know what it is. Tastes weird."

Weird? My slow-motion mind shifted into overdrive. I looked back to where Matthew was opening the door to the trailer. What if Shepard was right, and Matthew really posed a threat? He had gone to a great deal of trouble for the coffee, then insisted he had the right cream. And now Shepard thought it tasted off. Oh, nuts. Better safe than sorry.

I dropped my own cup of coffee to the ground and stood back from the splash as I grabbed Shepard's cup out of his hand. Inside the trailer, the lights blinked on. There was a whoosh and a bang, and Shepard's trailer exploded into flames.

Chapter Seven

A column of black smoke rose from the burning trailer, and the air crackled with the roar of the flames. The sound Shepard made as he screamed for Matthew sliced through me like jagged steel. Footsteps echoed on the boardwalk as horrified onlookers raced for the ramps leading down to street level.

I wrapped both arms around Shepard's waist, threw my weight against him to take him off balance, and forced him to move away from the blast.

"Let go of me!" he wailed. "No!"

"We have to move," I said.

"Get off me."

"Move!"

He stumbled left, and I pressed my advantage, using his momentum to turn him and get him headed away from the scene.

"Lorraine—"

"Keep moving."

He gave up the struggle and let me take him at a half run past the wooden police barricades, across the street where traffic had screeched to a halt, and through the street-side entrance to a casino.

We stopped just inside the lobby, within sight of a pair of security cameras, and turned to look back through the glass doors. Healthy flames licked the edges of the trailer despite the steady rain.

Shepard laid his forehead and palms against the glass, muttering, "Oh, my God, oh, my God." I pulled my hood from my head and took the cell phone from my pocket and hit speed dial 1 for the local police station.

The desk sergeant took exception to my calling the station rather than dialing 911 but connected me nonetheless. Maybe he heard the desperation I was trying to pretend wasn't in my voice, or maybe they're that good to everyone. In any case, I gave the location of the trailer and the nature of the emergency as I fought for a deep breath that would help keep the tears from falling.

Putting the phone away, I laid a hand on Shepard's shoulder, either to give him support or leech some from him—maybe a bit of both. Up the road a small crowd had gathered around the trailer, boardwalk police racing to keep onlookers back from the fire.

"We should be over there," Shepard said.

Though he couldn't see me, I shook my head. "You're safer here." For the time being we would rely on the casino's hyper-security and bank on the fact that we were likely already being watched by uniformed employees in their control room. And at any given moment we could move farther into the building, be big and bold and let their security force surround and protect the illustrious Shepard Brown.

"You think he's alive?" Shepard asked.

Again I shook my head. "I doubt it."

"It's my fault," Shepard said.

I stepped a little closer and ran my hand across his shoulders until I had my arm around him. "You didn't do anything."

He lowered his head and let his chin fall against his chest. "We shouldn't have let him go in first."

In the air-conditioned entryway, in wet clothes and saturated sneakers, I shivered. The alternative would have been for *me* to go in first. It could have—perhaps should have—been me trapped inside the burning trailer. Lord help me, I didn't want to trade places with Matthew.

I began to tremble and closed my fingers around a handful of Shepard's shirt, hoping the pressure would keep me steady against the adrenaline surge. I fought for a smooth breath, to not pant with the fear that threatened to level me. It could have been me in that trailer. I knew it. Knew the dangers, the risk implied in the job. But most protection assignments consisted of kidnapping prevention. Few people outside the purview of the Secret Service were likely to be targets for assassins. The concept of giving your life for someone else's was a bit . . . Hollywood. And yet there I was, facing it, facing a burning trailer, waiting for the scream of sirens, wondering if I were truly capable of laying down my life for Shepard's.

Maybe I had made a bad career choice. Maybe I wasn't cut out for this. Maybe I really was better off working the overnight shift at the Guggenheim warehouse, rats and all.

Slowly, as though he might be crumpling, Shepard turned to me and gathered me in his arms. "Thank you," he said. "I'm really glad you're here."

Alone in the police station, Shepard and I sat at a battered wooden table, me with the station's stained, loaner coffee cup, Shepard with a brand-new gleaming one emblazoned with the Atlantic City Police Department seal.

"Where do you think he went with the list?" he asked. The officer in charge of our case, Detective Holden, had asked Shepard to write down a list of any potential enemies he might have. It had turned into a good-sized list.

"I don't know," I said.

After a moment he asked, "You think he might question some of them?"

"Don't know. Would it bother you if he did?"

He lifted a shoulder. "I guess not. You ever hear of a person being mad because they thought you didn't like them?"

"Not until I met Catherine, I hadn't."

Easing back in his chair, he sipped his coffee, the sound amplified in the quiet of the room. "You don't suppose she had something to do with this, do you?"

I had no ready answer for him. I was wondering the same thing myself. "Someone sure doesn't like you," I said. I drank

from the coffee, trying to turn my mind to anything not connected to the morning's tragedy. A little tough when you've
been sitting in a police precinct answering the same questions
about it for three hours straight.

"Is it true Catherine set fire to your sports car?" I asked.

Shepard shook his head. "I never owned a sports car."

Detective Holden swung through the doorway, file folder in
hand. He smiled as he dropped the folder onto the table and,
lowering his balding head, fixed his gaze on me. "Would you
wait outside please?"

Shepard stiffened beside me, and I laid a hand on his arm
before he could voice a protest. "He's going to ask you some
questions about me," I said, leaning in to him. "I'll be right
outside."

Not waiting for Shepard to comprehend or respond, I pushed
my chair back with a screech that made Detective Holden wince,
and I headed out the door, coffee cup in hand. It had taken me
all morning to get a cup of coffee. All of a very bad morning.
No way was I leaving it behind.

I pulled the door shut behind me and let out a breath. I
couldn't very well stand around in the hallway waiting for the
detective to finish with my client, but neither was there anywhere to sit. I turned, hoping to find a battered chair at the end
of the hall or a hard bench shoved up against a wall. Instead I
found my boss.

Dave du Comte stood rigid at the end of the hall. Shoulders
against the wall, feet braced, he had his hands shoved into the
pockets of his dull brown trousers and the sleeves of his shirt
rolled up, suit jacket folded over his arm. If he'd worn a tie on
arrival, it was long gone, replaced by a scowl deeper and darker
than the abyss at the continental shelf. I didn't figure him as
too far into his thirties, but his eyes were a hundred and six.

His posture eased as he caught sight of me, and if I didn't
know better, I might have said he looked relieved. But even if
he went weak with relief at the sight of me, I went cold to the
bone at the sight of him. Bad enough I was beating up on myself over the episode at the trailer, but now the boss had taken

a three-hour car trip to chew me out over it as well. Oh, it just kept getting better and better.

I held his gaze and took a long, slow sip of the coffee, bracing myself.

Dave pushed off the wall and started toward me, his limp slightly more pronounced. "Let's go sit," he said.

He walked silently beside me as we made our way up the hall. A thousand rationalizations crowded my mind. He'd come to check on Shepard's well-being. He'd come to check on me. He'd come to see if he could help. If he had come to give me hell, he wouldn't be looking for someplace comfortable to get the job done.

He steered me into a ten-by-ten cell at the end of the hall and gestured for me to sit.

I gave him the dirtiest look I dared and dropped onto the only seat in the room—the slatted-wood bench within the small holding cell.

Dave hovered in the doorway, eyeing the bars of the cell as though locking me in might not be a bad idea. With a half shrug, he tossed his suit jacket onto the end of the bench and sat down beside me.

"So. What brings you to Atlantic City?" I asked, knowing full well what had brought him.

"I'm pulling you off this job."

I felt as if someone had punched the breath out of me. "Why? Is there some crisis at the Guggenheim that a surveillance system can't handle?"

"Don't joke, Rainny."

"Don't threaten me, then."

He sighed and pushed a hand through his hair, displacing his carefully combed locks. "A man died today, Lorraine."

His bald statement hit me with a weight I hadn't prepared for. I raised my coffee cup to my lips and held it there, trying to gather myself, keep hold of what little composure I had left. Every bit of my body wanted to give in to shouting and crying and shuddering denial. I wanted, if only for a moment, to let go. But this was not the time.

I took a sip of bitter coffee, feeling its heat slide from throat to belly. "Yes," I said. "Matthew's dead. But my principal isn't."

"By sheer luck."

"No." I shook my head, mentally grabbing hold of the spark of anger Dave's words had set off. "I'm only lucky that it wasn't me. Shepard never would have gone into that trailer first." I did my best to glower at him. "I'm not stupid."

"I never said you were stupid."

"No, just lucky."

"We can argue this some more at another time. Right now, I want you to go back to your hotel, pack your things, and wait for Frank to take over for you."

I'd like to pretend that I felt no relief at the prospect of being taken off the job and no longer jeopardizing my own life to protect Shepard. I suppose without that tiny seed of relief, I wouldn't be human. But that seed wasn't enough to make me thankful to be replaced, and it wasn't enough to make me rush off and do as Dave du Comte commanded. Because that contrary streak, that same "yes, I can" and "you can't tell me what to do" that made me deck Regis C. back in junior high had never gone away. In fact, at odd moments, I'd swear that streak had widened—especially when it came to my friends.

"I'm not leaving Shepard," I said, then thought I needed to provide some argument more practical than emotional. "This is my job. I brought it in."

"And the company thanks you. But your part is done. Time to let the big boys take over." He didn't look at me as he said this. Instead, he pinched the crease of his trousers at the knee between thumb and forefinger, as though my dismissal was one more housekeeping/grooming matter.

"The big boys, huh?" I said.

Dave blew out a breath. "Don't imagine something that's not there."

I slammed the coffee cup onto the bench beside me, the porcelain chinking ominously against the wood. "What's to imagine? You just said right out that you want the 'boys' to handle it."

"A figure of speech."

"A revealing choice."

He dragged in a noisy breath and smoothed his palms against his thighs. "Lorraine, you know this job gets kicked up to A-division. Right now, the only people I have in A-division are men. So can we drop the insinuation please?"

I rested my hand on the coffee cup. Was I overreacting? My nerves were a little raw, for sure. Maybe I needed to cut the guy some slack. He had come all the way to AC—had been almost nice in that he hadn't called me off the case over the phone. I could probably be nicer to him. Didn't mean I planned on leaving, though.

I lifted the cup once again and gulped down some coffee. "Look, get me more help if you want. Put more people on this. But only to help me. I'm not leaving."

"You want to keep your job?"

"You want me to quit right now?" The fact of the matter was, I needed that job. And I needed Dave. No one else would give me a shot in executive protection. I knew this because I'd tried. If I had spent five years or more on the city PD, they might try me out. But I'd never even been through the academy. Without that kind of experience, wherever else I went, whatever company I switched to, I'd be reduced to starting over, once again working my way up from night watchman. I wasn't keen on starting over. But more than that, I wasn't keen on trusting Shepard's well-being to anyone else. Yeah, I complain about the guy a lot. But he has a talent for weaseling his way into your affection. And staying there.

"You wouldn't quit," Dave said.

"Try me." I might have been bluffing. I was gambling on Shepard's continuing to employ me with or without oversight from Diamond Security.

Dave looked at me from the narrowed corner of his eyes, but the lift at the corner of his lips told me he wasn't quite as displeased by my obstinacy as he would like to appear. "You realize that if you stay, there's a good chance this psycho will target you, get you out of the way in order to get to Brown?"

I squeezed my coffee mug and hoped my nerves didn't show

too badly. "That's always a risk." I knew that; it was on page three of the *Girls' Guide to Bodyguarding.*

"So let's ask him," Dave said, pushing to his feet.

"What?"

"We'll ask Brown. If he wants you stay . . ." Dave sighed in a way that made him more human than I'd ever seen him. "If not, you're back to overnights at the Guggenheim for a while. Agreed?"

Now, probably I should have been thrilled by this deal. But Dave, while removing himself from the role of bad guy, had effectively asked me to put my future into the hands of a grown man who wears makeup and pretends to be fictional people all day long. The prospect didn't overwhelm me with confidence. Still, what choice did I have? In the end, it was all about keeping the client safe and happy and someday getting to the point where A-division had a healthy share of estrogen. "Agreed," I said.

Dave scooped his jacket up from the bench and gave me a weak smile. "Let's go see what he has to say."

I shuffled out of the cell behind Dave and followed him back up the hallway. Caffeine zinged through my system, charging up my already overworked nerves. My stomach growled, and my heart pounded. I needed sugar before I began to tremble.

"Got any gum?" I asked. "Breath mint, maybe?"

The crease in Dave's brow when he turned to gape at me said louder than words could have that he thought I'd gotten my priorities confused, but all the same he patted the pockets of his suit jacket and came up with a roll of wintergreen candies.

"Thanks." I moved out of the center of the corridor and placed my coffee cup on the ground. I pried two mints from the wrapper, popped them both into my mouth, and handed the roll back to Dave.

The door to the interview room was yanked open from within. Detective Holden stuck his head out into the hallway, looking, I guessed, for me. "Coming back?" he asked.

I kept my eyes on the detective, steadfastly ignoring Dave. "Yep."

Holden gestured me into the room. I grabbed my coffee and

went in, Dave at my heels. He introduced himself to the detective and to Shepard. "I'd like to listen in, if that's all right," he said. "I'll need to brief Miss Keys' replacement."

Detective Holden shrugged his unconcern. Shepard, on the other hand, looked as if someone had asked him to solve a quadratic equation.

"I don't . . . follow you," he said. "You mean Joe? You need to . . . well, Lorraine can tell Joe whatever it is that—"

Dave kept his gaze on me and shook his head as he slipped back into his suit jacket. "I'm taking Lorraine off this job," he said. And if I hadn't been staring at him, I would have missed the minuscule wink Dave shot in my direction.

"Taking Lorraine? No. No." Shepard came to his feet, knocking his chair over backward in his haste. "You can't be serious." He turned to me for confirmation. I wanted to say something, but I wasn't sure of my lines in Dave's little drama. Plus, I had a mouthful of mints. I shook my head and shrugged a little and hoped that passed for "It's out of my hands."

"I'd like to have someone with more extensive field experience take over for Lorraine," Dave said.

"No. You can't do that," Shepard said. "I want Lorraine. I specifically—what do I have to do? Do I have to sign some contract, some affidavit that says I insist on having Lorraine with me or the deal's off? Where is it? I'll sign it right now."

I bit down hard on a mint to keep the smile from showing on my face.

"I understand your preference, Mr. Brown," Dave said. He reached a hand out, palm down, as though to soothe Shepard. "But your safety is our number one concern. Please believe we can best execute our commitment to you by bringing—"

"Save it," Shepard said. He pointed a finger at Detective Holden. "They're going to have a couple of AC cops watching me too."

Dave and I both turned our attention to where the detective stood, arms crossed, leaning against the wall. His tired nod showed his agreement with Shepard's claim.

"And they're going to have the movie security cops watching

too. We're only here for six more days anyway." Shepard shoved a hand through his hair, forcing the wayward lock off his forehead. "It's my decision, right? It's my safety and my peace of mind. I want Lorraine to stay."

Dave slid his hands into the pockets of his trousers. He kept his head down, gaze somewhere south of the tabletop. I don't know what he had expected to hear, whether he'd thought Shepard would jump at the chance to have more experienced guards by his side, or whether he'd thought Shepard would reluctantly agree to send me back home. I didn't, in any case, think he'd expected Shepard's adamant defense.

Despite the fact that Dave and I had a deal, I didn't quite trust him to stick to it. I forced myself to continue to breathe while we waited for his verdict.

"Six days," Dave said.

"That's all. Six. We'll have a wrap party, and I swear, after that I'm headed home."

It started slowly, but the motion of Dave's head resolved itself into an absolute nod. "Very well, then. Any further incident and this agreement is void, understood?"

Detective Holden straightened. "We're on the job. There won't be any harm to Mr. Brown, I promise you that."

Dave pressed his lips tightly for a moment before answering. "It's not Mr. Brown I'm concerned for," he said. He met my eyes briefly, then nodded to the detective and to Shepard and strode out of the room, his limp, for the moment, concealed.

His absence left a subtle void. Luckily, we had Shepard's ego to fill it.

He turned to me with eyes wide as steel-belted radials. "What does that mean? He's not serious, is he? He would care if something happened to me, wouldn't he?"

I kept my gaze locked on Shepard's and bit down hard on a mint. The candy made a satisfying pop-and-crumble noise that I decided was enough of an answer. I didn't know myself whose safety Dave worried about more, but I didn't have time for conjecture.

Detective Holden gestured us back to the beat-up wooden

table and ran through his Next Few Days scenario. There would be an undercover officer assigned to Shepard around the clock. The officer would keep his distance, blend with the tourist and gossip crowd on hand, and wait for the perpetrator to strike.

While Shepard went about his business, the New Jersey Arson and Bomb Squad would continue to check the trailer for evidence that would lead them to the cause of the fire. If the fire proved to have been the result of malicious intent, the method of starting the fire would be fed into a computer and cross-checked with the MOs of known arsonists. Seems once an arsonist found a viable MO, he stuck to it. Made sense, in a twisted, mentally unstable kind of way.

Holden summarized by handing Shepard his business card and inviting him to call anytime with any concerns he might have. Shepard also got to keep the shiny new ACPD coffee mug. Hard to tell whether he got preferential treatment because of his job description or because his life was in danger.

A pair of uniformed officers escorted us from the station and helped me hustle Shepard past a gaggle of reporters shouting questions and cameramen shining glaring lights on us. The cops tucked us into the back of a squad car with the efficiency of a NASCAR pit crew, and the car sped away from the curb before any news crews could pursue.

"They'll call ahead," Shepard said. "There'll be another bunch of them waiting at the hotel."

"Hey, Officer." I waited for Officer Chauffeur to meet my eyes in the rearview. "I hate to sound like a passenger in a yellow cab, but could you drop us at the casino entrance?"

"If you sit back and put your seat belt on," he said.

I fought the urge to roll my eyes and did as I was told.

"I don't want to go to the casino," Shepard said. "I've had a rough morning. I want to go back to my room. I want to lie down and have a drink. I don't want to go to the casino."

"We're not going to the casino. We're going through it. They can't follow you with cameras into a casino." I tightened the webbed seat belt across my lap and checked the upholstery for mystery stains, but the vinyl looked shiny clean. "The reporters will follow you only as long as it takes for security to pick up the whole circus on the surveillance cameras. That is, if they're not already standing by."

I silently cursed my failure to program the phone number of the hotel security manager into my cell phone. A little advance warning might smooth some feathers. Seized by an idea, I reached into my jacket pocket for my phone. Matthew would have the number. In his job, he—

Reality hit, and my world tilted too far to the left. I pulled in a slow breath through my nostrils, hoping it would calm the crash of nausea in my stomach, the bitter coffee heartburn that threatened to gag me. Matthew. Damn it all.

"I'd really like to go home," Shepard said, his voice a whispered fraction above the hum of the tires and chatter of the police radio.

I reached out and patted his hand. "There's nothing to worry about," I said for both of us. And hoped with all my heart I was right.

Our arrival at Resorts' casino played out nearly the same as Shepard's arrival at de la Vega's had the night before, only faster. By the time we climbed into an elevator behind two security guards, my heart was pounding and I was fighting to catch my breath.

At Shepard's suite, hotel security waited in the hallway with Shepard while I did the canary-in-a-coal-mine routine inside the room. I flipped all the lights on and off, checked the TV, and peeked behind the drapes and inside the shower and closet in case an unimaginative killer had entered the room before us. To cover all bases, I peered under the bed. Having survived that long in the suite, I figured the air itself was safe. I sent the security guards back to whatever all-seeing room they had emerged from and allowed Shepard access to his room.

He went straight for the remote control and the couch. Feet up on scripts stacked on the coffee table, he switched the television on and began speeding through channels.

"How about we order up some room service?" I said.

Shepard paused on a beach volleyball game that had nothing to do with volleyball and everything to do with buxom girls and small bikinis. Good to see him revert to type. "No room service. Someone in the kitchen could be trying to kill me."

Judging by the amount of weight he was hauling around, I doubted that many such opportunities had been missed, but I figured it was best not to disagree with him. "How about we get someone we trust to bring the food?"

"Like Joe?" he said, sinking deeper into the couch.

"Yeah, like Joe. Or Barb." Maybe now wasn't the best time to introduce Barb to Shepard. But I viewed it this way: Barb was a great distraction. Plus, she already loved the guy. He wouldn't have to do more than smile once and shake her hand and she'd be happy. Moreover, she'd be happy and on her way home, and I'd have one less person to worry about.

Shepard nodded, and I shrugged out of my jacket and sat down at the little in-room desk and reached for the phone. "You have messages here," I said.

I could almost feel his sigh adding weight to the room. "Probably people calling to see if I'm all right."

Come to think of it, why hadn't anyone called me? Oh, right: I'd turned my cell phone off at the police station.

I fished the phone out of my jacket and powered it up.

"Hey, Rainny," Shepard said, as I watched signal bars grow one by one. "Would you do me a favor and go through those messages and let me know if there's anything important?"

I looked over at the guy, wisecrack at the ready. But he'd gone even deeper into the couch and had switched from semi-nude volleyball to a yoga program. I decided to be nice to him for a while, if only to prevent him from ordering something wildly inappropriate on pay-per-view. "Sure," I said.

As I scrounged through the desk for some hotel stationery to take notes on, my phone, sufficiently barred, chirped its voice-mail signal. I peered at Shepard, who was squinting at the pretzel pose the TV yoga teacher had tied herself into, and decided he could wait for his messages.

I had seven new messages. I found that disappointing, in a

selfish kind of way. After all, what if I had been seriously hurt? Only seven people cared enough to call?

Barb's third frantic how-are-you-where-are-you message set me straight. "Please," she said, "call me as soon as you get this message. No one's got your new cell number. Your mother's called me six times. Maybe call her before you call me. But call me!"

Mom. Crap. How was I going to explain this to my mom without worrying her? I punched the button for the next message, and the voice that typically rolled as slow as summertime came through at Earnhardt speed. "Hey. It's me. It's Eddie. Barb gave me your number. I'm worried to death about you guys. Everyone is. Will you call—one of you, call me, all right?"

Tears burned at the corners of my eyes. Barb had given Eddie my new number but not my mother. That's friendship.

I swiveled in my chair to face Shepard full-on. "Eddie Gale called," I said, knowing he had no clue what phone I'd been on. "He wants you to call him."

He seemed to think about this for a minute, then reached for his phone. "Good idea. He can bring some food. And he really knows his whiskey."

If Eddie was going to bring food, where would that leave Barb? Huh.

I listened, half to the last two messages she'd left and half to Shepard's conversation with Eddie.

My last message played on. "Rainny." A man's voice I couldn't quite place, even in the silence that followed it. "It's Dave." More silence. "Your boss." Oh, right. Well, okay, yeah. He sent the phone; he'd have the number. "I, uh . . ." Shepard clambered off the couch while Dave tortured me with pauses. "Just . . . be careful."

And then the voice mail voice instructed me on how to store the messages, and Shepard stood before me saying, "She's fine. She's right here. I'll put her on."

He handed me the phone. "It's Eddie. He wants to talk to you."

I stifled a snort and took the phone. "I just got your message," I said to Eddie.

"Y'all been with the police this whole time, huh?"

"It's been a tough morning. You guys keep working?"

"Nah. We thought about it, the schedule tight as it is, but it just wasn't right. We'll be back at it tomorrow."

"Bright and early?"

"That's the plan. Tonight, though, we're all getting together. Kind of an informal remembrance thing. I want you to think about coming and give me your answer when I get there."

"When you get where?"

"I'm bringing lunch. Brown wants a bottle of scotch. What would you like? And please tell me you're not one of those women who doesn't eat real food. You'll destroy my illusions."

Oh, the scotch sounded good. But my stomach seemed to be recovering from the day's upset faster than my mind, and it didn't want a drink as much as it wanted Italian. I asked for a meatball hero and hoped the growling wouldn't get any louder.

I said my good-byes and handed Shepard back his phone. I put in a call to Barb to let her know Shepard and I were fine and promised her I'd call when I knew when and where she and I could get together. A dinner with Barb held far more appeal than a "remembrance" for Matthew. I hadn't known him well, and the prospect of spending another evening in a room full of hot air and ego made my skin crawl.

And yet . . . In movies, the killer often shows up at the victim's funeral. If I attended the event for Matthew, would I be able to identify the person who had rigged the explosion? The person who wanted Shepard dead?

As with so many other critical choices in my life, there was only one way to find out.

Chapter Eight

Cursing under my breath, I snatched up the phone. "Shepard Brown's line. How may I help you?"

"Put Brown on the phone."

I looked over to where Shepard and Eddie lay passed out on opposite sides of the couch. A nearly empty bottle of whiskey, an assortment of chips, and a cluster of discarded cigars littered the table in front of them.

"I'm sorry," I said. "Mr. Brown is unavailable at the moment. I'd be happy to take a message for you."

"Fine. You tell that son of a sow that Karl Moyne called, and if he tries to use this mess today as an excuse not to show up for work tomorrow, he's in breach of contract. You got that?"

I'd maybe only been a secretary for an afternoon, but it didn't take long to get tired of being cursed at by every producer, agent, and director with access to a phone. I had to take my retaliation where I could get it. "Well, Mr. Moyne, I would tell him, but as I understand it, the best you could do would be to sue Mr. Brown for breach, and after the events of this morning, I doubt you'd get a conviction based on one day's missed work."

"One day? Listen, sweetheart, you have no idea how many days of work this guy has missed." I could picture Mr. Moyne going purple in the face, his beady eyes bulging out below his high, glossy forehead. "I knew this guy was a liability the day he signed on for the picture. Why do you think I had the jerk insured? So you tell that good-for-nothing, low-box-office piece of stale bread to have his game face on set on time tomorrow, or he's finished."

Mr. Moyne slammed down the phone, and I winced at the crack it made. I was going to have to work on the verbal thing. Without the guy face-to-face, I didn't know how to intimidate him.

The doorbell rang, and I looked over to the couch to see if anyone stirred. Shepard had his head thrown back over the arm of the couch, snoring like he was breathing through a tuba. Eddie lay crumpled in the other corner, looking not at all dishy with his hair smushed against the side of his head and a bead of spittle easing its way out of his mouth. Hollywood heartthrobs at their finest.

I checked my watch. Nearly seven o'clock. The doorbell rang again as I peered through the peephole. Joe stood on the other side, looking like a little bull in a blue suit and carrying a sack of takeout chicken.

"You're late," I said, as I hauled the door open.

"Late? Small potatoes. You screwed up today." He came sideways into the room and scanned the area.

"I did not screw up," I said. "The principal is fine." I pointed to Shepard, belatedly realizing he looked a whole lot less than fine.

"That's 'fine'?" Joe shook his head and crossed to the desk, leaving the scent of roasted chicken in his wake. He moved the list of phone messages to one side before putting down his bag of food. "Maybe time to consider other work?"

"Funny," I said. I grabbed my jacket from the back of the chair, trying not to get too close to Joe. "Did you fill out a job application at the chicken place? Or were you afraid you'd be underqualified?"

"Will you guys knock it off?" Eddie said from the depths of the couch. He swiped at his mouth with the back of his hand, then ran his fingers through his hair with the other. "You're likely to wake someone from a coma with your bickering."

"Sorry," I said, smoothing my jacket over my arm. I held my temper and faced Joe. "Brown's been out for well over an hour. He'll likely be hungry when he wakes up."

"I'll see he's fed," Eddie offered.

"Thanks," I said, sending a smile his way, and turned back to Joe. "They've got a thing later, a—"

"They'll tell me," Joe said.

"You're going to be there, Lorraine, aren't you?" Eddie asked.

I took a deep breath. "After last night, I really should spend the evening with Barb."

Eddie's gaze locked with mine. I hoped he was remembering last night for our friendly wager, not for my protracted separation from Barb. But then he seemed to relax, shoulders to toes. "Bring her along," he said. "Maybe hold her hand so you don't lose her this time."

"Yeah," I said. "Okay, I'll see if she's up for it."

As if that was really going to be a question. I couldn't wrap my mind around any concept that would include Barb turning down an evening in the company of Shepard Brown, Eddie Gale, Holly Bellinger, and whoever else decided to show, even if the event was more of a remembrance of the dead than a cocktail party.

Out on the boardwalk the rain had finally stopped. Bulky thunderheads pushed to the north, leaving behind trails of clouds brushed by the wind into soft streaks. The sun, having started its descent, lit the clouds from below, casting pink and lavender to the heavens.

I took a long, slow, deep breath, tasted the passing rain in the back of my throat. The air smelled clean and sharp, checkered with the fragrance of sand, sea, and damp wood. A gaggle of white-haired ladies laughed as they strolled along the boardwalk, straw handbags hanging from bent elbows. They shuffled out of the way of a rolling chair being guided in the opposite direction and paused to gaze into a storefront featuring imported oriental merchandise.

The door to the import shop swung open, and several members of the film crew emerged. Two held dark plastic bags and passed right by me without a glance. The next guy in line smiled and nodded. The last one stopped.

"Hey, Dutch," I said in greeting.

Dutch smiled softly and lifted his chin in the direction of Shepard's hotel. "How is he?"

"All right," I said, and I shrugged a bit. "I'm not sure how he's supposed to be, but he seems okay."

"It's not right, what happened," he said. "I've been around trailers and mobile homes. I don't figure that was any accident."

"I suppose you're right."

"But Shepard Brown . . . Who would do such a thing?"

"I'm open to suggestions."

He straightened as though I'd taken him by surprise. "What do you mean?"

"You've been on this set from the beginning, Dutch. You tell me."

He narrowed his eyes, looking to where his buddies had stopped beside an ice cream vendor's cart. "A lot of these folks got something against one another. And not too many of them are mentally stable. Hell, look at Catherine Dawes. She'd gouge Shepard's eyes out with a spoon if you held him down for her. But this is something else again."

I nodded and caught the scent of dough frying and hot dogs on a grill. "If anything's been out of the ordinary . . . if you've heard or seen anything . . ."

Sharp blue eyes captured my gaze. "I'll tell you," he said. "And then I'll tell the cops."

"In that order?"

"Sounds fair to me."

I grinned and watched as he moved off to join his pals at the ice cream cart. Maybe he'd think of something. Maybe he wouldn't. But he was one of the few people I trusted enough to ask.

Ice cream was starting to look like a really good dinner plan, which made it high time to call Barb.

We agreed to meet up at a burger shop, and I found her there, arms folded, people watching from just outside the entrance.

When she caught sight of me, she rushed me, throwing her

arms around me and hugging me tightly enough to force the air from my lungs.

"I'm so glad you're okay," she said, her voice carrying an intensity equal to her hug.

"You knew I was okay." I wriggled gently from her grasp. "I talked to you."

"It's one thing to talk to a person. Seeing you makes it real. You could have been lying to me. You could really have been hurt and lying about it. Once I see you, I can see for myself."

My brain hurt a little, trying to dope out that last bit. I nodded and smiled and pointed vaguely in the direction of the restaurant.

"So tonight," Barb said on our way through the door, "we should do whatever it is you want to do. You want to go gambling, we'll do that. You want to catch a baseball game, we'll do that. You want to stay in, order room service, and do makeovers, we'll do that."

"Actually, I already made plans for us." At the restaurant hostess' raised eyebrows I held up two fingers—two polite ones—and we followed her to a red vinyl booth with a view of the boardwalk. The air was thick with the aroma of grilled burgers and French fries. My stomach contracted, and my mouth watered, and I wondered if ordering fries *and* rings would make me look like a pig. Maybe if I ate them with a salad . . .

Barb dropped onto the bench like she'd been on her feet all day. "So, what did you plan?" she asked.

I had her. I knew I had her. She was going to flip. She was going to hug me and jump up and down and make me regret telling her in person. Which meant I had to remind her about the deal.

"Listen," I said, "we've been invited to this thing tonight. Everyone will be there. We'll go. And then first thing in the morning you are on a bus, a train, a boat . . . you are on the first conveyance out of here, okay?"

"Oh, no, I can't leave now."

"What? Barb, we had a deal."

"Yes, and I see where you're going with this." She pinched a handful of napkins out of the spring-loaded metal container. "You introduce me to Shepard tonight, and then I leave in the morning."

"Yeah, that was the deal."

"Well, we need a new deal."

"Barb—"

"I like it here. I'm having fun. It's not like I have anywhere else to be until school starts. So you'd better come up with a new deal, because I'm not saying hello to Shepard Brown and leaving town."

"There is no new deal. You meet Shepard, you go home. Very simple."

"Nope." She shook her head. "Not going to happen."

"Listen to me for a minute." I tried for a deep, calming breath, the sort that would give me patience and fortitude. "Things have gotten really complicated here."

"And by *complicated* you mean *dangerous*."

Rats. "Okay, yes, dangerous. You should go home, Barb. I've got to keep my eye on Shepard, and believe me, that man is exhausting. I can't do my job and look after you at the same time."

"And by *look after* you mean *keep me safe*."

We'd been friends for too long for me to sugarcoat anything for her. "I don't want to have to worry about you."

"Then don't." She picked up one of the bound menus the hostess had left. Across the room, a jukebox pounded out a Donovan tune. "There is no reason for you to worry about me. I'm a big girl. And whatever's going on with you and Shepard—"

"There is nothing going on with me and Shepard," I said.

"Okay, I'll rephrase. Whatever is happening that has you watching over Shepard has nothing to do with me. So there's no reason for you to worry. It's not like you're getting me caught up in some six-o'clock-headline-news drug deal gone bad."

"I know that," I said. "I know there's no connection between you and Shepard and the current state of affairs. My point is, I worry anyway. I'd feel a lot better if you were home."

"Your worry is your problem. You might think you were put on this earth to save mankind," she said, opening her menu, "but some of us are capable of saving ourselves."

"I'm . . . What?"

She sighed. "You have this thing, this attitude, like it's your calling in life to protect everyone you know. Well, you know what? A lot of us are capable of protecting ourselves."

I thought of Shepard, and Matthew. I wanted to point out that they, at least, had needed me, but would that prove my worth or prove her point? All that mattered, for the moment, right or wrong, was that I couldn't, regardless of my efforts, keep everyone safe in Atlantic City. If Barb were home, tucked away in her living room in Staten Island, I wouldn't have to worry about her. Nothing that happened in Atlantic City, not even the direst of Dave du Comte's scenarios, would affect her.

"The deal stays the same," I said, reaching for my own menu. "You meet Shepard, and you go home immediately after."

Her gaze met mine over the top of the menu. We stared at each other like gunslingers in sharp sunlight.

"Fine," she said at last, with a quirk of her eyebrows. "As soon as I meet Shepard, I'll go home."

I relaxed into my seat and let out any remnants of breath I'd been holding. "Thank you," I said.

She tipped her head and lifted one shoulder. "You're welcome. I'm afraid, though, that I'm unavailable to meet Shepard Brown tonight. I just remembered I have a prior engagement."

And then she closed her menu, flashed me a sickly sweet smile, and left the restaurant.

Lord, it just wasn't my day.

I shoved my ID case and room card into my back pocket. Time and again Barb would make me promise not to stick things in the pockets of my jeans because it "ruined the line." So maybe I did it for spite, or maybe I did it because I had failed to bring a purse suitable to my environs.

One last check in the mirror to be certain my hair in reality resembled what I thought it did in my imagination and I was ready to go. I hadn't seen Barb since she'd walked out of the restaurant. She hadn't been in the hotel casino and hadn't returned to our room while I showered and changed for the evening. A tiny shred of worry made the rounds through my central nervous system, but mostly I knew she'd turn up when she recovered.

I dropped the DO NOT DISTURB sign onto the doorknob and wondered for a moment if Barb would think I was inside. Then again, during our brief spell as apartment mates, she had shown a singular inability to respect all manner of I've-got-a-guy-in-my-room signals. Probably not much had changed.

Retracing my usual path, I made my way on foot past the Steel Pier, past the old, established casino hotels to the new de la Vega's Hotel and Casino. Each casino along the boardwalk had its own sort of personality. Some gleamed with gilt and glam, gold and mirrors. Vega's went soft: soft lighting, soft music, and European refinement.

The elevator took me to the fourth floor, where a harried-looking assistant stood outside the doors of a suite. She had a cell phone pasted to one ear and a private security goon yammering into her other. Clutched tightly against her chest was a clipboard from which, no doubt, hung the list of who may and who may not enter.

All at once I didn't want to be there, as though I had left my last ounce of energy on the elevator, and it was now plummeting down to the parking level. I stopped just outside the elevator foyer and felt an ache in my feet that radiated upward, past my ankles, around my calves, and sliced into the backs of my knees. In that moment the only thing I wanted in the world was to put my feet up in front of a television, a bag of microwave popcorn in one hand and a chocolate bar in the other.

The harried-looking assistant raised her eyebrows and demanded my name.

I checked my watch. Ten minutes to nine. The odds of anyone serving microwave popcorn in the Madrid room were pretty slim, I figured. The odds of vodka being served: considerably better. As in, a sure thing. "Lorraine—"

"Keys," she finished, nodding. "Go right in." In one blinding movement she crossed my name off her list and elbowed the security goon in the ribs. He opened the door and stood back to let me in without ever letting go of the doorknob.

I stepped inside the room and forced myself not to stand in the doorway and panic. Faced with a sea of people, actors I had seen in passing for the past few days or gazing out at me from newsstands, I became instantly aware of my otherness, my outsider status.

One drink, I promised myself. One drink, five minutes with Shepard, and then back to my hotel. What was I even doing there anyway? I'd known Matthew for a grand total of three days. Plus, if you looked at it from a certain angle, his death was my responsibility.

But this was a remembrance, even though it looked and sounded like a plain old party. Maybe the woman who'd been with Matthew when she ordered a poisoned pizza lurked somewhere in the room. Maybe I could end up lucky.

"Where is he?"

I jumped at the unexpected assault. "Good evening, Mr. Moyne."

"Don't give me that polite crap," Moyne said, beady eyes bugging out of his head. "Where is he? Where's Brown?"

No spittle had actually left his mouth as he spoke, but his vehemence and the drink he held made for a threatening combination. I eased back another step. "He's not with me."

"Well, where the heck is he?"

I forced my tired body into a square stance and spoke as firmly as I dared in a crowd. "Your issue is with Mr. Brown, not with me. I would appreciate it if you kept that in mind while you're talking to me."

His face rolled into layers of confusion. "What kind of crazy talk is that? I talk to everyone like this. Get over it. And make sure that yutz is on time tomorrow morning."

Moyne turned and shouldered his way through the crowd.

"Long day, huh?"

I spun at the sound and found Dutch behind me, his blond

beard freshly combed, his shirt clean and logo-free, a bottle of beer in each hand. "Long and crappy," I said.

He grinned and handed me a beer. "You look like you could use a hug," he said, lifting a shoulder and letting it drop, "but I don't think I know you well enough."

I swigged from the beer, a nice, cold, crisp, domestic beer. "Thanks," I said. "I think I need this more."

I scanned the assembled crowd, taking in who sat with whom, who shouted to whom across the room. "All these people knew Matthew?"

"Assistants know a lot of people," Dutch said. "And some of these people crave attention. Here they get to tell their stories about where they were when it happened."

It. Nice to be at the center of an event so seminal it could be referred to without definition. Maybe I should sit down; I didn't think the bottle of beer would hold me up, no matter how tight my grip.

"You know what?" Dutch said. "Screw it."

And he grabbed me in a hug that left me feeling like I was being cuddled by a teddy bear. He was all soft on the outside and strong as steel on the inside. He could no doubt hold me up while I fell asleep against his chest.

"Do you wear a sign that says Hug Me, or something?"

I lifted my face away from Dutch and stood eye to eye with Kim Lloyd, the pixie-blond assistant director.

"Where's Shepard?" she asked.

Disengaging myself from Dutch, I smiled past my fatigue and forced myself to appear cheerful. "So sorry, I haven't seen him this evening."

The dark eyebrow she lifted in response in no way matched the wisps of blond hair draped over her forehead. "Is he maybe with someone else? He and Holly looked pretty cozy last night."

"I don't know if that's much to go on. Last night, you and Matthew looked pretty close too. But obviously . . ."

Kim raised her hand to toy with her necklace, her tiny engagement ring a glimmer in the subdued lighting of the room.

She shivered a little. "Yeah, well . . . poor Matthew. Matthew was nice, but I'm engaged, you know? I won't risk my future."

"Of course." I took a swig of beer that did nothing to alleviate the pall of discomfort descending over our little trio. "So . . . uh . . . when is the wedding?" I asked.

Letting go of her necklace, she folded her arms across her belly. "We haven't set a date yet. Soon, though. Enough about me." Her voice rang a little too loud. "What about you? You're new. Union send you?"

I nearly choked on a mouthful of beer.

"Lorraine's not on the crew. She's a bodyguard," Dutch said.

Of course it was one of those horrible Hollywood moments where all conversation in the room had hit a sighing lull into which the word *bodyguard* boomed like an echo over a canyon.

"Oh, really? Interesting." Kim tucked her arms tightly against her body and leaned sideways a bit to peer around me. "And you know Shepard . . . how?" she asked, voice as tight as her arms.

"Professionally," I said.

"Good luck with that. Excuse me." She smiled, a little flatly, and slid away from us as if we were unpaid cast extras.

"She's wound a little tight, huh?" I said.

Dutch laughed. "She's got a tough job to do. Woman in a man's world. She's used to fighting hard to make things happen. Cut her some slack."

The testosterone-heavy roster of Diamond Security's A-division scrolled through my mind. So maybe I had an idea of what Kim struggled against. Maybe I'd been up against it myself twenty-eight out of thirty days a month. Didn't mean we were going to be best buds.

"Where's the rest of your gang? Those guys I saw you with this afternoon," I said.

"Didn't make it past the casino," he said, raising his beer to his lips. "They'll be here eventually, I guess. Look out."

Too late I registered that his "Look out" applied to the present, not the unspecified moment in the future when his friends tore themselves away from Texas Hold'em.

Someone grabbed my elbow and spun me around.

"Is it true?" Holly Bellinger asked.

I looked back to Dutch. Maybe he had an idea. But he grinned and shrugged and downed some beer to cover the laughter.

"What are you talking about?" I asked.

"You're really a bodyguard? I thought you were Shepard's long-lost friend from childhood or something."

"I'm both," I said. "I'm two mints in one. And I was never lost."

"Seriously? You're serious?"

The light in Holly's eyes didn't appear to be caused by any artificial substance. She seemed genuinely excited.

"Where do you work? Do you only work here in Jersey? Do you do work anywhere else? Are you with a company? What—"

"I work out of New York," I said in a hurry, trying to stop the waterfall of questions. "I mostly go wherever the company sends me." Like to banks, museums, and other boring places that require uniforms and hideous shoes . . .

"But you're a real bodyguard."

"She's the best," Dutch said.

I don't know where Dutch got that idea, but his endorsement made for good PR, so I nodded and thanked him.

Holly's perfectly white, perfectly blinding smile encompassed both of us. "That's so great. Would the company ever send you to California?"

"Ummm . . ." Face it, Dave barely let me go to Jersey. He might have a breakdown if my assignment involved getting on a plane.

"Maybe she could do some freelance work for you, Miss Bellinger," Dutch said.

Holly sighed. "You have no idea how great that would be. I mean, Shepard trusts you, so right there . . . and after today . . .

It would be so great not to have to deal with those smelly hulks my assistant always hires."

Good to know I didn't smell. "Their size is all about intimidation," I said. "It's a deterrent." And a distinct advantage I didn't have. What I lacked in size and testosterone, I had to make up for in attitude. It seemed to be working out.

"But it would be so nice to have a bodyguard who could come inside a lingerie shop instead of hanging around the sidewalk discouraging everyone else from entering, especially if that someone else happens to be the wife of a producer or director who's looking for a lead for his next project. Then I could chat the wife up over some panties, and then she could mention it to her husband or lover or whatever, *et voilà*. Do you have a card? What do you charge?"

"It's a sliding-scale fee," Dutch said. "See, first she'll do a needs-and-risk assessment, to establish where you're most vulnerable, and then work up a plan based on time and materials to meet those needs."

He went on a little while longer, until I understood he was talking about new-building construction, yet Holly nodded as if it all made great sense from a security perspective. I chugged some beer to keep from laughing, then reached into my back pocket where I shouldn't store things and pulled out my ID billfold. Behind my license, with the less-than-flattering picture of me as a blonde, were the cards Dave had sent down with my new phone. I handed a card to Holly.

"Thank you," Holly said, examining the card. "Do you have more? Dina will want one too. And Pam."

I kept two cards and handed Holly the rest. "Go to town," I said.

She took the cards and went off with the joy of someone who'd just been asked to hunt Easter eggs, and I turned to face Dutch.

"Needs-and-risk assessment?" I said. "What would you have done if she knew what you were talking about?"

"Told her I didn't know what I was talking about. But she

bought it, right? Now you can charge her whatever you feel like. And make her pay your expenses while you're at it too."

"I never said I would work for her." Not that I thought I'd refuse, but I wanted to keep my options open.

Dutch chuckled, and we shifted closer toward the center of the room to make way for a passing waiter. Whatever had been on his tray had long since been Hoovered up by the crowd.

We edged past a trio of electricians who, as Dutch had suggested, were telling their tales of what they saw when the trailer exploded.

"I bet it was C-4," one said.

"Nah, it was just some freaky accident. C-4 would need something to ignite it," the next said.

"Cell phone," third guy said, sounding bored and assured. "You can rig the explosive with a sound receptor and activate it with a tone from a cell phone."

A little wave of nausea rolled through my belly. There were a million clever ways to kill a man. How could I protect Shepard against them all?

I came up short at the sight in the center of the room.

Dressed in a dove-gray number that clung to every protruding bone, Catherine Dawes sat weeping beautifully on the arm of a wing chair. Sunk into the chair itself was none other than Shepard Brown.

"He was just . . . so kind to me. Always," Catherine said. Her voice was a strained whisper, yet it carried clearly to me and likely anyone else in a six-foot radius. "He never had a cross word. He was patient and good and everything the world needs today. I can't imagine . . ." Her words broke over a sob.

I huffed and rolled my eyes. This was the same woman who'd shrieked at Matthew the day I'd met her, calling him all sorts of holier-than-thou names. Who did she think she was kidding?

At my huff, Catherine sprang to her feet with the speed of a striking snake. "You!" she snapped, taking a step in my direction. "What are you doing here? How did you get in?"

I sneaked a quick look around in case she was addressing someone else, but most folks within earshot either ignored her or stared at me. Only Holly seemed interested; her seething gaze was fixed on Catherine.

Shepard stirred himself enough to reach for Catherine's hand and guide her back to the chair. He said something softly to her, something I couldn't catch, and she lowered herself to perch on the edge of the cushion beside him. She scanned the watchful crowd before, it appeared, giving in to her grief and collapsing with a sob.

Instantly alert, Shepard gathered her in his arms and whispered in her ear. I imagined his words to be soothing, meant to calm her. But knowing Shepard and their relationship, he might have been urging her to stop making a scene.

Where was Barb when I needed her? She would eat this up. Of course, she'd run off to heaven-knew-where, angry at me for wanting to keep her safe—

Joe. Where was Joe?

I scanned the crowd, gave Dutch a description, and had him looking too, but I didn't see Joe anywhere. The only person who might have an answer to his whereabouts had a hysterical starlet on his lap.

Dutch and I split up to search the room. Panic ignited an adrenaline surge as I shoved my way through the crowd. He had to be there, had to be lurking somewhere nearby. He was short; maybe that accounted for why I couldn't spot him. Maybe he was standing in the center of a group of really tall people.

But no. He was nowhere to be seen. After I convinced a waiter with an empty tray to check the men's room for me, I ran out of options.

I forced a path back to Shepard.

Catherine sat sniffling prettily on his lap, and Shepard seemed a bit past caring.

"I've lost control of my life," he said when I knelt beside him. "Nothing, nothing is in my power anymore."

"Yeah, whatever. Leave the drama to Blondie there, huh? Where's Joe?"

"I . . . I used to be in charge of my destiny. I used to get up in the morning—"

"Shepard, where's Joe?"

"—and decide, this is what I'm going to accomplish today, and I made it happen."

"Shepard!"

"Get. Out," Catherine snarled.

"Hush," Shepard said. "See? You upset her."

I wasn't sure which "her" he was referring to and didn't much care. Crouched beside his chair, I couldn't kick any sense into him. I used the beer bottle instead, slamming it into his shin with enough force to make him sit bolt upright and drop Catherine.

She tumbled to the floor with an undignified shriek, and Shepard yowled and clutched his shin. "What was that for?"

"Where is Joe?"

"He's outside, in the hallway."

"You left him in the hallway? He's not a coat, Shepard; you don't check him at the door."

"He wasn't going to let me drink any more."

Catherine pushed up onto hands and knees. "I said, get out."

I stood and reached for Shepard's shoulder without looking and ended up patting him on the head. "I'm going to get Joe," I said.

Since most folks had been watching the recent Shepard-and-Catherine show, I had only to squeeze through the perimeter of onlookers before my path to the doorway lay clear.

I deposited my empty beer bottle on a passing waiter's tray as I caught sight of Joe, having a laugh with the security goon. No doubt every ounce of my anger showed on my face. After giving me crap about the events of the morning and acting so superior, Joe could stand around, laughing it up, while the principal went unwatched into a crowd of people? I don't think so.

Having apparently dismissed me as a harmless female, the security goon made no move to stop me as I clamped onto Joe's shoulder and yanked until he faced me.

"What are you doing out here?" I asked.

"Chill."

"Why aren't you inside with Shepard? Are you insane?"

"The cop's inside," Joe said.

Of course. The undercover cop. At least that explained why I hadn't seen him. It didn't, however, change my opinion of where Joe should be.

"You need to be where Shepard can see you," I said.

"He's fine."

"How would you know? Get inside."

"Hey. Don't order—"

"Get. Inside," I hissed, in my best impersonation of Catherine Dawes.

I suspect a measure of insanity shone through my anger and scared Joe into motion. He told the goon he'd catch up with him later, then skirted past the harried-looking assistant without meeting her eyes.

With Joe back where he belonged, the adrenaline rush that had carried me to the hallway abated, leaving me sweaty, exhausted, and vulnerable to all the emotions I had suppressed throughout the day. The painful awareness of losing Matthew broke from somewhere deep within me.

I sniffed back threatening tears as I pushed the call button for the elevator, then slumped against the wall. Hauling in a deep breath, I promised myself a good cry when I got back to my hotel room. In the meantime, I unclipped the cell phone from my belt and dialed Barb.

She answered with, "What is it now?"

"Where are you?" I asked, somewhat pointlessly. I could hear the cheerful bells and whistles that meant someone had hit it big on the slot machines.

"I'm still in Atlantic City," she said.

Too tired to spar with her, I said, "Fine. Look, I'm going back to the room, and I—"

"Okay," she said, and she disconnected.

I guessed that meant she was still mad at me. Which stank. I could have used a friend.

The elevator dinged its announcement of an arriving car as I closed my phone and fought back more tears. The doors slid open, and Eddie Gale stepped out.

Oh, he looked good. Black shirt hugging every muscle, slim trousers caressing every curve—every inch a heartbreaker. He was also staring at me, brow creased above those crystal-blue eyes.

"Are you okay?" he asked. "Were you—?"

"I'm fine," I said, sniffling back tears and edging behind him and into the car. "I was just power-yawning."

He turned quickly. Bracing his arm against the door to prevent it from closing, he said, "You're not leaving, are you? Don't tell me you're going back to your hotel."

"Okay, I won't." I pushed the button for the lobby. "I'll let you guess my destination, and in the morning you can tell me your guess, and I'll tell you if you were right."

With a surprised huff, he lowered his arm and stepped back into the elevator with me. The doors closed with a *thunk,* and we lurched into motion.

"Are you sure you're all right?"

"Fine."

"You don't look fine," he said, voice laced with gentle concern.

"How thoughtful of you to say so."

"I don't mean it like that," he said, smiling softly and reaching for my hand. "You've had a heckuva day. The strain is maybe starting to show a little."

His hand felt warm on mine, strong, something substantial to hold on to. Half of me wanted to cling tighter; the other half wanted to shake him off.

"I'll stay away from the poker table, then. Thanks for the warning."

He shifted his weight, easing closer to me. "Let me walk you back to your hotel."

"Thanks, I'm fine on my own."

"I know you are," he said, with a firm nod. "But maybe for

a little while you can pretend you're not, and I can pretend to be gallant."

The offer tempted me. But Eddie was forgetting a few valuable elements in the equation. "You think you can walk with me all the way down the boardwalk without drawing a crowd?"

He reached past me and pushed the button for the parking level. "You have to know which roads to take. What do you say? Up for a little more risk?"

"I don't know," I said. "I'm pretty tired."

He smiled. "Leave it to me. I'll see that you're safe."

In the parking garage Eddie dropped my hand and slung his arm around my shoulders. We walked, heads bowed, out of the garage and down Pacific, talking of topics as widespread as baseball and the afterlife and learning where our common interests lay. On occasion, passersby would stop and narrow their eyes at Eddie, as though trying to place him. Eddie would nod sharply, a silent "Good evening," and turn to me and say things like, "This is why I don't want to work nights at the plant anymore" or "I believe it's time I leave the Post Office. What do you think?" Most of his questions allowed me to answer with the generic, "Are you crazy?" I guess it worked, because we arrived at my hotel unmolested and leaning on each other as if we'd been walking arm in arm for years.

"This is my stop," I said, as we neared the hotel entrance.

But Eddie shook his head. "Nope," he said. "I've come this far. I'll see it through."

We rode the elevator to the tenth floor, Eddie's back to a pair of girls who might have been college age, or who might have been carrying fake IDs, but who appeared drunk already in either case.

"You ever do that?" he asked, lips close to my ear, hand on my waist.

"What?" I asked. I had a handful of his shirt, my knuckles resting on the waistband of his trousers. Lord, he smelled good. Being so close to him made me feel a little drunk myself.

"Get all liquored up, hit the casinos."

"That was my plan for tonight, actually."

"Yeah? What went wrong?"

"Oh, you know, the usual." I peered over his shoulder and watched the illuminated numbers tick off floors as we passed them by. "Weeping starlets, intoxicated leading men, domestic beer."

"Just another day at the office."

"Maybe. But I've never worked in an office before."

He smiled, slow and slightly rueful. "You get used to it. It has its moments."

"And its perks," I said. The elevator lurched to a stop and the maybe-twentysomethings staggered into the fifth-floor hallway and pulled each other in opposite directions. They came back together like two ends of a stretched rubber band, consumed with laughter.

The doors slid closed, and rather than turning to face front like a well-behaved elevator passenger, Eddie edged closer to me.

"Tell me something," I said, still speaking softly, though no one remained to overhear. "What are you doing seeing me to my door when you could be off with any number of sleek, stunning women?"

"I tried sleek and stunning. Not my style," he said in his soft, slow way. "I prefer a woman with curves and confidence, the kind who's not afraid of getting her hair mussed." He ran his hand around the back of my neck, fingers reaching up into my hairline. "A woman like you."

And then came the kiss. Soft and searing, tender and hungry. Through the fabric of his shirt I could feel the heat of his skin, the steel of his muscles. The elevator was going up, and I was falling.

When the bell sounded for my floor, we jumped apart like guilty teenagers. Eddie chuckled and cleared his throat, and I moved to cover my eyes with my hands, but I was too late. As the doors slid open, I locked gazes with the stunned woman standing in the hallway: Barb.

Chapter Nine

Barb stood in the maroon-carpeted corridor, credit card in one hand, umbrella drink in the other. In an instant she spotted Eddie beside me in the elevator. Her eyes went as wide as saucers, and her jaw slowly fell open. "Holy heartthrob," she said.

Oh, good. At least for the moment she had forgotten her anger.

I held my thumb against the DOOR OPEN button. "Barb, this is Eddie Gale. Eddie, my good friend Barb."

"Pleasure to meet you."

"Holy cow."

Eddie strode from the elevator and relieved Barb of the drink she was ready to drop. "Here, let me take that for you."

I stepped out of the elevator as Eddie sniffed at the drink and recoiled. "Whoa. What are you drinking here, girl?"

"Holy . . ."

At last, she blinked. And stumbled to her left. I didn't have to get any closer nor smell her breath to know she was plastered.

"Zombie," I said. "She'll pound four of them and then pass out standing up."

Eddie took hold of her elbow. "How many of these you have, darlin'?"

Tears took up residence in the corners of her eyes. "You're Eddie Gale."

"That's right," he said over a laugh. "And you're lit."

"Come on," I said, taking hold of her other arm. "Let's get you inside."

She tore her gaze away from Eddie to eye me up and down. "Aren't I mad at you?" she asked.

"You're furious with me."

"Oh." She nodded. "That's what I thought. I'll go with Eddie, then."

"It's okay," Eddie said, talking around Barb. "I've got her. Where are we going?"

I pointed to my right and started up the hall. Leading the way, I fished my room card from my pocket.

"I've seen all of your movies," Barb said.

"Thank you," Eddie said. "I appreciate your support."

"I didn't like most of them."

"Funny, I didn't either," Eddie said, laughter in his voice.

"I like you better with your shirt off," she said.

"Hey, Barb, vow of silence, huh?" I suggested, peering over my shoulder.

She narrowed her eyes at me. "Aren't I mad at you?"

"No," I said. "You're mad at my mother."

"Oh."

I unlocked the door to 1004 and shouldered my way into the room. Flicking on the light switch, I was relieved to see the room in no great disrepair.

"Here we are," Eddie said, guiding Barb into the room. "Right where you belong."

Barb catapulted away from him and threw herself onto the nearest bed. "I am kind of tired."

I looked at her prone form, strung across the blue and beige comforter, and then looked at Eddie. His half smile held a hint of resignation. "Sorry," I said.

He nodded. "Is she really mad at you?"

I took a deep breath. "Yeah," I said. "Spitting mad."

"What'd you do?"

I shook my head, unwilling to dredge up all the dinnertime drama, unwilling to examine her accusations to see if they had merit. "You'd better go," I said. "I've got to—"

Barb sat bolt upright. "Oh, my God, I'm gonna puke," she announced, and she took off for the bathroom.

"I've . . ."

Eddie nodded, then took hold of my hand. "Tomorrow. You, me, dinner. Deal?"

"Deal," I said.

He kissed me firmly, then headed for the door. It had barely closed behind him when Barb began her prayers to the porcelain god.

I sighed and headed for the bathroom to prep a glass of water and a cool cloth. Not exactly feet up with the remote, or relaxing with Eddie Gale, but a poetic end to the day all the same.

The storms of the previous day had blown out to sea, leaving behind a sky so brilliantly blue, it appeared a work of Hollywood magic.

At six forty-five I relieved Joe on the set. Coffee in hand, I listened as he briefed me on the events of the night before. From what he said, I'd been at the remembrance for all the important bits. The only thing to transpire in my absence was Holly B's indignant departure. Speculation had her angry at Shepard. Or Catherine. Or both. But that, the gossips maintained, was nothing out of the ordinary and had been going on since the day rehearsals began.

I returned mentally to the question of why Catherine and Shepard would appear in the same film while embroiled in personal differences. A contractual agreement? Could Catherine think proximity would allow her to weasel her way back into Shepard's good graces?

Sipping my coffee, I watched the ant farm of activity on the set slow into stillness. I had to hand it to them, back to work the very next day after such an upset. Talk about professionals. Then again, these particular professionals were running behind schedule and facing the inevitable shortage of funds, so maybe I was witnessing desperation.

The director commanded the cameras to roll, then shouted,

"Background!" Extras walked in preset patterns along the boardwalk, some alone, some in pairs, replicating the regular comings and goings one would ordinarily find there.

"And action," the director said.

Shepard and Eddie walked side by side into the shot.

"You've been running that pawnshop since your old man died," Eddie said, his speech rapid and not at all like his usual easy drawl.

Shepard shuffled along, his shoulders slack and his off-diet belly leading the way. "So? That's supposed to mean I know right away who it is keeps trashing my store?"

"The odds of these being random hits are astronomical. I'm willing to bet you know who it is, even if you don't want to admit it, even if your ego might get bruised."

"What are you saying? You saying Eva had something to do with this?"

Eddie reached into his pocket and pulled out a soft pack of cigarettes. "You gotta stop thinking the women you meet are incapable of anything more underhanded than lying about their age." He tapped the bottom of the soft pack, and two cigarettes shot into the air and dove for the ground. "Whoops," he said.

Shepard barked out a laugh. "Ten bucks you can't do that again."

"Cut," the director called. "Let's go again, from the top."

The anthill sprang to life. Extras crossed back to their original starting points, Shepard and Eddie took up their positions at the edge of the shot, and one of the assistants scrambled along the boardwalk on her knees, picking up the cigarettes Eddie had dropped.

They went again. And again. Nine times before Eddie got the cigarette out of the pack, into his mouth, and lit. For shots three through seven the director suggested new dialog. By eight they returned to the original lines.

I leaned toward the electrician standing next to me. "Who's playing Eva?" I asked, eyes on the director as he conferred with Shepard and Eddie.

"Holly Bellinger."

"I see. And Catherine Dawes? Where does she fit in?"

"She's the cop's wife. Eddie's wife."

That meant Eddie would probably have to kiss her at some point. For the first time ever I felt nothing but envy for Catherine.

The cell phone in my pocket vibrated to life, making me jump with surprise.

I didn't recognize the phone number that came up on the readout. I gave a proper name-plus-corporation greeting.

"Miss Keys, this is Detective Holden."

I could picture him easily, hunched over a desk strewn with paperwork, cold cup of coffee in a none-too-clean mug at his elbow, suit jacket off, and tie askew.

"We have a report from the Arson and Bomb Squad."

So much for pretending yesterday was no more than a bad dream. "That was fast," I said.

"Now, there might yet be secondary causes. The guys are still looking. But they're fairly certain of the cause of the main blast."

He went on to explain that the device that had caused the blast was no bomb, hardly a device at all. Rather, Matthew's death had resulted from a simple electrical wire plugged into a wall socket and passed through the propane tank affixed to the trailer. When Matthew had turned the lights on, the electrical charge ignited the propane, and the rest was pyrotechnic history.

"We're checking the database," Detective Holden said. "So far we've got five guys who have used methods similar to this. None of them is in the state. One of them is doing time. But we're still looking."

I looked briefly at Shepard and Eddie, returning to their marks for the top of the scene, and shivered a bit. "You say 'guys.' You mean 'men'?"

Holden's impatience carried across the phone lines. "Guys, men, whatever."

"What if it's a woman?" I said softly. The director called for background action.

Another sigh from the detective. "The database is only giving us men. If you know something that makes you think it's a woman, I'd like to hear it. Now."

Though he couldn't see me, I shook my head. "Nothing concrete," I said. "I was just thinking of the list of enemies Mr. Brown wrote up and his history with jealous women."

"Miss Keys, I appreciate your thoughts, but women prefer other methods. Very few choose arson."

Maybe, but women aren't averse to hiring people to do their bidding. On the whole, women are pretty okay with paying someone else to do a job they themselves don't have the knowledge for. We have no testosterone to get in the way of admitting we need help.

"Other methods," I said. "You mean like poison or vehicular sabotage?"

Holden sighed. "You're still convinced there was something sinister about that pizza. Something more than a confused old man and a fouled-up order. Look, Miss Keys, I'm going to keep you and your boss up to date on how this investigation is progressing, but leave the theories and investigating to the professionals, okay? You just make sure Mr. Brown continues to live and breathe."

I thanked him for the information and said a polite goodbye, even though I wanted to throw the phone to the ground with enough force to make Detective Holden wince at the sudden pain in his ear. Leave it to the professionals, my foot. What did he take me for? A cocktail waitress?

Just because I hadn't had formal police-department training in investigative techniques didn't negate the fact that I have a brain. And I may not have had my own forensics team sifting through the crime scene, but I had the results of his. The trailer had been rigged. Anyone inside the trailer when the lights were switched on was doomed. Right away I knew two things. First, the person who'd rigged the propane tank was not necessarily an explosives expert. Second, the deviant in question would have had to be inside the trailer to set up the explosion, which meant he had to have a key.

All right, maybe he had picked the lock. That left us with either someone who could pick a lock or someone who had access to the keys.

Prior to my arrival, Shepard didn't have a key to his trailer. But someone kept keys. Someone locked up at night. So who did Shepard get the keys from?

I started toward where he stood but stopped when I spotted Dutch heading in my direction. He had a folding canvas chair in one hand and a foam cup in the other.

He half smiled and handed me the cup. "Coffee. I wasn't sure how you took it, so I just made it regular."

"It's fine. Thanks."

"Have a seat," Dutch said, smoothing out the canvas.

As I scooted back in the seat, Dutch leaned in close. "You remember yesterday you asked me to tell you if I saw anything unusual?" he said.

His whiskers tickled my ear, and I tried not to shrink back and giggle. "What about it?"

"Karl Moyne's been spending a lot of time in Catherine's trailer. I don't know if that's the kind of information you're looking for . . ."

My memory scrolled back through my brief encounters with Moyne and with Catherine. "Is Moyne not the type to visit the trailers?"

Dutch shook his head and solemnly stroked his beard. I sifted swiftly through the information in my head, wondering if time spent together meant Catherine and Moyne were uniting forces against Shepard or merely talking business.

"Tell me something," I said instead. "Who has keys to the trailers?"

"You mean the stars' trailers?"

"Yeah, those."

"The stars, I guess."

I shook my head. "Shepard didn't have one until he asked for it. Someone keeps them."

Again his fingers went to his beard. He stroked it as he pondered, eyes on the director, who was doing a lot of pointing again. "You're thinking someone let themselves into Shepard's trailer and wired it up."

A curious choice of words. "It's a place to start," I said.

He nodded. "I'll see what I can find out." With a little wave, he ambled off, and I settled back into the chair.

Why would Dutch refer to the trailer as being "wired up"?

I shook my head against the absurdity of the thought and took a large swallow of coffee and reality. Dutch had nothing to do with the threats against Shepard. Thinking he did smacked of paranoia.

By lunch I had my Windbreaker tied by the arms around my waist, the day having warmed to its midsummer standard. I felt a layer of perspiration between my skin and my shirt, and beads of sweat collected behind my knees. All I wanted was a shower and a drink with an umbrella in it. What I got was lunch with Catherine Dawes.

With Shepard's trailer a pile of cordoned-off rubble, and its neighboring trailers damaged and useless, we had little choice but to accept any hospitality offered. That is, we plunked down at a resin patio table outside Catherine Dawes' trailer, chowing down on an assortment of salads and deli sandwiches her downtrodden assistant had been sent to fetch.

In Catherine's eyes, I was truly only the hired help. It was a lucky thing I'd been allowed to sit in the six-dollar chair. I certainly wasn't expected to speak, which suited me just fine.

I shoved a fork into a chicken-walnut salad I'd gotten stuck with because Catherine's assistant botched the order, and tried not to growl at Catherine. She had one hand on a Diet Coke and the other on Shepard's thigh.

"It's still all so terribly upsetting, don't you think?" she asked.

Shepard took a super-size bite of the eggplant parmesan hero that should have been mine. "I'm trying to stay focused," he said.

Catherine recoiled. "I've asked you a dozen times not to speak with your mouth full."

"I'm hungry."

"That's no reason to appear barbaric."

He lowered the sandwich to its paper-wrapper-cum-plate. "Back off, will you?" he snapped. "This is just as tough on me, so give it a rest. Let me eat in peace."

She straightened as if he'd struck her, nostrils flaring at his impertinence. When she caught sight of me staring, she channeled the full force of her anger into a withering grin that failed to wither me. I knew her type. Any woman who survived high school knew her type. It may take some time, but eventually they fail to intimidate you.

"If you'll excuse me for a moment," she said, pushing her chair away from the table. She stood, ramrod straight. "I have a few business matters to attend to."

Diet cola clutched bludgeon-like in her hand, she walked into the trailer. Anyone else, I would have been inclined to describe the movement as flouncing. But Catherine lacked the minimum body fat required to flounce. Probably the most she could do was storm and stalk.

Shepard opened a second can of soda and downed half of it in one gulp. Then he burped like a teamster.

"Tell me something," I said, setting my fork down and fishing out a walnut half with my fingers. "What impact does this stunning meal have on your legal action?"

"What are you talking about?"

"Wilkinson, Hershowitz and who's his name. You've started harassment proceedings against this woman, and now you're letting her hang all over you?"

Eyes wide, he glanced over his shoulder. "Shh. Quiet. She'll hear you."

"She knows about the proceeding," I said. "She's seen the paperwork, remember?"

"She's just upset right now. I know that it's hard to see, but she really did adore Matthew. She actually tried to get him to come work for her." He smiled a bit and hefted the hero. "All this has her pretty upset."

I decided to go for the silent thing, staring at him, waiting for more.

"She needs a friend right now, all right?"

I reached blindly for my bottle of water and unscrewed the cap.

"She needs someone to lean on," he said, exasperation in his voice. "And you might have heard that we have a history. Supporting her right now is the least I can do."

He took a he-man-size bite of the hero, and I chugged a good deal of water while trying to digest his attitude toward Catherine. But really, friends made an effort for each other, right? Should his behavior really surprise me? And even if it did, he was being kinda sweet, right? I mean, there was a reason the guy had friends in the first place, right?

"Got another question for you." I set down the half-empty bottle of water. "Who knows about Kelly?"

"What?" he asked through a mouthful of eggplant.

"Kelly. Who knows? Does Catherine know? Does everybody know? Who knows?"

His brow furrowed. "You want a list?"

"Is the name common knowledge?"

"It would be a stupid alias if everyone knew, wouldn't it?"

The list was remarkably short. Cell phones must have had a noticeable impact on the volume of calls being routed through hotel switchboards. Shepard's agent, manager, publicist, and business associates of that sort all contacted Shepard by cell, as did anyone associated with the production of the film—the director, the producer, the assistants. No one even needed to know the alias.

"Matthew said *she* knew, and you must have told her," I said. "Who could 'she' be?"

Shepard shook his head and swiped his chin with a napkin. "I don't know. Why does it matter?"

"Because the pizza you had Matthew order the other night was ordered by Kelly, and according to the guy in the shop, a woman placed the order."

"The voice was that memorable?"

"Maybe," I said. "But I think the shop doesn't do that much business."

"So you're thinking . . ." Shepard began.

I waited, but he didn't finish. Clearly, he wasn't tracking and needed me to fill in the blanks.

"The woman who placed the order knew enough to use the name Kelly without Matthew telling her."

"But I asked Matthew to get the pizza. So Matthew . . ." He furrowed his brow, trying to put the events together. "Matthew told someone else to place the order?"

I flopped back in my chair. "I don't think so. I think someone offered. Matthew would know enough to order food that wouldn't kill you."

"So he was with someone when I called. He was with a girl, and I probably ruined his night," Shepard said, pivoting to face me. "Man, do I feel like a jerk."

"Yes," I said, nodding. "Matthew was with someone. He went and got the pizza himself, so he didn't delegate the whole thing."

I could play the scene in my imagination. Matthew cozied up in his room with some faceless woman when Shepard calls, making his demands. Not surprisingly, Matthew is beyond annoyed. The woman soothes him, tells him not to worry, she'll call, she'll get the pizza. She orders the pie with its strange I'm-pregnant-and-I-have-a-craving ingredient. But Matthew's a gentleman, and he insists on picking up the pizza himself.

Okay, so my imagination relied heavily on guesswork. The scenario seemed plausible. And without Matthew around to give us the details, guesswork was all I had to go on. Until I could find the girl.

"What if . . . ?" I started. Shepard ignored me as my thoughts took shape.

My mind was on the trailer, on the explosion, on Matthew being the first one in. Matthew was always the first one in, wasn't he? It was part of his job to be in there, set things up, make sure Shepard didn't have to worry about basic life issues. So what if the trailer explosion wasn't meant for Shepard in the first place? What if Matthew was the target all along?

Catherine emerged from her trailer, making it impossible to question Shepard about my theories.

And still I wondered. How far would Catherine go in her quest to get Shepard back? I bad-mouthed the guy a lot, but I knew he was soft at heart. His support of Catherine during a rough time was the least he would do. She would know that. She would know he wouldn't freeze her out, regardless of what his lawyers advised. He was sweet and pigheaded that way. But would she force that situation once pleas and fancy gifts had failed?

Once I returned Shepard to the care of the stressed-out director, I put in a call to Barb, checking up on her well-being, what with that shiny new hangover and all.

"Oh, my God," she said. "I had the weirdest dream, and it's all your fault."

"Mine?" Someone had removed the chair Dutch had brought me. Just my luck.

"That story you made up the other night about Eddie Gale and the horse racing," she said. "It must have stuck in my mind, 'cause last night I dreamed he was here, in our room."

"You still think I made that up?" I scouted around for a chair and thought I saw the one I had been sitting in under the butt of Kim Lloyd, the assistant director.

"Lorraine, you're my friend, and I love you, but let's be honest here."

"Why is it so hard for you to believe? You who came down here for the sole purpose of throwing yourself—"

"I have no intention of throwing myself."

"Right," I said, eyes on where Kim sat in my chair, having a very intense cell phone conversation and fingering her engagement ring. The wind carried sentence fragments to me—here an "amazing opportunity," there a "can't let."

"You know, I've been thinking about this," Barb said. "What if I did manage to hook up with Shepard for a night or a weekend or, God willing, two weeks on a private island? Once that's over, how would I ever go back to thinking Rudy the bagel guy is sexy?"

That got my attention. I'd met Rudy the bagel guy. He was sexy. His bank account . . . most likely not that attractive.

But Barb's theory deserved at least a moment's pause. If the theory of being spoiled for other men was true as it pertained to Shepard, it would have to be true pertaining to Eddie, right? What if by some miracle I hooked up with Eddie? How could I go back to dating the typical guy next door?

The moment's pause needed to be over. I shook my head to call myself back to the present and took a bracing look around. Catherine sucking hard on an impossibly skinny cigarette. The director Riley Jacks waiting to talk to Kim, his arms folded as "not a good time" took to the wind. Holly savagely chomping at a celery stick and shooting daggers at Catherine. Shepard and Eddie oblivious. Business as usual.

"Okay, so I called . . ." I said firmly, to bring Barb back into the moment with me. "I need you to do something for me."

"I'm not going home. We covered this."

I sighed. "No, I was hoping I could put you to work."

"Helping you? Really? Can I buy handcuffs?"

Whatever. "Yeah, okay, if you think you're going to need them."

"Well, you want me to guard something, right?"

"Not quite. I need information and was hoping you could dig it up for me."

This time Barb sighed. I pictured her clearly, strewn across the comforter, her hair wrapped in a towel turban while she watched twenty-four-hour news and waited for her nails to dry. "What do you need?" she asked.

I retreated from the milling crowds and, speaking as softly as I could, gave her a list of names I wanted her to check out. Maybe Barb thought I was crazy. Probably she thought I would have known half the stuff if I'd listened to her tabloid updates for the past six months. But she made no complaint. Thankfully.

"Will you remember all that?" I asked Barb when I finished my list.

"Not a problem. I'll see what I can find out by dinnertime."

"Great, see you then."

I know. I should have warned her my schedule called for

dinner with Eddie, but what was the point? She wouldn't have believed me anyway.

Eddie finished for the day by four o'clock. Shepard had to stay as some twisted punishment for failing to show up to work the day he'd spent hiding out at the shooting range. Okay, no one said "punished." But that's how he looked, and that's how I felt.

Before he left, Eddie stopped by to advise me he'd be calling about dinner after he took care of a few things, and I should keep my cell phone handy. Despite the brain-melting effects of an afternoon in unbroken sunshine, I managed to assure him I would do that without adding any shade of sarcasm to my voice. I think.

Joe arrived to relieve me while a handful of cast and crew huddled under the tent watching the playback monitors. I waved good-bye to Shepard, and he met my gaze over the head of the director, giving me a thumbs-up. What he meant by the gesture I didn't know, but I'm fond of thinking he was happy about making it through the day without bloodshed.

Feeling pretty good about things myself, I swung by the sweet shop and picked up a few one-pound boxes of Atlantic City's famous saltwater taffy along with a handy snack-size package that would tide me over till dinner.

I checked my phone as I left the shop. Past seven thirty, but no word from Eddie and no messages. Huh. But on the bright side, no further calls from the police or my boss.

Cheering myself with that thought, I popped another bit of taffy. My mouth watered at the welcome sweetness, and I held the candy on my tongue and let the flavor seep into my blood. With a smile on my face I entered Bally's and made my way to my room.

Barb sat at the little convenience desk in our room, cell phone pinned to her ear. She waved a hello, and I dropped the snack package of taffy in range of her reach and headed for the bathroom to shower.

She was still there when I came out. I checked my cell phone. No messages. No blinking light on the room phone either.

Had I hallucinated the whole Eddie Gale thing? It had happened, right? No matter what Barb thought. Then again, maybe what Barb thought was right. Maybe Eddie really wouldn't be interested in plain ol' me, and I should stick to Rudy the bagel guy.

"Okay," Barb said as she switched off her phone. "Get dressed, and we'll go eat, and I'll tell you everything."

"Everything? You really found out stuff?" The pinching around her eyes activated my instant guilt. "That's great!" I said quickly. "I can't believe you did that so fast."

The hurt pinch continued to deepen until it morphed into annoyed. "I'm so glad I impressed you. Put some clothes on. I want dinner."

Good thing I'd never told her about dinner with Eddie. Not only would she have called me a liar, but he wasn't exactly banging down the door to prove my claim, was he? So I did the only thing I could do. I threw on some clean clothes and some understated makeup and walked out onto the boardwalk with Barb.

"I'm absolutely craving Mexican," she said. "Okay by you?"

A tingle started in the back of my head. Mexican. Something to do with Mexico. Something I needed to remember but that dangled just out of my reach.

"Rainny? Mexican?"

And the tingle faded to nothing. Nuts. "Yeah," I said. "Mexican sounds great."

We wandered into a kitschy little Mexican place where boldly colored serapes covered the walls and the air smelled strongly of corn chips and ground cumin.

Many hours had passed since I'd inhaled the power bar Dutch had brought me around three, and the taffy had betrayed me and only made my hungrier. It was all I could do not to dig into the complimentary tortilla chips like a Rottweiler on a diet. On the off-chance this was going to be my first dinner of the evening, I didn't want to gorge myself.

"Should we get some sangria, do you think?" Barb asked.

Here are words you should never utter on an empty stomach: "Sure. Let's get a pitcher."

She wouldn't tell me anything she'd learned until the waiter had brought the sangria and we'd done a proper toast, which, for us, meant simply "Cheers."

"So, what have you got?" I asked, the alcohol going down as easy as water.

A mischievous glint brightened her eyes. "Well, you were right about Catherine Dawes," she said. "She's not all that stable."

"Everyone knows that—doesn't give me any great powers of deduction."

"True. But what everyone doesn't know—or she wishes everyone doesn't know—is that she's spent a fortune trying to keep the press from getting too close to her high school years."

"Did she used to be a man?" I asked.

Barb gave a delicate giggle. "All woman. As far as I can tell. What she keeps having to bury is a scandal that accuses her of poisoning the class salutatorian."

I sipped a little more sangria and tried to wrap my mind around the consequence of a salutatorian. "Not the valedictorian or the prom queen? What's the point?"

Hands held palms out, Barb shook her head. "I have no idea. Probably you'd have to ask her."

"Pass. What did she use for poison?"

Barb had her mouth open before she realized she didn't have the answer. She snapped her jaw shut and shrugged. "I could see if I could find out."

"I don't get it," I said. "You live for this stuff. How did you not know about this?"

The look she gave me spoke volumes about what she thought of my mental aptitude. "Ask me any question about any hot guy in Hollywood, and I'll have the answer for you. Ask me about women, you take your chances on what I know."

"Okay, fine." Boy, that sangria tasted like a dream. "What else you got?"

"Not much on Holly Bellinger. A lot of charity work, a little plastic surgery."

"You mean 'enhancement procedures.' "

"Whatever. She was hot and heavy with the special-effects guy who started with that Kiss tribute band, you know, the one who does the commercial for that retro T-top car?"

I knew exactly which commercial she meant. I couldn't tell you the name of the car or its manufacturer, nor could I recall the name of the band, but I knew the spot. Brand-new candy-apple-red vehicle bursting through a wall of flames, coming toward the camera along a tarmac straightaway and igniting explosions on either side as it progressed. Swell. Holly had her hooks in one of those guys. This was just getting better and better.

I downed half a glass of sangria in one go. "What about Karl Moyne?"

"Just like you said," Barb said. "In debt up to his laser-corrected eyeballs, but then, half the population's in debt these days. Maybe he insured Shepard, and maybe he didn't."

"He told me he did."

She grinned and raised her glass. "I can neither confirm nor deny that rumor. I posted the question to a couple of my Internet forums, see if anyone knows for sure. But so far, no one's talking. Could be hush-hush, could be small change. Who knows?"

Warm and fuzzy from the sangria, I stretched out a couple of kinks in my neck and eyeballed the tortilla chips. I figured I could have a couple. They wouldn't affect my appetite too much.

I cussed quietly and crunched a chip. "There's got to be something I'm missing," I muttered.

"Ask me about Eddie Gale," she said.

I met her gaze so quickly, I gave my eyeballs whiplash. "Why do you mention Eddie?"

With perfectly manicured fingernails functioning as pincers, Barb lifted a chip from the bowl. "You failed to put him on your list of suspects," she said with mock innocence. "I figured it was an oversight."

"Suspects?"

She relaxed into an eyeball roll. "Duh. I'm not stupid, Rainny. You're trying to figure out who's after Shepard. I can put two and two together, you know."

"All right, fine. I'm trying to figure it out." Sangria was like truth serum. "But Eddie's got nothing to do with it."

Even as the words left my rapidly numbing lips, a sliver of uneasiness snaked up my spine. Barb wouldn't mention him if she didn't think he fit the bill somehow. Even before I heard what she had to say, I was telling myself she was way off base. But I squirmed against that sliver all the same.

"Did you know," Barb said, "that Eddie Gale was up for the last three films Shepard starred in? And each time the job went to Shepard?"

I waved a hand, dismissing her speculation. "They're friends. They're with the same agency or something. Of course they see all the same scripts."

"Yeah, but three films? That's a lot."

"So? It's not like they're both competing for the same job now."

Barb nodded. "Yes, they are. They're both being considered for some espionage action-adventure thing. It's supposed to be the next big franchise, you know, like Bond and Bourne and—"

"Batman?" I said.

"Funny. Maybe you should eat more and drink less."

"No, I'm fine," I said. In fact, to prove it, I refilled my glass without spilling a drop.

"I think you really have to put Eddie on your list," she said.

"Based on that? I don't think so. Compared to rehab and a poison past, Eddie just doesn't stack up. Got anything else?"

She pushed a stray hair away from her face, then cast her eyes to the ceiling as though seeking answers there. "He rides a motorcycle. Has a big place in Wyoming. He's left-handed."

"Oh, well that's it, then. He's left-handed. He must be guilty."

"Would you cut it out?"

I held up a hand in mute apology and nodded to show I'd keep my mouth shut. It wasn't tough; my brain was hiccupping on an image it didn't want to let go of. "Eddie rides a motorcycle?" I could just picture him, legs stretched out alongside the engine of an Indian Chief, sun shining on his hair, dark sunglasses, torn T-shirt . . .

"Apparently that's his preferred method of transportation aside from classic cars. Here. Eat more of these." She pushed the bowl of chips closer to me and moved the pitcher of sangria clear of my reach.

Letting her have her way for the moment, I munched and took a minute to review. If I assembled the pieces that Barb laid out, I had Catherine Dawes with a background in poison, Holly Bellinger with access to a demolitions expert, and Eddie Gale, who knew a thing or a thousand about cars. Not to mention Karl Moyne and his incredible invisible bank account. What if they all had a hand in it? What if everyone together was after Shepard? How does one newbie bodyguard protect her subject against that? What does it take for a single woman to successfully stand between an old friend and his imminent murder?

Chapter Ten

The phone was ringing.

I lay in bed, unable to open my eyes as I slowly came to consciousness. One by one, different body parts checked in with my brain, doing their little anatomical updates. Either because my arm was ready or because my ears didn't want any more of that noise, I reached for the phone.

The recorded voice on the other end identified itself as my wake-up call. Couldn't be. Couldn't be five thirty already, could it?

Forcing my eyes to open, I pushed up onto my elbow and felt in immediate danger of my head falling off. I flopped back onto the pillow and continued taking stock.

All my body parts and critical systems seemed to be functioning, but I was definitely a quart low on brain fluid. I hadn't felt that bad since the morning after Barb's Aloha Alaska party. I had sworn back then to never drink that much again. So why was I hungover again?

Ah, yes. Someone wanted to kill Shepard, and I had been stood up by Eddie Gale. That explained the pain.

I levered myself out of bed and went through my morning routine with one hand braced against my head to keep it from moving too much and thus causing me more pain. From the dusty corners of Barb's purse I extracted a single-serving size of aspirin while she slumbered away, blissfully unaware.

I dressed, put my ID in my pocket, pulled my Windbreaker on, and felt a little heartsick for my gun. I wished it were with me on the adventure instead of stuck in the floor safe at my house. Then again, maybe it was best there where it couldn't do Eddie Gale any harm. The swine.

He probably had a good explanation, I reasoned as I made my way out of the room. As I continued out of the hotel and down the street to a drugstore, I tried to arrive at that reason. Short of "I was attacked by a roving pack of alligators, and they bit my hands off so I couldn't dial a phone," I decided he had no excuse. Unless he was dead. I might accept that as an excuse.

Under normal circumstances, dead wasn't a genuine concern. But I was operating in Shepard's world, where nothing was normal and there was a potential killer on the loose, so the possibility of Eddie standing me up because of death lost all humor in a hurry.

I paid for two bottles of water charged with electrolytes and downed half of one before I returned to the sidewalk. What if Eddie was dead? On the plus side, that would mean Barb was wrong about Eddie being a suspect. On the minus side, it would mean I'd never get to have dinner with him.

Okay, so that last bit leaned to the selfish side of things. Sue me.

My phone bleeped twice, and Joe's voice burst forth. "Lorraine, you there?" I fished the phone out of my pocket, cursing its walkie-talkie, point-to-point, everyone-can-hear-this-conversation functionality.

"What?" I snapped.

"Ocean Pier. Fast."

"Joe? Hey, Joe?" No response. Which way to Ocean Pier?

As soon as I broke free of the cover of the hotels and hit the boardwalk, I had a solid idea of the location of Ocean Pier. Unless I missed my guess, it was right there where all the police cars had gathered at a construction site, lights flashing in the hazy, early-morning glow.

Shepard.

I tossed the empty water bottle into the nearest receptacle and sprinted toward the scene. Each heavy footfall jarred my brain, threatening to split my head open. I should have stayed with Shepard. Shepard was my friend, my responsibility. I never should have trusted Joe. I never should have let Dave talk me into letting Joe help out.

As I got closer, I could hear the crackling of police radios. A pair of uniformed officers moved to intercept me. I dragged the lanyard full of pass-cards from my pocket and slung it around my neck. The officers failed to back off. Over their shoulders I spied a gaggle of familiar faces, crewmen and makeup artists mingling with construction workers. The feeling that cast and crew were my people surprised me, as did the sensation I had been cut off from them.

"Sorry, miss, you'll have to step back," a tall cop said.

"Where's Shepard Brown?" I demanded.

"You have to step back."

I took one neat step backward and grabbed my cell. I dialed Joe's point-to-point and keyed up. "They won't let me pass," I said.

"Give me a minute."

The cops stared at me, expressions carefully blank, as only police officers can manage.

I paced, caught my breath, and eyeballed the massive construction site that comprised Ocean Pier. Some new company owned the area now and was in the process of renovating a former shopping mall to make it a shopping/dining/nightlife venue that would draw more visitors to the area and keep them there. Walls made of plywood blocked access to the site itself. But to the north, where the police cruisers had driven right onto the boardwalk, trailers and Porta-Pottys and assorted construction equipment were kept safe behind a gated cyclone fence.

Joe didn't come fetch me. Detective Holden did.

"Where is he?" I called as he neared.

He waved back the two uniformed officers, and I double-timed toward him. "Where's Brown?"

"Relax. Mr. Brown is fine. I'm told he's still in his hotel, sleeping."

I wanted to see him with my own eyes, wanted to hear his voice. But for the moment, I had to trust Holden. If Shepard was safe in his room, why had Joe directed me to the pier?

"What's going on, then?"

"Come with me," Holden said.

He gestured for me to walk with him and led me past the cluster of murmuring onlookers and under a waist-high strip of yellow crime-scene tape. Holden gripped my elbow and propelled me forward until the reason for the cops and the tape and the chattering crowd became clear.

"You know this guy?" Holden asked. "Peter Johannson?"

Sprawled on the packed-dirt ground beside an excavator was Dutch, motionless and unseeing. The handle of a knife protruded from a circle of dried blood on his shirt, the bulk of the blade buried in his chest.

My head expanded, and my stomach contracted. The bottle of water I held slipped from my grasp and rolled toward a puddle of mud. I tried to turn away from the sight of a vibrant man brought to nothingness, but the detective held me firm. The best I could do was close my eyes and keep my face averted. But the nausea and heartache were too much.

Tears burning my eyes, I sank to my knees and let out a sorry moan. Dutch was gone. Dutch was dead. I clapped a hand over my mouth but let the tears fall and dampen my fingers. Oh, my God. Dutch was dead. He was killed—murdered. Someone had rammed a knife into his chest and left him to die.

A full-on sob escaped, and Holden finally released my arm. After a moment, he knelt beside me, elbows on his knees. "So you do know this guy."

"This is Dutch," I said, keeping my eyes on the ground beneath my feet.

"We pulled ID off him that says his name is Peter Johannson," Detective Holden said.

I shook my head, short motions, not a full-out refusal. "Everyone called him Dutch. Everyone . . . How could . . . ?"

Holden tipped his head and sucked some air through his teeth while he pretended to consider how much he should tell me. "We thought at first it was a random mugging gone a little sour."

"A little?"

"In fact, that's what we're telling anyone who asks."

"You're going to tell me differently?"

A uniformed officer approached and set my bottle of water down within my reach. Holden waited until the officer had fully retreated before he answered me.

"Your friend here wasn't mugged. He still has his wallet. He was a union member, a volunteer fireman, and a Mason." He shook his head. "It's going to be a helluva funeral."

Again I looked away, looked to the stretch of pale sand and breaking waves, anything to stop the visions Holden inspired from forming in my mind.

"But this," he said, reaching into his pocket, "was not in his wallet. It was stuck to his chest."

He held forth a plastic baggie. I squinted at its contents, a smallish piece of paper stained with dried blood. A little blue glob occupied the lower left-hand corner, the Diamond Security Services company logo. And in the center of the card, I could just make out my name.

"The blood held it in place," Holden said.

A chill rushed through my veins, washing away the sorrow and leaving behind stern resolve. Whether dropping the card on Dutch's body was an attempt at making me look guilty or a warning that I might be next made little difference. Only one thing mattered: Shepard was in danger, and come heck or high water, I was going to keep him safe.

I pounded on Shepard's door, impatient for Joe to let me in. Sleeping Beauty was still abed, but his bulldog bodyguard, Prince Charming, was wide awake and his cordial self.

"So?" Joe said. "You been?"

I held a hand up to silence him—not that he was running off at the mouth, mind you—and headed straight for the bathroom. I set my water bottle on the wide marble countertop and scrubbed my hands and face as though enough soap and water would wipe away the shock and sadness of the morning.

"What's going on?"

Shepard stood in the doorway, hair on end, bleary-eyed, and shirtless. If I looked closely, I could just make out the form of the well-made man lurking beneath the added pounds.

I dragged a hand towel across my face. "I needed to wash up."

He nodded as though that almost made sense. "I have to use the toilet."

My stomach took a threatening turn. "I'll just get out of your way."

I got out of the bathroom in a hurry before the man's bladder failed. Joe lounged in the living area, feet up, watching television, volume down around two.

"Any news?" I asked.

"Gold's up."

Right. Good. Well.

Sitting at the desk, I grabbed the phone and punched the number for room service. Before I could take a breath, a serene female voice at the other end said, "Good morning, Mr. Kelly. What can we get for you today?"

I caught myself before I corrected her; the suite belonged to Mr. Kelly, World War II hero and Hollywood target. "Coffee," I managed to say. "And some rolls or bagels or whatever you have down there—an assortment, I guess."

"Very good. Will there be anything else? Shall I send up some juice?"

"No. No juice. Just the coffee."

"Very good. And would Mr. Kelly like the call hold removed from his phone at this time?"

"Not at this time, thank you," I said, mimicking her happy-pill tone.

I dropped the phone back into its cradle and stared at the red blinking message light. It looked frantic and more than a little ticked off. If I hadn't wasted my money on the slot machines,

I would bet half a dozen profane messages from Karl Moyne waited there. And probably Catherine had a few things to say. And—

Like a scene in a bad horror film, I turned to face Joe. "This phone's been off," I said.

Joe aimed the remote at the television. "All night."

"So how did you know that . . . ?" I choked on the words. I couldn't say "Dutch was dead." "About the pier? Was it on the news?"

He settled on a television station and slowly angled his head so that his eyes met mine. "Dave called my cell."

The fact that Joe chose to include all the pertinent words gave the statement a ton of impact. Dave knew about the pier. How did Dave know?

"Cops called him," Joe said.

All sense of proportion lost, I steamed. Why had the cops called Dave instead of me? Detective Holden had my cell phone number; it was printed right on the bloody card. But no, he had to call my boss first. And my boss—the man who had given me the cell phone in the first place—called Joe. Old-boy buddy network crap. I should have been out looking for a job where the staff was 98 percent female. Instead I was stuck in a luxury hotel suite babysitting a Hollywood hunk and waiting for room service.

Okay, so maybe that sort of evened the score.

I shrugged out of my Windbreaker and tossed it onto a chair.

Shepard yanked open the bathroom door. He'd combed his hair and wrapped himself in a bathrobe that looked fluffier than my pillow. Shuffling out of the bathroom, he looked me up and down. "What's that on your knee? Is that blood? Something happen? You're all tense."

The TV switched off with an audible pop. "Gotta bail," Joe said, coming to his feet.

"You didn't tell him?" I asked Joe.

"He was asleep. You were late. Your problem."

"I'm late because I'm a suspect."

He moved his hand in a motion somewhere between a good-bye wave and a brush-off. "Your problem," he repeated, and he slammed the door on his way out.

"Rainny? You're a suspect?" Shepard's voice was approaching girly pitch.

"Not—yes—no." I sighed. "Someone . . . someone killed Dutch. They left my business card at the scene. That wins me a place on the suspect list."

"But you didn't do it, right?" he asked, voice creeping into the higher octaves.

"I did not do it," I said. "I wouldn't wish a moment's ill on Dutch."

Shepard nodded, shoulders relaxing. "Good. That's what I thought. So, who's Dutch?"

"He was—" I began. But something caught in my throat, something scratchy and uncomfortable, and it made my eyes water. "He was on the crew. Electrician. There was no reason for him to be killed."

"There's no reason for any of us to be killed," he said, and he turned away.

I watched him go, staring, unseeing, at the hairy legs protruding from beneath the white terry robe. For me, for Shepard, even for Joe . . . there was no reason for anyone connected to this film to die. Someone out there saw it differently. I needed to find out who.

Fortified by half a pot of coffee and an extra large cinnamon-raisin bagel, I accompanied Shepard to the set for his ten A.M. call. Once again I waited outside the makeup trailer, watching the back and forth of the crew. Their pace hadn't slowed, but the atmosphere felt subdued. Less chatter, less shouting, less laughter, almost as if there had been a meeting where they all agreed to buckle down, get the most work done in the least amount of time, and get the heck out of Dodge.

Emerging from the trailer, Shepard squinted against the glare of the sun and took me by the arm. "They're saying this guy Dutch was mugged," he said quietly. "But no one believes it."

I didn't blame them; I wouldn't believe it either. "The cops say it was a mugging."

"But you said the police think you're a suspect," Shepard said, eyes on me. "Why would they accuse you of a mugging?"

"Okay, first off, I'm only technically a suspect. I spent half the night in the casino with Barb. There must be a dozen different surveillance tapes chronicling my drunken attempts to operate slot machines." We reached the ramp to the boardwalk, and Shepard brought our progress to a halt. "Second, if I was actually a suspect in poor Dutch's death, would I be walking around with you right now?"

Shepard smiled. "Nah, you'd be at the police station, wishing your boss would go away."

My boss. I hadn't heard from him. Not once had my phone chirped to life. Which could only mean the man was speeding toward Atlantic City to chew me out and drag me home personally.

As long as we stayed on the set, I was safe. Dave didn't have a magic necklace of pass-cards to get him onto the set. As long as I didn't set foot on the civilian side of the barricades, Dave couldn't touch me.

"Let's go," I said, stepping onto the base of the ramp.

Shepard pulled me back. "Gotta go talk to Eddie first."

Facing Dave suddenly sounded preferable. More than anything at that moment I wanted to be able to tell Shepard, "You go on ahead. I'll meet you at craft services." But my job was to stick with Shepard, which meant I had to go make nice with the guy who'd stood me up. The day just kept getting better.

We found Eddie outside his trailer, crouched, screwdriver in hand, beside a Harley. When he caught sight of us, he came to his feet, and his eyes melted with apology. "Lorraine, I am so—"

"Dude, where've you been all morning?" Shepard asked. "You were supposed to call me."

Eddie looked from me to Shepard and back as though trying

to decide which conversational thread to pursue. "I did call you," he said to either or both of us.

I folded my arms, huffed, and looked away—basically, that's my impersonation of Barb doing her haughty thing.

Eddie shifted to face Shepard. "The hotel's got a hold on your calls," he said. "What's the story? You have a hot date last night?"

I felt my own cheeks flush, but no way could they have been as red as Shepard's. Even through the pounds of makeup, his blush blazed.

"Let's not go into that right now," Shepard said.

"Oh, I think we should," I said. "Why did you have a hold on your calls last night?"

"It's personal," he said.

"Please don't tell me you were with Catherine," I said.

Eddie shuddered and pulled a sour-lemon face.

"It's none of your business. In fact, none of this is anyone's business. Can we just drop it please?"

"I don't think so," I said, reaching to pull my phone from my pocket. Shepard's discomfort proved a great distraction from my own. I had no intention of letting him off the hook. "Joe's probably still awake. I'll just give him a call, and he can tell me all about what you did last night."

Not that Joe would have two polite words for me. But sometimes bluffs worked.

I punched in three numbers before Shepard grabbed my hand and tried to pull the phone away. I twisted free of his grasp and stepped back. My wrist stung from where he had held it. To look at him, you'd assume his weight made him out of shape. But he was as strong as an ox—which I probably should have guessed from all the bone-breaking bear hugs.

"What did you do last night?" I asked again, finger poised above the number pad.

"I was with someone, okay? Can we leave it at that?"

Not really. I was on a roll. I turned on Eddie. "And what did you do last night?"

"I want to explain about that," Eddie said.

"Explain about what?" Shepard asked.

"Come on inside, though," Eddie said, grinning at me. "I picked you up something, kind of an apology."

Oh, Lord, let me not find out that this man had bought me flowers. Flowers made an unimaginative apology.

Shepard and I trooped up the trailer steps behind Eddie into a space that duplicated Shepard's trailer, with the exception of the color scheme—tan and cocoa here.

A chill danced down my spine as I thought of Shepard's trailer. I did a quick prowl around the space, looking for anything out of the ordinary, like a block of C-4 on the kitchen counter or in that toolbox on the table.

"What brings you by anyway?" Eddie asked, dropping the screwdriver into the toolbox and moving the box to the side. He hefted an overstuffed messenger bag onto the table.

"I wanted to talk to you about tomorrow night," Shepard said. "You still chartering a plane out of here?"

Eddie pulled a trio of film scripts from the bag and plopped them onto the table. "Yeah, me and Riley and Karl so far," he said, then looked to me. "It's in here, I swear."

He hefted out one more script, this one well-thumbed, with red-ink notations across the cover page. "You need a ride, man?"

"You still got room?" Shepard asked.

Feeling a bit ridiculous standing around waiting for Eddie to hand me an apology, I picked up the script and read the title. *The Whispering Gallery.* Why did that sound familiar?

"Here it is," Eddie said. He pulled a black plastic bag from the confines of the messenger bag and handed it to me. "It's a little unusual, but I thought you should have one."

I set down the script and reached into the bag. My hand closed around a long, square cardboard tube, and I pulled out a glossy box. The words 16-INCH EXPANDABLE BATON were printed across the box in wide black type.

"Comes with a pouch so you can keep it on your belt," Eddie said.

"What is it?" Shepard asked. "And why does she get presents?"

"It's a baton," I said, not sure whether to be touched or deeply freaked out. "It's like a portable lead pipe." The bag still held some weight, so I set it down carefully before pulling the baton from the box. The cushioned handle on the baton helped to maintain a better grip, and with a proper turn of the wrist, the compact device telescoped to sixteen inches. Wielded properly, it could bring an opponent to his knees. It was a very thoughtful and bizarre gift, coming from a guy who'd stood me up.

"She gets presents because I saw this and thought she'd like it," Eddie said. "I was supposed to give it to her last night, but I got hung up on a conference call with some guys over at Tanglewood Studios. By the time I was done there," he said, looking to me, "there was no answer at your room. I figured you were out for the night."

I shrugged. "It's no big deal," I said. I might have been lying.

"There's more in the bag," he said.

I collapsed the baton and laid it down while I reached into the bag once again.

"What? Did I miss something?" Shepard said. "You guys were going to get together last night?"

I came up with half a flashlight. "Hey, you had your own little secret rendezvous you won't tell us about," I said. "So no throwing stones."

"It attaches to the baton," Eddie said. And suddenly he turned into a kid, thrilled by gadgets. He reached for the baton and the flashlight while Shepard sank into a chair, pouting.

"I can't believe you didn't tell me about this," he said.

"Nothing to tell," I said.

"Yet," Eddie said, affixing the flashlight head to the end of the baton. "Check it out. See? Makes it all-in-one."

Indeed, it was a very cool tool. And very cool that Eddie Gale had gone and bought me a weapon. Also very weird, but I tried to overlook that part and focus on the thoughtful and practical. Plus, it beat the crap out of a dozen red roses. Literally.

Disgruntled, Shepard fingered the stack of scripts on the table, laid his hand on *The Whispering Gallery,* and froze. "What is this doing here?" he asked. "Where did you get this?"

Eddie looked up from the toy. As he spotted Shepard with his hand on the script, Eddie's brow folded in confusion. "I heard you passed."

"Where did you hear that?"

"From my agent, when he sent the script. He said you passed."

"I didn't pass," Shepard said. "I sent back some requirements. That's not passing."

I took the forgotten baton from Eddie with one hand and shook the nylon sheath free of the box with the other. Of course I wasn't wearing a belt, so I couldn't actually hang the baton from my person despite the loop integrated into the sheath. Maybe I could call Barb and ask her to pick me up a belt.

"Well, what were you asking them for?" Eddie said. "Maybe they thought you were being unreasonable."

"The usual stuff," Shepard said. "Back end, some casting approval . . . I have some doubts about the director."

I tested the baton, to see if a gentle flick of the wrist would get the thing to open.

"Look, man, I don't personally have any doubts about the director," Eddie said, hand to his chest. "But you have first refusal on this, so I'll just—"

"According to you, I've already refused," Shepard said, voice tight.

"I'm just telling you what I was told."

"Why would you think I'd passed?"

"Why would I think otherwise?"

"Oh, for the love of carbs," I said. "Would you two knock it off?" I retracted the baton and glowered at the boys. "Shepard, do you want the part or not?"

He pressed a thumb to his lip and began gnawing on the edge of the nail. "It's a good part," he said. "But van Weer hasn't directed anything more than a couple of car commercials and a handful of music videos."

"Sounds to me like you're leaning toward a 'no.' Eddie, what about you?"

Arms folded across his muscular chest, Eddie shrugged. "I have no problem with van Weer. And I would love to dig into that part."

I looked at Shepard, then nodded my head in Eddie's direction. "Let him have the part."

"You like him better than me, don't you?" Shepard said.

Oh, for heaven's sake. "The fact of the matter is, it sounds like word's already out that you passed. Now, I don't understand too much about how your business works, but my guess is, if you want the part, you're going to have to get on the phone pretty quickly with a yes."

Shepard huffed and stood. "I'll think about it," he said. "I'll know for sure by tomorrow night. How's that?"

Again, Eddie shrugged. The body language he was shooting for was unconcerned. But he came off too relaxed, too "hey, whatever, dude" to be convincing.

"What's so special about this part anyway?" I asked, pulling the script closer. I riffled through the first few pages, hoping they would jog my memory.

"It's an adventure," Shepard said.

"You know, bad guys, ancient secrets, explosions, hero saves the world," Eddie added. "That kind of thing."

It all came back to me—the next Bond-Bourne franchise that Barb had been talking about. Eddie had summed it up well. I understood why they both wanted the part. But really I thought the role called for an Angelina Jolie type.

"All right, then," Shepard said. "I'll definitely come to some decision on this. And you're going to save me a seat on that plane, right?"

After a moment's surprise at the shift in topic, Eddie nodded. "You got it."

Shepard moved toward the door. "Good. We'll do details later."

"Hey, Shepard," Eddie said. "Before you go, you might want to check your hair, man. I don't think the stylist got it right."

Instantly outraged, Shepard stomped into the tiny bathroom, and Eddie put an arm around me and hauled me up close against him.

"Sorry about last night," he said.

I thought of a few dozen polite demurrals but decided on: "You should be."

"I am." He kissed me, in his slow Eddie way, while Shepard huffed and cursed in the bathroom, clearly finding some non-existent flaw in his hairstyle. "Let me make it up to you. How about tonight?"

"I think tonight I—"

His kiss shut me up but good. "I'm on set till eight, and then I've got a two-hour turnaround. How about dinner? Say, eight fifteen, at Bruni's? In the hotel."

Probably I should have refused him. But I stood nose to nose, scant inches from his deadly blue eyes, and the spot on my waist where he rested his hand burned beneath his touch.

"All right," I said. "But only because you bought me a really cool present."

He grinned. "I thought about flowers, but I wanted you to have something to remember me by."

"Good choice. I'll think of you anytime I'm forced to beat the living snot out of someone."

He laughed and released me. "Lorraine, you are a true romantic."

At the sound of the bathroom door coming open, I stepped out of his grasp, reluctantly.

"Is this better?" Shepard asked, emerging from the bathroom.

"It looks way better than it did when you got up this morning," I said.

"Is that good?" he asked.

"It's great. Let's go. You're going to be late."

We clattered out of the trailer, and Eddie waved good-bye from the steps as though waving farewell from the porch of a country estate.

As we started up the ramp to the boardwalk, Shepard said, "He likes you."

I nodded, lost in the memory of his kiss.

Shepard sighed. "Last day on the boardwalk," he said. "I almost thought this day would never get here."

"Wait a minute," I said. "That's it? Just 'He likes you'? No 'Watch out for him'? No 'Be careful, Rainny'? None of that?"

"No," he said. "Eddie's as harmless as the next guy. Besides, he's leaving tomorrow night with the rest of us. How much havoc could he create in such a short time?"

Oh, please, let him give me a whole lotta havoc.

Inside my pocket, the phone rang, instantly dashing my improving mood. It had to be Dave. He was overdue to call and chew me out.

I pulled the phone from my pocket and flipped it open. "Lorraine Keys."

"Keep your questions to yourself, and leave the crew out of it," the electronically masked voice said.

"Who is this?"

"Dutch didn't have to die. Stay out of my way, or you're next."

Chapter Eleven

My knees weakened enough to prove my body understood the threat, and I stutter-stepped onto the boardwalk.

"I want to stop for a cup of coffee," Shepard said.

I nodded and tried to focus. "Sure," I said. I looked at the phone in my hand. With the incoming number still displayed, I hit DIAL. A cheery recording informed me I'd reached de la Vega's Hotel and Casino and I should pay attention because their menu had changed. Silently swearing, I punched the DISCONNECT key. I needed to call someone—the police, Dave, Joe even. Someone should be told. Someone should do something. I needed protection.

Problem was, other people called *me* for protection. How would it look if I went crying for help? If I admitted to being scared, I risked looking like what every narrow-minded man thought me to be: a frail little woman who needed a man to keep her safe. I'd worked too hard for too long proving myself capable. I didn't want to surrender any ground I'd gained.

And then reality hit. I didn't need to give ground. If I knew how to protect other people, I knew how to protect myself. The same principles applied, right? I had knowledge, experience, and a dandy new baton with which to hold back any opponent. I would be fine. I hoped.

I slid the phone back into my pocket, forcing myself to appear unconcerned. A little too much late-night television had me thinking that whoever had placed that call was watching me, watching for a reaction. I decided I should look cool, as if this sort of thing happened all the time and didn't scare me.

Beside me, Shepard helloed everyone as we neared the hub of the on-set action. I spent the time scowling at people. Matthew was dead. Dutch was dead. Someone was threatening my life. Who? Guys on the crew went about their business with stone faces. Folks associated with the production of the film had a different sort of grim demeanor, born of disasters on and off the set and the rapidly ticking clock, counting down to the cessation of funds, expiration of permits, and end of contracts. No one looked happy. Everyone looked as if they'd like to kill someone.

A few deep breaths and a Boston-crème donut and I could think a little clearer. Okay, so someone was threatening me. I decided to take it as a compliment. Maybe the threat meant that my presence prohibited the bad guy from getting at Shepard, which meant I was doing a good job.

Okay, maybe "compliment" was stretching things. Maybe I'd really pissed someone off. Someone who had my phone number. My brand-spanking-new cell phone number that even I had to get from my business cards.

"Where's Holly?" I asked one of the gazillion producer-types clustered near the craft services table. "Is she due this morning?"

His face a mask of exhaustion, producer-type guy tipped his head in the direction of the playback tent. "Check the call sheet."

I fought down a rising aftershock of grief. Over the past few days, Dutch had hooked me up with a copy of the call sheet soon after I'd arrived on set each day. I didn't miss having my own copy of the call sheet. But I missed Dutch, missed the idea of having a friend nearby.

Shepard sank into deep schmooze with one of the assistant-something-or-others, and I edged away to check the call sheet tacked to a support beam of the playback tent. Holly was due soon. I had to settle in and wait.

Baton protruding from my pocket, I poured myself a cup of coffee and watched as the chaos around me slowed to stillness and the cameras rolled on the first of the scenes that needed to be shot.

Halfway through the coffee, I was fighting to keep down the boredom-induced panic, when Catherine Dawes arrived on set—quietly and in the company of Karl Moyne.

Heads bent toward each other, the two most volatile people I'd encountered looked as if someone had slipped some Valium into their lattes. It chilled me to see them both so serene.

My eyes met hers. She lifted one eyebrow and flared her nostrils like an Afghan hound on a scent. Beside her, Moyne tried to follow her gaze and, in doing so, glanced right over me. Not to say he couldn't decipher which direction Catherine was looking off in, but he looked dead at me and kept on searching, dismissing me as unworthy of Catherine's attention.

The director called "Cut" and sent everyone "back to one." From the corner of my eye I spotted Kim, the assistant director, creeping onto the set. She moved quietly and swiftly toward the hub of the action, pulling a headset into place as she went. I didn't think I'd ever seen her arrive late before. And apparently, late was frowned upon.

In front of the cameras, Shepard and the gentleman who was portraying his father leaned against the boardwalk railing and walked through their scripted heart-to-heart. When Shepard got to "You did the best you could after Mom died," Riley Jacks sprang from his chair and whirled on Kim.

"Where have you been?" he demanded.

Apparently surprised by his volume and vehemence, Kim flinched visibly, but only once. She stood her ground, feet braced, chin level, as the director informed her and anyone within a hundred-yard radius that this was no bleeping time for her to bleeping show up bleeping late.

"And now," Jacks went on, "you think you can just show up late with no explanation? No apology? You got anything to say?"

She smiled—not a Mona Lisa smile, a Hannibal Lecter smile—and said, "You're still rolling."

"Cut!" He ripped off his headset, took Kim by the arm, and hauled her off past where Shepard stood. Everyone involved in the film gave them a wide berth, pretending to work while watching what transpired.

Judging by body language and the occasional "bleep" the wind carried in, the director was more than somewhat put out. But I had to hand it to Kim. She didn't shrink; she didn't look away, didn't fold her arms or bite her lip. She met his attack head-on and gave him some of his own back. Seemed she, too, had developed the attitude necessary to thrive in a man's profession. More power to her.

I did a quick scan of the onlookers and spotted Eddie Gale coming toward me, with his arm around Holly Bellinger. Her shoulders drooped, her spine sagged, and she barely lifted her feet when she walked, yet she didn't look like a slob. She looked . . . sad.

Eddie gave me a wink and a smile and steered Holly in my direction. "What's going on?" he asked.

I nodded toward Jacks and Kim. "The director and the AD are having some artistic differences."

"Involving?"

"Punctuality and etiquette." I swirled the coffee in the cup and turned my attention to Holly. "I have a question for you," I said, then downed the last of the coffee. "The other night I gave you a bunch of my business cards. Who'd you give them to?"

Holly went blank, and Eddie took the cup from my hand. "Let me refill that for you," he said. "How d'you take it?"

"Black, one sugar. Thanks." I turned back to Holly. "Do you remember?" I began. "At the get-together, I gave you a bunch of my cards. You said you were going to give one to . . ." Nuts. She'd told me their names.

Holly's eyes lit. "Pam and Dina," she said.

"Yes. Who are they?"

"Did one of them call you?"

A shiver of panic gripped my heart. I took a breath. "Who are they?" I asked again, trying not to hear the "you're next" echoing in my head or picture Dutch's lifeless body. "Can you point them out to me?"

"Sorry, they left already," she said.

"When?"

"Yesterday morning."

And then I curled my hands into fists to prevent myself from strangling Holly. I realized—I hoped—she had no idea why I was asking these questions, but that didn't give me any extra time to stand around reviewing useless information.

"Whom did you give the cards to who is still here?" I asked.

She took a deep breath and seemed to struggle into a more upright stance and focus on my question. "Well, I gave one to that horrible Catherine, and one to Kim, and then I just left a bunch on the table for anyone to take. Why? I'm sorry. Was that wrong?"

"No," I said. Rats. Way to narrow down the suspects.

Finished with their argument, Jacks and Kim returned to their positions behind the camera. Jacks dropped into his chair, and Kim snatched up her clipboard with enough drama to send some loose papers flying.

"Did you ever get that garment bag I had sent?" Holly asked.

Eesh. Probably I should have sent a note. "I did. Thank you. That was really nice of you." I fought back a grin at the sight of Kim scrambling to collect papers fluttering in the breeze.

"You know that little black dress is couture. One of a kind," Holly said.

"It's gorgeous, honestly. But it's really too kind of you. I mean, you hardly know me," I said.

"I know," she said over a sigh. "But I was hoping."

"Hoping?"

"That you would put in a good word for me with Shepard. But it's useless," she said. "He's back together with the creature."

"With whom?"

"Catherine. That back-stabbing . . ."

"No," I said. "They're not together. He has a legal action pending against her. Even he's not that stupid."

Holly gaped at me as though I were the stupid one. "He was with her last night," she said. "And the night before that. Ever since Matthew . . ." She drew in a deep, steadying breath. "She stayed in his suite but left while it was still dark so no one would know. Well. Whatever. It's hopeless now."

I looked to where Shepard stood, earnestly running the "You did the best you could after Mom died" line, and I felt the bile rise from my belly. How stupid could he be? Holly might be a little on the . . . surgically enhanced side, but she was a whole lot nicer than Catherine Dawes. What had he been thinking?

I took a step closer, trying to get into position to grab him and shake some sense into him as soon as the director called cut. But even as he did, and I got ready to move, Eddie's voice stopped me. "Look who I found," he called.

I glanced quickly over my shoulder and froze as I saw Eddie approaching, coffee cup in one hand, Barb in the other.

She grinned like she'd just arrived in hostile territory and was trying to soothe the natives.

"What's up?" I said, meeting her eyes.

"It wasn't a dream," she said.

Eddie handed me the coffee. "Black, one sugar," he said. "There were no more Boston-crème donuts."

"How did you know I—"

"Shepard told me," he said, and then he smiled. "I found your friend hanging around the other side of the barricade and figured you wouldn't mind."

Barb fought to maintain her smile.

I shrugged. "I don't mind at all." And smiled. "Maybe we can finally introduce her to Shepard."

"She hasn't met Shepard yet?" Eddie said.

"He's a slug," Holly pronounced, and she sidled away, head bowed.

"No, she hasn't met Shepard," I said. "And she'd really like to." And then she'd finally go home where she'd be safe and couldn't gamble legally.

"Do you think you could keep it down?" Kim the AD planted herself in my path. "Otherwise I'm going to have to ask you to leave the set." She looked like she might enjoy ordering me away.

"Ah, Kim, cool it."

"And now who is this?" she asked, eyes on Barb.

I tried for a smile. "This is my best friend, Barb. Barb, this is Kim, the assistant director."

Kim shot Barb a weak smile. "Are you a bodyguard too?"

"Oh, I'm way tougher than that." Barb laughed. "I'm a high school teacher."

"Did I hear right? You want to meet Shepard?"

Barb smirked at me, then smiled at Kim. "Yes, I would."

"Right now we're a little behind schedule," Kim said, "and I don't want any of my actors distracted. But I tell you what. You're a friend of Lorraine's? You come back tomorrow early, and I'll have a pass for you to come watch the shoot from this side of the barricades, okay?"

"Seriously?" Barb squealed.

Kim nodded. "Right now, though . . ." She pressed a finger to her lips, and Barb nodded rapidly.

Kim hustled back to Riley Jacks' side, and Barb gazed longingly at Eddie for a long moment and said, "I should go."

Eddie waved away her concerns. "Don't worry about her. She'll forget about you any second now."

"I just stopped by to tell Rainny . . ." Her eyes went wide as she looked from me to Eddie.

He watched her, patiently waiting for her to finish.

"Umm . . . to tell Rainny about this great . . . Internet café I found," she said.

It took a moment before I was able to crack her code. Trusting that "Internet café" alluded to her getting pertinent information online, information she couldn't share with anyone but me, I turned to Eddie, forcing my face into what I hoped was a concerned expression. "Holly's gone," I said. "I think she's upset about something."

He sighed. "I'll find her," he said. "Eightish, right? At Bruni's."

I nodded and even managed a smile. "Eightish."

"Nice seeing you again," he said to Barb, and he ambled off in search of Holly.

"Again," Barb said in a voice just above a whisper. "Oh, my God, I can't believe that really happened. I thought I dreamed that he was in our hotel room, but . . . it was real, wasn't it?"

"'Fraid so," I said, edging her away from the small cluster of people behind me. I sipped the hot coffee.

"Why didn't you tell me?"

"You wouldn't believe me."

She took a breath and looked closely at me. "I'm sorry. I'm sorry I didn't believe you," she said. "But what's this about eightish? You're seeing him tonight?"

"Dinner," I said. "You know, if he shows."

"But, Rainny, what if he's the guy? What if he's the one who's after Shepard? The one who made the trailer blow up?"

"Barb, he's not."

"You don't know that for sure. You don't know where he was. He could have done it."

And the night prior he should have been with me but had never showed. He'd had a lame conference-call excuse, and Dutch was dead. Maybe Barb was right.

The headache I thought I'd beaten with aspirin and electrolytes flared to life. I couldn't think about Eddie now. I had Shepard and Catherine to worry about. And Dutch and my boss and the police. Ugh. I pressed the heel of my hand against my forehead. "I really have to get back to work," I said. "So quick, tell me what you found out about Karl Moyne and the insurance thing."

"Nobody knows for sure—it's all gossip, you know—but word is Moyne has Shepard guaranteed for twice his salary. If Shepard doesn't finish the movie, Moyne stands to collect tens of millions in settlement."

"And that would take care of his debt," I added.

Barb nodded.

"Well done, Tonto," I said.

She grinned. "What next, Fearless Leader?"

I sighed. My priorities at the moment were hopelessly inverted. "I need shoes. Think you could find me a pair of plain black pumps to go with that dress Holly sent over?"

Barb smiled and saluted. "Anything I can do to help the cause."

"I need to have a word with you," I said, taking Shepard by the arm.

"Can I get some water first?" he asked.

"No." I hauled him to what could only be called the far end of the set. We skirted past a painted statue of George Washington, and I rested one elbow on the railing dividing the boardwalk from the beach. Grass-covered sand dunes rose before us, and beyond, the ocean thundered into the shore with an ageless constancy.

"What kind of an idiot are you?" I demanded, whirling on him and scaring off one of the many black-and-white cats living along the boardwalk.

"A thirsty one?"

I gave him a shake. "What are you doing spending your nights with Catherine Dawes?"

"C'mon, Rainny. We covered this. It's none of your business."

"It is my business. The woman is a mental case. You were well rid of her, but no, you had to drag her right back to your bed."

"Hey," he snapped. "Who I drag to my bed does not concern you."

"How long?"

"What?"

"How long have you been sneaking around with her?"

He turned away, his gaze on the grass growing along the dunes and the bathers along the beach. "A few days. Since—"

"Since you called me about the pizza?"

He shook his head. "No."

"No? Then where were you the night before I found you at the shooting range? Eddie left you in the casino. Where did you go after that?"

"I . . ." He kept his focus on the dunes and let his sentence trail away.

"You . . . ?"

"I was with Holly."

"You were with Holly?"

"No," he said, all manner of annoyed creeping into that one syllable. "I wasn't with her in the sense of holding her close and swearing my devotion. I was with her in the sense of sitting around her suite drinking and talking till I finally took a sleeping pill and passed out from exhaustion. When I woke up, she was already gone."

I shook my head, hoping to make the information therein settle into a recognizable pattern. "I don't get it. If you were with Holly, what the hell have you been doing with Catherine? How did you end up—"

"At the . . . thing for Matthew. Catherine was upset. I was—"

"She was upset?" I ran a hand through my hair in frustration. "Shepard, this is the woman who managed to pour scalding coffee all over Matthew, call him an insignificant peon, and walk out without an ounce of concern. The whole broken-up-over-Matthew thing is an act. How do you not see that?"

"You don't understand."

"No, I don't," I said. "I don't see how you could get on track for a relationship with Holly Bellinger and then completely derail it for Catherine Dawes."

"You're not part of it," he said, enunciating each word. "This is my private, personal life, and it does not affect you. Stay out of it."

I blinked against the sudden shock of his words. I'd known Shepard for too many years to count. In all that time, despite the total disparity of our lives, he had never set me apart, treated me like an outsider, or closed me out of his life. To have him do it now, when we needed to stay together and stay in agreement, hurt so much, it shortened my breath.

Damn, but this whole Atlantic City trip was testing friendships. Or maybe it wasn't the trip, maybe it was the job, or, more to the point, me in the job. How much personal loss was

I willing to risk to see this man safe? Could I let go of the friendship, do the tough-love thing? His life was at stake. If he ended up hating me . . .

"Shepard, listen to me," I said, struggling to keep my voice both soft and firm at the same time. "You've got me and Joe here because you think someone's trying to kill you. God help me, you're probably right. This is not the time to sidle up to a woman who would be better off stripped of all sharp objects and locked in a padded room. What if she's behind the attempts on your life? What are you thinking?"

He leaned in close, green eyes dark with resolve. "I'm thinking if she's responsible for this, if she's attacking me because she's angry, then if I make her happy, she stops. This is self-preservation. This is me thinking I'd like to get out of this city alive."

He straightened, tugged at the tails of his shirt so that the fabric pressed tightly against his chest, and glared at me. "I'm going to go get some water now," he said, and he turned sharply away.

Still smarting from my impromptu showdown with Shepard, I took up my post with my arms folded and a pained scowl on my face. If he wanted to make the mistake of hooking up with a crazy woman, so be it. He was right. It was none of my business. Didn't make my job any easier or any harder. In fact, I never even had to deal with Catherine Dawes. Joe was the one who had to pretend to neither see nor hear what happened between Catherine and Shepard, and in my opinion, he deserved it.

The trill of my cell phone put an end to my silent grousing. "Lorraine Keys," I said into the speaker.

"Dave du Comte. You've got another dead body down there, Lorraine," he said.

A chill ran through me so fast, I shivered. "Who's dead now?"

"Report here says Peter Johannsen. Unconscious from a Taser and then stabbed to death."

I went a little weak, sorrow and relief making me sigh. "Everyone called him Dutch," I said. "And exactly why do the Atlantic City police feel the need to inform you of everything going on here? How come no one told me about the Taser?"

"Semper Fi," he said, his voice unusually gruff.

Another old-boy network. Should have known. Maybe I needed to get to work on an old-broad network, even the score.

"This voids the deal I made with your principal," Dave said.

Oh, I could just see him, sitting behind his massive wooden desk, shirtsleeves rolled up, tie tucked between the second and third buttons of his shirt—big boss man cutting a cream cheese bagel and sipping a cup of tea.

"You might want to take that up with my principal," I said.

"It's time to pack it up and head home."

"You cannot do this," I said. "Dutch was not my responsibility. I have done nothing to warrant my being removed from this assignment."

"You've become a target."

"You don't know that." Did he? Did he know about the "you're next" thing? Did he have my phone tapped?

"Joe will relieve you at noon."

No, no, no, no, no. "You know, I'd like to head home," I sputtered, "but the police have advised me not to leave town."

"The police will know where to find you," Dave said. "You're relieved at noon. Say good-bye to Mr. Brown."

Chapter Twelve

I said nothing to Shepard about the changing of the guard. I'd like to think my frustration over the Catherine thing caused my silence and that my removal served him right for telling me his personal life was none of my business. But I'd probably be closer to the mark to admit I was afraid I'd cry when I told him why I was leaving. Best to let Joe deal with explaining things. He wouldn't put all the words in to begin with, so my being upset about the situation would never come through.

A few minutes shy of noon, Joe strolled onto the set, and I walked off, with one last look at the undercover cop laying out chocolate chip cookies on the craft services table.

On the street, I pulled out my phone and called Barb.

We met up at a club table in the bar area of a chain restaurant. I briefed her on the events of the morning while I sucked down a particularly delightful mudslide that did more for my headache than four aspirin had.

"Rainny, that just plain sucks," Barb said. "How could your boss order you off the job like that?"

"Because he's my boss," I said, pulling a menu close. Opening it and reading seemed like too much work at the moment.

"You wouldn't consider quitting, would you?"

I shook my head. "And do what, Barb? I can't start over someplace else and continue to make rent. Can you see me back in my parents' house?"

"Without a court order? No."

"Besides, I like my job. It's the job I want," I said.

"Well, what would happen if we stayed here in Atlantic City? As long as you show up for your next shift back home, you can stay here as long as you want, right? I mean, we still need to try to figure out who's after Shepard, don't we?"

" 'We'? What 'we'?"

"Besides, you've got a date tonight with"—she paused and glanced furtively around the room—"Eddie Gale."

"Who you think might be a little shady. Can we get back to the 'we' thing?"

She opened her menu but kept her eyes on me. "All I'm saying is, now we can devote some time to really figuring out what's going on. We've already missed checkout at the hotel, so we'd have to pay for another night anyway. So why not stay? You go on your date and see what kind of information you can get out of the guy, and I'll see what else I can dig up on Catherine and Holly and Mexico and all the rest of it."

"Does it matter?" I asked, huffing. "The police are here; they're working on it. Dave will send someone else to take my place. Let them figure it out. I'm done." I didn't even want to think about the way Shepard had shut me out.

Barb laid her forearms against the vinyl-wrapped menu and leaned in to me. "What happened to you? I thought you were going to be the first female bodyguard on the A-team."

"A-division."

"Fine. Division."

I sank back in my seat, away from her glare. "I'm still hundreds of hours away from even applying, Barb. That has nothing to do with today."

"If you stay with this job," she said, her voice intense, "and you finish your hours, what do you think will set you apart from the thirty or forty or however many other guys applying to A-division?"

I lacked the energy required to make a rude remark.

"Don't you think solving the question of who wants to kill

Shepard Brown is going to count in your favor? Don't you think that might give you an edge?"

The first time Shepard called on the point-to-point to ask me where I'd gone, I stood half-naked in a dressing room trying to decide on underwear.

"This really isn't a good time," I said into the phone.

"How come you're not here? Why is Joe here? What's this noise about them sending someone to replace you?"

I tugged the bra strap tighter. "You made a deal with Dave. Don't you remember?"

"For crying out loud, I make deals all the time. I didn't sign anything, and we didn't shake hands on it. I want you back here. Now."

"Now's bad," I said, and I turned my back on the mirror. It creeped me out just a little to be talking to Shepard with my cleavage showing. "And I believe you and Dave made what the guys in legal like to call a gentleman's agreement. Or a verbal contract. Or something like that."

"So what? You're saying you won't come back unless Dave tells you to?"

"Dave is my boss," I said, snatching up my shirt to cover myself. "For right now, what he says goes."

"Oh, that's a load of crap, Rainny. Just come back. I'll pay you."

Not "I'm sorry." Not "I need you." Just "I'll pay you."

"I can't," I said, pushing down the bitter taste in my mouth. "I'm not insured. The company is."

"Well, what do I have to do to get you back here?"

"Take it up with Dave."

He swore soundly. "I'll call you back."

By the time I settled on underwear befitting a designer dress, Shepard and I had repeated the same conversation three times and resolved nothing. Barb was waiting for me outside the fitting room. "Brown's having a breakdown," I told her.

"I thought I heard his voice," she said wistfully. "All right. Let me see what you picked out."

I held out the hanger draped with little black nothings, and she tipped her head, considering. "What?" I asked. "What's wrong with them?"

"It's just . . . you couldn't find anything sheer? Maybe something with a little lace at least?"

I looked at the black demicup bra and matching panties. "Give me a break," I said. "I'm going on a date in a dress. One milestone at a time."

Bruni's boasted Italian cuisine, low lights, Roman sculpture, and a water feature. Miraculously, no noise from the adjacent casino filtered past the maître d' podium.

I spotted Eddie seated at the bar, white shirt, dark jacket, glass of scotch in hand. He looked good enough to drizzle chocolate over.

Drawing a deep breath for courage, I nodded toward the bar so the maître d' understood my destination, adjusted the purse on my shoulder, and walked toward Eddie.

Each step confirmed the appalling lack of support offered by the strappy sandals Barb had called "so chic," to say nothing of the way the little black cocktail dress hugged so tightly, I felt every stitch on my underwear. At least I had a purse; knowing it was weighed down by the inclusion of an expandable baton made me feel more like myself.

Okay, probably wearing sexy underwear and carrying a weapon on a date could be construed as having mixed emotions. But the lingerie was my idea; the baton was Barb's. I thought I'd have one night to spend with Eddie before he went back to LA, so I ought to be dressed for it. Barb thought I'd have one night before he went to jail, so I ought to be armed. Really, I wasn't conflicted, just . . . impressionable.

I eased into Eddie's peripheral vision, hoping he'd spot me before I needed to speak. Every possible greeting running through my mind sounded lame. "Hello" seemed unimaginative. "Hi there" struck me as cheesy. I thought about going with "Haven't I seen your face before?" but I was really no good at humor.

I slid onto the vacant bar stool beside him, watching the railing to make sure I didn't bang it and accidentally knock my shoes off. When I looked up, Eddie's gaze was making slow progress from my legs to my eyes.

"Well, have mercy," he said. "You, darlin', look amazing."

I shrugged and silently begged the heavens to keep me from blushing.

"You need something to drink?"

I ordered a glass of wine and did my best to remember to sit up straight and keep my knees together.

"You disappeared today," he said. "Everything all right?"

On the verge of telling him precisely what had happened, I heard Barb's voice in my head, insinuating Eddie's involvement in the anti-Shepard activities. "I just needed the afternoon off," I lied. "Had some things to take care of."

"But you've got the night off too, don't you? Not running back to look after Shepard anytime soon?"

"Shepard's covered," I said, and then the evil Barb-in-my-head implant made me say, "Why do you ask?"

He smiled his slow smile, and his eyes brightened with good humor. "I just wanted to make sure you wouldn't have to disappear anytime soon and cut our evening short."

Did I believe him? I believed him, right? It was just Barb making me paranoid.

I reached for the wine the bartender had left and sipped the white, telling myself as I swallowed that I trusted Eddie. Barb had put wicked ideas into my head. All I had to do was ignore her as thoroughly as I planned to ignore my conscience, should the opportunity arise.

"I promise I won't go running off. But what about you?" I asked. "Didn't you mention having a turnaround? You could be running off at any minute yourself."

"Nah," he said, palming the glass of scotch, "it's not so immediate that I'd have to leave in the middle of something. There's time for me to finish up."

Oh, mama. I took a big gulp of wine and got hit with a sangria flashback. "You know, I should probably eat something," I said.

"I recently was reminded that drinking on an empty stomach can lead to deadly mornings."

Too late, the image of Dutch lying dead in the dirt flared in my memory, and I closed my eyes as though that might erase the image.

"Well, we can't have that," Eddie said gently. "Come on." He laid a hand against my shoulder and turned me away from the bar. "The nice thing about being me is that my table is ready when I am."

With a nod from Eddie, the maître d' bowed and led us to a table in a far corner of the restaurant. Our waiter appeared in seconds with the drinks we'd left at the bar. He laid a pair of menus on the table's edge and promised to return.

We studied the menus, discussed our options, and finally ordered. My hero the waiter left a basket of warm bread and a plate of soft butter. I didn't even try for ladylike as I snatched a heel of Italian bread from the basket.

"Did you eat at all today?" Eddie asked over a laugh.

"I did, actually," I said around a mouthful of bread. "It's funny, though. When I'm working, I don't get to eat much. So I kind of make up for it in the off-hours."

"How did you get involved . . . ?"

I told him my story, and he told me his. He'd been raised in Oklahoma (which Barb had told me), gone to college in Texas (which Barb had told me), and gotten his first movie role—a bit part—at the seasoned age of twenty-four (which Barb had gotten wrong, and I could hardly wait to lord that one over her).

"So, may I ask you something?" I said. "How long has this rivalry been going on between you and Shepard?"

Both eyebrows shot up, and he reached for his nearly empty glass of scotch. "We're not rivals. Brown's a good friend of mine."

"Yeah, I know, you go way back. All the way back to *The Memphis Mission,* where Shepard stepped in and took the part you would have played if you hadn't separated your shoulder in a motorcycle accident."

He looked shocked and a little disheartened.

"Barb told me," I said.

"Now, that's not fair. You can just dig up all kinds of dirt on me."

I shrugged. "Think of it like a setup date. I've been completely briefed on you."

"But I haven't been briefed on you."

"I get to stay an enigma."

His smile in return was downright seductive. "I'm going to learn all your secrets."

"Oh, you think you can ply me with a little fancy wine and good food and I'll tell all?"

"Darlin', I have not yet begun to fight."

Have mercy, but I was ready to melt right there in the restaurant. "I need more wine," I said.

He sighed and let the mood go. Turning, he signaled a waiter with the briefest crook of his finger. "I intend to make good on my threat," he warned, but lightly, more of a tease than an intent.

"I look forward to it. But first we eat, and you tell me how you and Brown got to be rivals."

"I told you, we're not rivals."

"What about *The Whispering Gallery*? You wouldn't consider the fact that you both want that gig so badly, you'd lie or steal to get it grounds for rivalry?"

He chuckled and handed the waiter my empty wineglass without taking his gaze from mine. "I don't know about stealing," he said. "Lying is an occupational hazard."

"Why is it so important to you? To both of you?"

"It's a great part."

"Big-time award stuff?"

"Action franchise stuff. Sword training. Stunt work."

"A testosterone job."

"Exactly."

I smiled. "Would you want it so much if Shepard wasn't interested in doing it?"

He huffed and sat back, looking at me through narrowed eyes. "Shepard put you up to this?"

"What? What are you—"

"You're going to ask me all these questions and then go on back and tell Shepard—"

"Unbelievable. You're as paranoid as he is." And *he* thought lying was an occupational hazard? "I am not here because Shepard asked me to be."

"That's why you got the afternoon off, isn't it? So you could spend your time getting yourself ready to pull this act on me? And then you'll run right back to Shepard and tell him everything, right?"

"Believe me when I tell you that Shepard had nothing to do with my being here now. And no way would I leave here and run and tell him anything," I said. "I got the afternoon off because my boss pulled me off the job, and I spent my time shopping for nice underwear, okay?"

I wasn't sure what to be more embarrassed by, being pulled off the job or talking about underwear over dinner.

"You were shopping for underwear?" he said quietly, skipping right over the part about my getting fired. Sometimes the predictability of the male of the species wasn't at all comforting.

"If you don't mind, I think I'd prefer to not say anything for a while." I grabbed a roll from the basket and shoved a most unladylike portion into my mouth.

"Ah, Lorraine, I'm sorry," Eddie said, shaking his head. "I'm a little on edge. It's . . . well, you know it's been a tough week. And now this argument over *Gallery* and whether it's going to go to me or Shepard and whether or not they're going to let van Weer direct . . . I guess I'm just kinda keyed up."

The waiter returned with a full glass of wine and two plates of green salad.

I leaned low across the table, getting as close to him as I could without dropping the bustline of my dress into the salad. "Eddie, Shepard wants approval of the director, right? So what happens if he says he doesn't want van Weer?"

He leaned in to meet me. "Then van Weer's out of his first shot to direct a full-length film. And he might be a tough sell in the future."

"Just like that?"

"Maybe not just like that, but like that, yeah."

Huh. "He's not involved with this project, is he? With *Boardwalk*?"

Eddie shook his head. "Nah. As far as I know, he's still in LA."

Of course, that was only as far as Eddie knew. This van Weer guy could be in Atlantic City. Or he could have someone else on the cast or crew looking out for his interests.

Was being denied a shot at directing enough of a motive for murder? More important than the prospect of earning thirty million dollars on an insurance payout? More than revenge against the man who cheated on you in front of the world and then started a legal action against you? Or did there need to be some other angle to really tip the scales?

"Why do you ask?" Eddie said.

I let out a frustrated sigh. "Just trying to put some pieces together. Trying to make some connections between Shepard and . . . whomever."

He smiled warmly. "It's a big business. There are connections all over the place, and not always positive ones."

"Oh, really? You mean there are people other than me in the world who don't adore Shepard Brown?" I said over a laugh.

"One or two."

Of all the people I had met in the past few days, half a dozen people came to mind who had a beef with Shepard. But the first name on someone else's I Hate Shepard Club roster might prove interesting.

"Really. Name one," I said. "Name one person who doesn't adore Shepard."

"Besides you?"

"Naturally." I might have been the founder of the club.

He popped a grape tomato into his mouth and considered while he chewed. "Kim, for one."

"Kim the AD? She's not that charming to everyone?"

Fighting a grin, he shook his head. "Kim hates Shepard. You may have noticed."

I noticed they never seemed to be in the same square footage at the same time, but the same could be said of me and Derek Jeter. "He can be a jerk sometimes—I'll be the first to admit that. But *hate*'s kind of a strong word. What makes you use it?"

Eddie straightened in his seat. He slid half the forkful of salad into his mouth and chewed quickly. "I can't gossip about friends," he said.

"Don't grow morals on me now, Eddie."

He grinned. "Let's just say that's one of my secrets."

"So what are the odds," I said, "of my getting that secret out of you?"

He froze midchomp, and his eyes lit with mischief. "Odds, huh? A little gambling, a little seduction? That what you planned for the evening?"

"It's the new and improved plan," I said.

"Same underwear?"

"How do you know I didn't go out and buy granny panties?"

"With that dress?" He shook his head. "Not a chance."

"You know dresses?"

"I know women."

"You don't know me."

"I will."

With the salad course finished, I snuck off to the ladies' room to try to call Barb to ask her to check out Ko van Weer. She didn't answer her cell, so I left a voice mail and hurried back to Eddie and some serious flirting over the entrée.

By dessert, me and Eddie waking up side by side was a foregone conclusion. It had nothing to do with the wine or the secret he was laughingly keeping. The decision had been made somewhere between his eyes on my lips in the morning and my credit card on the counter at the lingerie store in the afternoon.

As we rode the elevator to his floor, we barely touched and

never spoke. We stood side by side, facing forward, fingertips colliding periodically, setting off sparks and making the air around us buzz with the thrill of newfound affection.

Inside the room we made it only as far as the entrance hallway before he was on me, all heat and hands and hunger. And, Lord, it had been so long, and he felt so good.

My purse slid from my shoulder and thunked to the floor. Free of the weight, I ran my arms under his jacket, felt the firm muscles of his chest beneath my palms. I grabbed at his chest, his shirt, his belt, and hauled him close against me.

His hand skimmed up my back, fingers caressing the melting point at the nape of my neck.

"Lorraine!" Shepard shouted.

Eddie froze.

"Lorraine, are you there?"

I thought about weeping. "It's the phone," I said, trying not to let go of Eddie as I reached for my purse. "I'll switch it off."

"Rainny, answer the damned phone!" Shepard demanded. "Barb's in danger!"

Chapter Thirteen

Eddie practically threw me off him, and we both dove for the bag. I tore the zipper open, and Eddie upended the purse to spill its contents onto the floor.

I grabbed the phone and keyed it up. "Shepard. What's going on?"

His voice at the other end of the point-to-point sounded tight with strain. "I just got a call. Some strange, computer-sounding voice said Barb wouldn't be able to meet me tonight, that she's tied up watching the tide come in. And then the voice laughed and said there's a great view from under the pier."

My world rocked sideways, and I would have fallen to the floor had Eddie not been there to hold me up.

"I don't even know what it means," Shepard wailed. "I mean, I think I know what it means."

"It means they got Barb," I said. "I have to go find her."

"Not without me," Eddie said. "I'm going with you."

"Was that Eddie?" Shepard asked. "If he's going, I'm going."

"No. You stay where you are," I said. "Stay with Joe. Call—"

"Oh, I fired Joe."

"What!"

"Rainny, I told you. I want you to be my bodyguard. I didn't want Joe; I wanted my friend. You're the one I trust. "

Leave it to Shepard to say exactly the right thing at precisely the wrong time.

"You're insane," I said. "Just stay where you are, then. Call the police and tell them that Barb's . . . that she's . . ." Words caught in my throat, and I choked back tears.

179

Eddie grabbed the phone from my hands. "Tell them just what you told us, and tell them to send someone to the pier."

"Which pier?" Shepard asked.

Eddie and I gaped at each other, as if in so doing we might figure out which of the four piers Barb would be beneath. "They'll have to check all of them," he said. "We gotta go."

He pocketed the cell phone and hauled me to my feet. "Come on," he said. "We'll start at the top."

"No," I said. "I'll be fine. You go stay with Shepard."

"Like hell."

"Eddie."

"No running off on me, remember? Besides, you know how I enjoy being gallant. This is an outstanding opportunity. Grab the baton."

I wanted to argue with him, but there wasn't time. Plus, I kind of liked the idea of not going it alone. "Thanks," I said, lifting the baton from the floor. "Let's go."

I took a step toward the door and fell off my shoe. Pain shot through my ankle. "Argh! I cannot go saving people in these stupid shoes!" I cried.

Ignoring the pain, I tore the shoes from my feet but was still stuck standing in a black lace cocktail dress. I thought longingly of my jeans and kicks, and then it hit me. "Holly," I said.

"Holly?"

"Where's Holly's room? Do you know?"

We raced down the hall to the suite of rooms assigned to Holly. "Open up," Eddie said, pounding on her door.

"She's not answering. We don't have time. We have to go," I said.

"Holly!" More pounding.

The door swung open, and a mud-masked Holly stood gaping at us, hand on hip. "What do you people want?"

Eddie pushed past her into the room. I followed, trying to explain as quickly as I could that I needed to borrow something more suitable than a cocktail dress for a triumphant rescue.

"It's not just any cocktail dress," Holly said. "I told you, it's one of a kind."

I felt a bead of hysteria break loose in my belly. "Unless it's got secret compartments with the kind of life-saving devices favored by superheroes, it's a *schmotta*. I need something I can run in."

Eddie, already tearing through the closet, tossed me a pair of pink velour sweatpants. "Try these," he said.

Holly confidently informed me of the designer's name. "Super easy to move in."

"Great." I tugged them on over my legs and dragged them over my butt.

"Black silk," Eddie said, wistfully. "Really nice."

Beyond decorous, I hauled the dress over my head and reached for the matching top Holly held out.

"And matching bra," Eddie said. "Wow, this night has gone the wrong way."

I shoved my arms into the jacket and pulled it down over my head. "Sneakers!" I shouted.

Eddie dove back into the closet while Holly shook her head. "I don't think that's going to work."

"Do you not have sneakers?"

"Sure, I do," she said as Eddie reappeared. "But I have feet like a kangaroo."

Eddie held forth a pair of sneakers that looked like standard NBA equipment.

"Got any flip-flops?" I said.

The flip-flops weren't a big improvement over the sneakers, but they were hugely better than the strappy stiletto deals I'd left in Eddie's room.

"Holly, listen," I said, as we prepared to leave. "Go to Shepard's room, will you? Sit with him. Stay with him till I get back. Can you do that?"

She rolled her eyes so masterfully, I had to admire her. "I'm not a child. I understand what you're saying."

Good. Okay. Safety in numbers. Maybe I could ask someone else to sit with Shepard too. I turned for the door.

"But I'm not going," Holly said.

"Why not?"

"He's a swine—I told you."

"He also might be in a great deal of trouble. Please, Holly, go. And get anyone else you can think of to go with you."

She pulled her lower lip between her teeth, considering.

"Holly," Eddie said sternly.

"Okay," she said. "But I have to wash my face first."

"Fine. Just be as quick as you can, okay?"

Back in the hallway Eddie and I jogged to the elevators. He punched the call button, and we waited.

In the growing seconds I hugged myself and tried not to panic. Eddie came up from behind and wrapped his arms around me.

"She'll be fine," he said. "Don't worry."

"It's my fault," I said. "I should have made her go home. Hell, I should never have let her come in the first place. But I was stupid. I was in a rush. I didn't have time to argue with her, and now . . ."

"Stop. Don't blame yourself," Eddie said, his voice mellow and soothing. "The only person you can blame is the person responsible for this."

I took a deep, steadying breath and ran the short list of suspects in my mind.

"Who do you think it is?" Eddie asked.

"I don't know."

"But you have an idea."

"I have a few."

"What if I told you," he said as the elevator dinged its arrival, "that Kim was the one who put the press on to Shepard and Malena while they were in Mexico? Would that help you narrow things down?"

I stepped out of his embrace and into the elevator. "That's the big secret?" I asked. "That Kim called the press? How much do you think that matters?"

He followed me into the confined space that smelled of the last occupant's designer cologne and punched the button for the lobby. "It matters because while Shepard was dallying with Malena, Catherine wasn't the only woman he was cheating on."

The doors slid closed while I tried to make sense of his words. "Shepard said he had a *fling* with Kim while he was in Mexico."

Eddie shook his head and sucked air between his teeth. "I don't think Kim took it so lightly."

"Oh, no."

"And then Malena came along, and it was adios, Kim."

"Unbelievable," I said. "It takes a special kind of jerk to cycle through women like that. I think I'll kill him myself."

"You don't think you'll have to get in line?"

Disgust cut grooves into my forehead. "And you're friends with this guy?"

"Hey, now. You are too. Careful with those rocks in your pretty glass house, huh?"

The elevator shuddered to a stop. When the doors slid open, they revealed a lobby jam-packed with the matching-T-shirt-clad women of the Mount St. Clair Choir and Bible Study group.

"Oh, my Lord!" one of them shouted. "It's Eddie Gale!"

Oh, crap.

One quick thinker snapped a picture; the flash blinded me and angered me. I had no time for diversions. I felt Eddie wrap his arm around my shoulders and guide me forward. Another flash from a camera. How did he live like this?

We eased out into the surrounding crowd. Women reached to shake hands with Eddie, profess their undying devotion, and beg him to stand for pictures. Eddie's responses consisted chiefly of "Thank you, not right now, sorry," and "Excuse us."

Not nearly so polite nor restrained in any way by a public image, I shouted as loudly as I could, "Back off!"

Nobody actually backed, but I shocked them into momentary stillness.

Eddie and I made a break for it, dashing to the right and out through the lobby doors. Past the valet circle, we headed left along the road.

"Which way?" I asked as we double-timed it toward the boardwalk.

"Your call," Eddie said.

We came to the top of the ramp and paused. Up and down the boardwalk, shops, hotels, restaurants, and casinos beckoned patronage with alluring lights. An adult-carnival atmosphere enveloped us, and the ocean that could be heard but not seen on the darkness of the beach added an ominous sound effect.

Off to our right, the construction site stretched over the water along Ocean Pier. Lights blazed over the area tonight, and a pair of uniformed patrolmen stood post at the entrance to the site; they still controlled a crime scene in there. One of them turned his head, lips moving as he angled the radio clipped to his shoulder toward his mouth.

"Looks like they've got their eyes on this one," Eddie said.

"Left."

We jogged north along the boardwalk, weaving in and out among people who had nothing better to do than stroll. Under other circumstances the retired couple holding hands would be heartwarming, the drunk construction workers incapable of pronouncing Bally's accurately would be funny, and the kids awake past their bedtime eating ice cream with their parents would be sweet. With Barb in trouble, they were infuriating.

"Beach," Eddie said, and we cut off the boardwalk to follow the annoyingly winding wooden path onto the beach.

Within seconds of hitting sand, I left Holly's flip-flops behind. Bad enough they were too big; they also spewed sand up the back of my legs with each step I took.

We ducked between the cement pilings of the Central Pier, where the whine of go-carts on the track above us failed to drown out the thunder of breaking waves. The sea gobbled up beach, the water higher beneath the pilings than I'd yet seen. An incoming wave reached to swell above our ankles, and Eddie cursed as he fought his feet free of his shoes.

I pulled the end of the expandable baton from its sheath and switched on the flashlight. Light against the pilings made them glimmer where the ocean had touched them and revealed tide markings that warned how deep the water would get.

"What's Barb's number?" Eddie asked. He had my cell phone out, poised to dial.

"Speed dial two," I said.

"Two? Who's speed dial one? Shepard?"

"The police."

I turned the light toward the boardwalk, surprising an amorous couple with other things on their mind, and illuminating a trio of gentlemen who appeared to be engaged in a drug deal.

"Rats," I said. No sign of Barb. The panic I had been working to keep down threatened to break loose.

Eddie snapped the phone shut and took hold of my elbow. "She's not here and not answering her phone. Let's keep going."

Switching off the flashlight, I let him lead me out from under the pier and back onto the beach. A quarter mile ahead of us, the Steel Pier with its brightly lit rides and carnival noises stretched another quarter mile into the ocean. Subtle shifts in the wind carried shrieks from people on the thrill rides.

The beach, as we neared, grew more populated. By the time we reached the pier, it was evident any goings-on beneath it would be witnessed.

"Now what?" I said, nearly shouting to be heard above the thrash of the ocean. "Was this just some wild goose chase? Some sick joke to . . . to . . . ?"

"To keep you away from Shepard," Eddie said. "Startin' to look that way." Breathing heavily, Eddie pulled off his jacket, rolled it into a ball, and threw it in the vague direction of the dunes.

My head swam, and my stomach threatened a repeat presentation of my dinner. Was Eddie right? Had this all been some scheme to get me away from Shepard? But I hadn't been with him, wouldn't have been even if Dave hadn't pulled me off the job.

Flashing lights drew my attention back to the boardwalk. A police cruiser rolled slowly toward the Central Pier, its progress hampered by pedestrian traffic.

"One?" I screeched. "They send one car?"

I turned to head up there and give them a piece of my recently addled mind, but Eddie caught my arm and held me in place.

"Leave them. Let's keep going. There's one more," he said. "Garden Pier."

"No, there's only . . ." My eyes followed the direction of his gaze.

Of course he was right. One more pier remained, farther north from where we stood. Rather than stretch into the ocean, this one had yielded to it. Its silhouette in the moonlight gave the illusion of the pier diving into the sea, though with a section missing midway, it appeared jagged rather than graceful. The pier threw a very contemporary Gothic shadow. Very Hollywood.

A good quarter mile separated Eddie and me from that pier. What if the phone call about Barb had been a diversion? What if, for reasons I didn't grasp yet, I was meant to be as far from Shepard as possible? If I had gone home when Dave ordered me off . . .

"Phone," I snapped at Eddie.

He pulled my cell from his pocket. "What are you doing?"

"Shepard's in trouble." I took the phone and flipped it open.

"What about Barb?" More than a hint of frustration edged Eddie's voice, making me think he might be a little put out about my dragging him down to the beach and ruining his shoes, his jacket, and our evening. But I could cope with only one crisis at a time—which was proving to be a problem.

Search for Barb, or go back to Shepard? Technically, according to Diamond Security, I was no longer responsible for Shepard. No legal action would stand against me if anything happened to him. That fact wouldn't make living with myself any easier, though.

But Barb had been my best friend since forever. And even

though I had no legal responsibility to her either, her presence in Atlantic City was absolutely my fault. She was only implicated because of her relationship to me, because hurting her would do something to me—stop me, get me out of the picture, keep me away . . . from what?

"Lorraine. What are we doing?"

My head throbbed with the crowding of thoughts. One thing at a time, I told myself. Get all the facts.

I punched the number for Shepard's point-to-point into the phone and turned for Garden Pier. "You coming?" I said to Eddie.

His mouth twitched into a smile quickly replaced by white-lipped determination. "Let's go."

I keyed up the phone. "Shepard," I said into it as we started to jog toward Garden Pier. The incoming tide dampened more and more of the beach, leaving the sand beneath our feet firm and cold—better by far than trying to run through the loose, dry version.

"Shepard," I said again.

"Dial the right number?" Eddie said.

I ignored him and keyed up one more time. "Shepard!"

No answer. Crap.

I shoved the phone into my pocket and picked up the pace of the jog, edging into a sprint and trusting that Eddie would keep up.

We slowed within feet of Garden Pier. Pilings of lichen-coated concrete struggled to hold up what remained of the pier. The noise of the waves receding made it sound like the pilings were groaning with the effort.

And then there was shouting. And I knew I wasn't hearing things.

"Barb!" I shouted, dashing under the pier.

Eddie grabbed the baton from me and switched on the flashlight as a wave on steroids crashed through the pilings and threatened to take us off our feet.

Sputtering and coughing split the air as the water raced back to the sea, but the coughing had a very girly sound.

"Barb!"

Eddie played the light against the pilings. "There," he said, and he moved.

We slogged through moist, sucking sand and knee-deep water, gripping each other for support against the potential of the next wave.

Barb stood lashed to the final upright piling, her body facing the oncoming ocean.

Tears of relief stung my eyes, and I did my best to hug her. Probably if she hadn't been bound against the piling she would have hugged me back. As it was, she sobbed with relief.

"Rainny, Rainny," she said.

Eddie thrust the flashlight at me. "Hold this. I'll untie her."

"I'm so glad you're here," Barb said, her voice deep and husky from shouting.

I shone the flashlight on Barb's arms, following back until the light centered over her hands. "Barb, what happened?" I asked, as Eddie went to work on the knot.

Barb ducked her eyes and shook her head. "I'm so stupid."

"Hang on," Eddie said. I thought for a moment he wanted Barb to wait to tell her story. But when a wall of water caught me from behind, I knew better. Unprepared, I pitched forward and stumbled up against Barb. Thank heavens she—and the four-foot-wide concrete piling—prevented me from going down.

We both gasped as the ocean caught us well above the knees, spray rising above the rolling wave and slapping us in the face.

"Jesus, get me out of here," Barb said.

"Don't worry, sweetheart," Eddie said. "Lorraine, the light."

"Sorry." I righted myself and got the flashlight back in place, biting back the need to urge him to hurry. "Don't you have a pocketknife or something?" I asked.

Eddie gaped at me as though I'd gone mad. "No," he said. "Sure you don't have wire cutters stuck in your bra?"

"Fair enough." I turned my attention back to Barb. "Tell me what happened. How in God's name did you get here?"

With the flashlight trained on Eddie's hands, I couldn't get a clear view of Barb's expression. But the tone of her voice made me think she'd gone past blushing.

"Kim Lloyd called me," she said. "At the hotel. She said she knew I really wanted to meet Shepard and so she was inviting me out for drinks."

"Underneath a broken-down pier?"

"No, of course not. She told me they were getting together on the beach and I should meet her at the museum and she'd walk down with me."

"Wave," Eddie said.

I stepped toward the piling and got one arm around Barb and one around Eddie as the wave crashed into me from behind. The water swirling around my legs was creeping higher on my thighs.

"We have to hurry!" I shouted over the roar.

"Almost there," Eddie said.

As the wave receded, I took a step back, and Barb fell forward against me.

"There," Eddie said.

"Oh, thank God, thank God, thank God," Barb murmured, sliding to her knees.

"No, you don't," Eddie said, catching her under the arms and hauling her to her feet. "We've got to get you out of here."

When he had her upright, he picked her up bodily and carried her out from under the pier and farther up the beach, well clear of the incoming tide.

Ahead of us, on the boardwalk, the police cruiser edged nearer in its slow progress, lights flashing. Pedestrians slowed, no doubt trying to determine what all the fuss was about. We didn't have much time.

Eddie set Barb on her feet and eased her down until she was sitting. He crouched in front of her, one hand on his knee, one hand in the sand. "You're okay," he said.

She nodded and sniffled as she started to cry.

I settled in beside her and put my arm around her shoulders. "I'm sorry you got caught up in this," I said.

She let out a shuddering sigh. "We were just walking along,

chatting," she said. "Then we got underneath that pier, and I felt like I'd been hit by lightning. When I came to I was . . . I was . . ."

I pulled her close to me, making the sort of noises used to soothe crying children.

Eddie was shaking his head, eyes narrowed.

"What is it?" I said, keeping my voice down.

"She might be a skinny thing," he said, tipping his head at Barb, "but she's pretty heavy dead weight."

Under my arm, Barb gave a little wail. In her mind, I am confident, Eddie Gale had just called her fat.

"And?" I prompted.

As soon as he opened his mouth to explain, it hit me. "No way Kim could lift her," I said.

Eddie shook his head. "Not get her upright and tied to that piling, no. Not a chance."

I jostled Barb a bit. "Who else was there, sweetie? You remember seeing anyone else?"

She rolled her head slowly from side to side.

"Had to be someone else," Eddie said.

I agreed. Because Barb hadn't seen anyone besides Kim didn't mean Kim had acted alone. Nuts. All this time I had worried about the threat against Shepard coming from one person. I hadn't taken seriously the idea there might be one source comprised of many people. How badly had Shepard screwed up his life that more than one person wanted to help facilitate his demise?

"You've been here for a while with Kim," I said to Eddie. "Who is she friendly with?"

As Eddie opened his mouth to speak, my cell phone chirped to life. I leaned left and pulled the phone from my pocket, every nerve in my body awake with the hope that Shepard was on the other end of the call. "Shepard?" I said into the phone.

"Lorraine?" Definitely not Shepard.

"Who's this?"

"Lorraine, it's Holly. Shepard's gone. What do you want me to do?"

Please, Lord, let me have heard her wrong. "Can you repeat that?"

"He's gone."

My body language must have transmitted my fear. Barb stopped sniffling, and Eddie laid his fingers lightly against my knee, eyes gone sapphire with concern.

" 'Gone' as in not answering his door? Or 'gone' as in he packed up, ran off, and didn't bother to close the door behind him?"

"What's going on?" Barb asked.

The area around us instantly flooded with light. Eddie reached up to shield his eyes with his forearm. I didn't have to turn to know the police cruiser had come to a stop behind us and now shone their nine-jillion-candle-watt spotlight in our direction. Our little huddle cast a long shadow over the beach.

"Please stay where you are," someone, no doubt the cop snug in his car, advised over an enunciator.

I didn't have time to stay put. I wondered, insanely, what my odds were of sneaking away without the police noticing, and if anyone along the three-mile stretch of the boardwalk would take action to stop me.

"He was on his way out when I got there," Holly said.

"And you didn't follow him!"

"What's wrong?" Eddie asked. "Where's Brown?"

"Catherine was with him," Holly said.

Behind me, the *thunk* of car doors shutting and the sudden squawk of radio traffic announced cops on the move.

Eddie shook his head while Holly's explanation rattled into my ear. "He went off with that stick," she said. "Catherine came along and told him they had to go back to work, and I could see how proud she was, getting him to do what she asked, carting him around like he was her private pet, and we all—"

"Where did they go?" I shouted to cut her off.

"That's what I'm telling you," Holly said. "He and Catherine went back to the set."

"Back to the set?" I repeated so Eddie would hear.

He furrowed his brow and checked his watch. His raised

eyebrows and the tilt of his head said there was a possibility it was the truth, but the possibility was slim.

"Police are here," Barb said.

"Thanks," I said into the phone. "I gotta go." I snapped the phone shut as the toes of beat-up black shoes sent a spray of sand into our circle of light.

"You folks see anything unusual out here tonight?" the cop asked.

Barb, Eddie, and I all shared a glance, a fraction of a second during which we all silently asked if we should fess up or take the opportunity to make a break for it.

Neither one of them spoke. Both watched me as though awaiting my decision on how much, if anything, we should divulge.

I peered up at the uniformed cop. "We found my friend tied to a piling. Someone tried to kill her."

Beside me, Barb sniffed so loudly, it sounded like she was snorting something. "But I can't tell you about it right now," she said. "Right now we have to go save Shepard Brown."

Eddie and I both turned to gape at Barb.

"Shepard Brown, the actor?" the cop said.

"Yes. Kim Lloyd, the lunatic who tied me to the pier, is trying to kill Shepard Brown."

The uniformed cop made the face all cops learn to make in their rookie year; he'd heard every color of crazy, and Barb was just a new hue.

"I'm serious," she said.

I pushed myself to my feet and took a couple of steps toward the cop. "It sounds insane, but it's true. I've been working as Shepard Brown's personal bodyguard. The woman who's been making attempts on his life lured my friend here as a diversion."

The cop looked me up and down, no doubt weighing my wardrobe against my words.

"Why would this Kim person want to kill Shepard Brown?"

I could only speculate. "Lovers' quarrel," I said.

"Because Shepard Brown has the power to end Kim's fiancé's chance as a debut feature-length director," Barb said.

I spun to look at Barb.

"Her fiancé is Ko van Weer. They've been living together for the past eight months."

Eddie nodded, following along. "Shepard is the one guy who doesn't want Ko to direct *The Whispering Gallery*."

"Right," Barb said. "Remember how you didn't understand why Shepard would do this *Boardwalk* project with Catherine if she was causing so many problems for him? It was part of the deal he made with the studio. He does *Boardwalk* with Catherine, and in return he gets all this background power on *Gallery*."

"Folks, this is all fascinating," the cop said. "But I need to hear what happened here tonight, okay?"

"And Kim, as AD, can call Shepard back to a set . . ." I began.

"That may or may not still be working," Eddie finished.

"I told him to stay put," I said.

Eddie shook his head. "He'd have to go to work."

"Folks," the cop said.

"Look, officer, my name is Lorraine Keys. Detective Holden is fully briefed on my involvement with Shepard Brown. Call him, talk to him, do whatever you have to do. But Mr. Brown is in trouble, and I have to find him."

"No, *we* have to find him," Eddie said.

"Yeah, we," Barb said.

Of course, the cops weren't about to let Barb go anywhere, certainly not away from a crime scene where she was the victim. After frantic negotiations and radio calls to Detective Holden, I clambered into the back of an undercover cop car.

"Good luck," Eddie said, leaning in through the window. He kissed me soundly and reached in to slide the expandable baton beneath my thigh. "Think of me when you beat the crap out of her," he teased.

I shifted a bit in my seat, making sure the baton stayed

well-concealed below the fabric of the sweatpants. "Will you stay with Barb?" I asked.

His smile was staggering. "You got it."

A detective and a patrolman joined me in the car. The detective started the engine, and we peeled away from the curb. I waved good-bye to Eddie and commenced crossing my fingers.

During the short drive to Gardner's Basin, where filming had moved to following the morning at the boardwalk, I filled in what details I could for the police and got a whole lot of wet sand on the backseat.

We rolled into the small parking lot at the basin, headlights flashing across the empty tarmac and against the private cabin cruisers tied stern-in to the pier. The only sound was the crunch of tires against loose bits of gravel and the quiet chatter on the police radio.

As we circled the lot, the knot of anxiety in my stomach twisted tighter. What if we were wrong? What if Kim had lured him off somewhere else? Mercy, where else could they be? The boardwalk was too crowded. The casinos were too protected. Where . . .

"Got movement on a boat," the detective said.

The patrolman lifted a spotlight from the floor of the car and shone the beam along the line of boats.

"Go right," the detective said.

I had one hand on the door handle and one hand wrapped around the baton, ready to burst from the car the moment we stopped—if not sooner.

The light came to rest on the black-and-gold lettering on the back of the *Affair to Remember*. Slowly, the patrolman lifted the light and revealed Catherine Dawes, sitting on the back of the boat, bawling her eyes out. In the harsh flare of the spotlight her face appeared blotchy red, raw with grief. I suspected real tears.

Kim Lloyd stood above her as though she had been shouting down at Catherine but froze for the moment, eyes turned in our direction. Kim's lips moved in profanity, and she dove for the first line tying the boat to the pier. I saw no sign of Shepard.

The detective brought the car to a rocking stop.

The patrolman with the light struggled to get out of the car while keeping the light on the boat. "Wait here," he told me.

Right. That would happen.

I slipped out of the car.

"Stop right there," the detective commanded. Luckily, he wasn't looking at me at the time. His gaze and his gun were directed toward the boat.

Kim shrieked at Catherine, perhaps telling her to do something. Nothing but frantic intent reached us.

"This is the police. Stay where you are, and put your hands in the air."

Catherine rocked with sobs. Kim, fighting a losing battle unwinding the line from the cleat, gave up, hurried to the bow of the boat, and dove into the bay.

"Oh, heck," the detective said. "Now I have to swim. Call for backup." He kicked off his loafers and made a run for the pier. The patrolman raced to get the light on the water while shouting into the radio clipped to his shoulder.

Bits of loose gravel bit into my bare feet as I dashed across the narrow stretch of tarmac toward the stern of the boat. Dim light radiated from the cabin, spilling enough light on the fantail to show Catherine sinking to the floor in hysterics.

I hit the dive platform and vaulted onto the boat. Catherine screamed, and I spun on her and snarled, "Where's Shepard?"

She shook her head and sobbed something I couldn't make out through the blubbering.

I grabbed her by the hair and raised the collapsed baton high above my head as though ready to whale on her. "Where is he?"

"Inside," she managed to say. "I swear, I didn't have any idea—"

I released her and stepped back. She scrabbled off the deck and onto land, calling to the waiting officer for help. Good, he could deal with her. All I wanted was to find Shepard.

I hauled open the sliding door to the cabin, calling for Shepard. No response.

I came around the thin wall that divided the sitting area from the kitchenette. Shepard lay on his side on the floor. Gagged. Hands and feet bound. Perfectly still.

Panic hollowed me. Heart in my throat, I fell to my knees. Oh, God, please no. Not Shepard. Dropping the baton, I reached for him.

His skin felt warm beneath my fingers, but I could find no pulse. Frantically, I searched along his jawline, then worked my way lower on his neck, back and forth, murmuring prayers I thought I'd forgotten as tears welled in my eyes. I was not ready to lose a friend.

I jammed my fingertips along the length of his windpipe, and a gurgle rose in the back of his throat. His head rocked back, and his eyelids fluttered.

"Shepard!" I shouted. Gripping his shoulder, I rolled him onto his back. I tapped his cheeks. "Shepard, wake up. Wake up. Come on, Shepard. Wake up. You can do it."

He opened his eyes, slowly, as though being called back from a comforting dream.

"That's it. Come on. Wake up. All the way." I fumbled behind his head, trying to untie the tight knot in the gag. "Come on. I've got you. We've got you. Come on."

His eyes, fully open, went wide, and he tried to speak.

"Soon," I said. "Soon. I've almost got it."

He made a noise of alarm, gaze fixed on some point over my shoulder.

Understanding hit me in the last possible second. As I tried to push myself to my feet, a blunt object struck my left shoulder. One more second's hesitation and it would have been my head.

I spun to find Kim standing over me, soaked from head to toe, a piece of wet wood the size of my arm in her hands.

"Get away from him!" she said, raising the makeshift bat.

I grabbed for the baton and wrapped my fingers around the handle. Bringing it forward, I gave it one hard flick of the wrist. The comforting sound of expanding steel filled me with confidence.

I swung at her, catching her around the knees. She tumbled backward, landing on her butt with a surprised cry. The wood flew from her hands.

Quick as I could, I got to my feet and braced myself. I knew she'd come at me again; all I had to do was wait.

Sure enough, she scrambled for purchase, got her legs under her, and went for my knees.

I raised my foot—quickly, and in a direct line toward her chin.

Pain shot through my foot and into my ankle as I caught her in the chest.

She bounced backward and landed sideways, the wood now within easy reach.

I took a step toward her, baton at the ready. I had no intention of beating her as she lay there. I had no intention of beating her at all. But if she came at me again, or so much as touched Shepard with her breath, I'd have no qualms about kicking her up one side and down the other.

Shepard grunted and stomped his feet. Outside, the cops shouted back and forth at one another, apparently unable to locate Kim in the water. Probably I should have let them know she'd returned to the boat, but first things first.

Kim had her hands around the driftwood and was dragging herself up, using the side of the little dining table for leverage. "Bitch," she said, breathless. "Get out of my way."

Shepard did some more stomping and muffled shouting.

"Girl," I said, "you will not lay a hand on this man while I live."

Snarling, she lifted the wood to shoulder level, looking ready to swing for the outfield. A drop of seawater trailed down her arm.

I kept the baton at waist height, mentally prepared to duck her blow. I'd been too gentle with her earlier. I needed her to go down and stay down long enough for me to shout for help.

With a noise that sounded like a growl, Kim stepped in and

swung. I tried my best to duck out of the way, but watching marathons of Jackie Chan movies is not the same as training. The wood grazed the top of my head, taking what felt like a good deal of hair with it.

Tears filled my eyes, and I let out a yowl. Swinging as hard as I could, I caught her again in the knees.

As the baton contacted, light filled the cabin, and the boat pitched hard to port. I caught myself against the low dividing wall. Kim crashed against the table.

She squeezed her eyes shut and cried out.

Letting go of the baton, I tackled her. One hand on her waist, the other on the arm holding the wood, I dropped to the deck with her beneath me.

"Freeze. Police."

I looked up to see the detective, gun drawn and dripping seawater, standing braced in the doorway, the patrolman two feet behind him, similar stance. Relief flooded my veins.

Kim writhed beneath me. "Get. Off. Me."

"Can you cuff her please?" I said to the cop.

The detective got the cuffs on Kim while the patrolman helped me untie Shepard. No great surprise, the first thing the guy did when free was hug me till I feared internal injury.

It felt pretty good.

Chapter Fourteen

Turned out director Ko van Weer had promised to give Kim the wedding of the century and a mansion on Mulholland Drive as soon as he got his first big Hollywood deal. The assistant director was trying to guarantee her future and Ko's and had conned Catherine into acting as accomplice under the guise of revenge for the Malena affair.

I settled back into the hard plastic chair in the interview room at the police station and adjusted the ice pack against the back of my head. "But I don't get it. Why try to kill him before filming on *Boardwalk* was finished?"

Detective Holden opened his mouth to answer, but Eddie spoke first. "The shoot was close enough to done. With what little was left, the computer wizards could CGI him in, like they did Oliver Reed in *Gladiator*." He looked to the detective. "That about right?"

Holden nodded. "And time was running out for her. This was her best chance." He handed me coffee in a plain beige mug with a chip on the side. Beside me, Eddie sipped from a shiny new mug with the ACPD shield on it.

I wrapped my free hand around the mug and took a moment to let all the information sink in. "So she really was the one who ordered the pizza," I said.

"Yup," Detective Holden said, and he chuckled a bit. "I can't believe you were right about that."

"What about the car?" Eddie asked.

"And the trailer?" I added.

Holden shook his head, lips a grim slash across his face.

"The car she had help with. We got a couple of uniforms picking up the mechanic now. But the trailer . . . that was her handiwork, all right. She had a duplicate key made for herself when Brown asked for one, then helped herself to an extension cord from the movie equipment. Your pal Johansson figured it out and tried to get her to turn herself in before he called us." He drew in a noisy breath. "She had other plans."

My pal Johansson. Dutch.

My chest hollowed, and my throat ached. I took a slug of coffee to wash down the grief. Dutch had been a good man. I wished he were there to give me a hug; I could have used one.

A uniformed officer stuck his head in the door. "Jim, telephone."

Holden sighed and pushed himself to his feet. "Excuse me."

I watched him go and focused on feeling a little sorry for him that he'd been dragged out of bed to come back to the station on our account. It was easier than thinking about Dutch.

"Well, I'll say this," Eddie said, turning to me. "This is the first date I've ever had that ended in a police station."

Pulling the ice pack away from my head, I could barely look at him. "Sorry. Not how I pictured it ending either."

"So it's over?" he asked, grinning as he checked his watch.

The face of his watch was visible from where I sat—nearly four in the morning. "You don't have to wait, you know," I said. "I'll be fine here till they're done talking with Barb."

"I know," he said, taking the ice pack from me. "I choose to wait. Let me do this." He shook the pack to redistribute the cold, then laid it gently against my head and held it there.

"You don't have to—"

"Stop. Drink your coffee."

I turned the cup so I wouldn't have to drink out of the chipped side. "Hey," I said. "If it's okay with you, can we skip the whole tender moment where I thank you for helping with everything tonight and just leave it with me saying that was pretty great of you, and I really appreciate it?"

He smiled, slowly. "No."

"No?"

"You owe me one, Lorraine. And don't think I won't collect."

"Fair enough," I said, fighting hard not to grin like an idiot.

"Speaking of which," Eddie began, but Holden returned to the room, Barb and Shepard in tow.

Barb rushed toward me, and Eddie pulled the ice pack away in time for Barb to bend down and hug me in my chair. "I'm so sorry," she whispered in my ear. "I should have listened to you and gone home."

I hugged her back as best I could. "Don't worry about it."

"We got a couple of cars out front," Holden said. "The officers have volunteered to drive you all back to your hotel."

Free to pursue our own business, we said our good-byes and promised we'd be available should the police need us.

"Miss Keys," Holden said as I headed for the door. "That was your boss on the phone."

Oh, nuts. "And?"

"Says he needs you at the Guggenheim on Friday."

"Great," I said, forcing a smile that I knew without a mirror came out looking like I was nauseated. "Night shift?"

"I'm not your social secretary. Call him yourself."

I left Detective Holden with the ice pack and headed outside to the squad car, where Shepard Brown stood waiting by the back door.

"Eddie and I are over there," he said with a nod to the other car. "I just . . . tomorrow might be kind of crazy and . . . I wanted to say thanks. You're the best."

"Oh, well, I . . ." I folded my arms across my belly, uncomfortable with the praise.

He reached for me and took me gently in his arms. "There's no one else I'd rather have on my side," he said on a sigh.

Then he released me and guided me into the backseat of the car, where Barb sat quizzing the driver/patrolman on the best places to buy donuts. Don't know why she thought he'd know.

Shepard shut the door behind me, and I shrugged into the seat belt.

"I got to meet Shepard Brown," Barb said softly.

I nodded, happy for her. "Yes, you did."

"He's amazingly nice," she said.

I nodded some more, holding my smile in place.

"He said any friend of yours is a friend of his and that we should go out to LA to see him soon."

More time with Shepard. Good idea or bad idea?

"We should go," Barb said. "I want to go before school starts and I have to go back to work. Man, the other teachers will be green when I tell them. We should go. Soon."

I carefully leaned my head against the back of the seat as the car rolled away from the curb. "Maybe," I said. "We'll talk about it in the morning, okay? Right now I really need a decent night's sleep. I haven't had one since this all started."

Barb reached out and patted my knee. "In the morning," she said. "We'll go get donuts."

LA didn't sound too bad. I could take a few days, figure out what my career choices were, lounge on the beach . . . maybe hook up with Eddie. I might even do some shopping. Buy girl clothes—you never know. Maybe a little trip was just what I needed to recover from my little trip. After all, it couldn't be as crazy as Atlantic City, right?